I0537124

Margaret at Barnard

Part Two: Deliverance

Also by R. L. Rhyse

Margaret of Greenwich

Margaret and Erika

Margaret at War

Margaret in Tokyo

Margaret and Eve

Margaret and Velda

Margaret and Emily

Margaret and Hillary

Margaret in London

Margaret at Barnard

R. L. Rhyse

Margaret at Barnard

Part Two: Deliverance

Book Eleven in the
Margaret of Greenwich® Series

Wyston Books, Inc.

Wyston Books, Inc.

www.margaretofgreenwich.com
www.wystonbooks.com

R. L. Rhyse

Margaret at Barnard/Part Two: Deliverance: a novel
Book Eleven in the Margaret of Greenwich® Series

1. Margaret of Greenwich (Fictitious character)
2. Teenage Girls Fiction

Library of Congress Control Number: 2016931696
ISBN 978-0-9903920-6-4
eISBN 978-0-9903920-7-1
Cover Photograph by meshaphoto/E+ Collection
Licensed from Getty Images
BISAC: JUV014000 (Girls & Women)
JUV028000 (Mysteries & Detective Stories)
JUV026000 (Love & Romance)

Love is more likely to deceive a woman than a man.
–Margaret

Real love and goodness can guide you home.
–Margaret

Chapter 1

"I've been playing with house money since I was twelve. What I most want is to be known and understood. It's not so terrible to die young if you're been part of the pattern of life and loved," Kimberly, a fellow Barnard student, had told me as I visited her in jail.

She had been damned by a nation that demanded her execution. There *must be* a way to save her, I hoped. But I couldn't imagine how.

Just months before, my second year at Barnard began more quietly than my first. This was because I had lucked out. I was the first student to pounce after the announcement that a single room was available.

I had valued my past roommate, Missy, who now lived off campus. But grades were more important for me than for her and I needed the peace of a single room to achieve them. She came from a wealthy family while mine survived on my father's Social Security Disability payments.

I couldn't have attended Barnard if not for my scholarship. It covered tuition, housing, and the meal plan. I paid for my clothes and other necessities with earnings from my babysitting jobs.

The Barnard Babysitting Service found me work with wealthy Manhattan families. They would often expose my humble status by labeling me ("This is Margaret. She does chores."). You get my point.

In Manhattan, just as in Greenwich, poverty had condemned me to a lowly place on society's hierarchy. But I didn't mind. I was loved by my boyfriend, Randy, and by my family and that's what really counts. I had long told myself this and still believed it.

During my first year, my grades were good enough to keep my scholarship but they weren't as high as they could have been. I had become too involved with Missy's problems, as roommates tend to do. Things will be different this year. When not in class or working, I will spend my time studying, I vowed.

My new single room was on the fourth floor of the Brooks Hall dormitory. It was half the size of my previous double room and came with half the furniture: a twin size bed, a desk and chair, a dresser, and a closet. There was no air-conditioning or TV. You could have cable but only if you paid for it. A TV lounge is on the first floor.

I hadn't purchased much during my first year and my move-in went quickly. Afterward, I lay on my bed, luxuriating in the quiet of my new room. But I had made the mistake of not locking the door.

Chapter 2

Soon after arriving at Barnard, I learned that New Yorkers go overboard with locks. Homes in Greenwich usually have one lock and rooms other than bathrooms often don't have any. Not so in Manhattan where "locking up" has become an art.

Charlotte, the Manhattan doctor with whom Missy and her baby live, has *three* locks on her apartment's door. This, in a building with a doorman and video security too!

My background doesn't excuse my unlocked door but does explain it. "Locking up" hadn't yet gained the importance for me that it does for other New Yorkers.

I had been lying on the bed, fantasying married life with Randy, when I sensed a change in the room. Opening my eyes, I saw that I was no longer alone. I sprang up, instantly on guard. Crime occurs everywhere, even at snooty Barnard. Several years before, a girl had been murdered by her roommate.

"I wanted to see this room," the girl said, as she stood by the opened door.

"I just moved in," I replied calmly.

"My room is down the hall," she said.

Her statement made no sense. If she lived down the hall, why was she interested in my room? I gave her the benefit of the doubt. Maybe she had a double room and sought a single but had not yet learned of its

9

unavailability. Or she might simply be looking for a new friend.

I'm tall, 5' 10", and this girl looked taller. I'm thin and she was more than thin, resembling a newly released prisoner from a really bad place. Her face was stark white from pallor and makeup. Her eyebrows and eyelashes were black. Her lipstick was the shade of the Maybelline Red Sensational Creamy Matte that I had a coupon for but still couldn't afford.

I gave my best smile to the striking image before me.

"Hello, I'm Margaret," I said, in a cheery tone, walking forward and extending my hand.

The girl came closer.

"I just wanted to look in. I thought I smelled something, that someone could be dead," she said.

Her voice was toneless as her limp cold hand barely touched mine.

Chapter 3

We spend most of our time in our own heads so to catch someone's attention you must say something startling and this girl did. Instinct had told me to ignore courtesy. Run from her fast, it said.

But curiosity ruled. It is like when you force yourself to watch a horror movie to learn its ending though being sure that doing so will cause a nightmare.

Forgive yourself for everyone has dumb moments, I might have told myself later. But I had felt fearless, having just survived my first year at college which everyone says is the hardest. I was healthy and my boyfriend loved me. Nothing bad could happen. My thinking returned to the girl.

"Why did you think that someone here might be dead?" I asked.

"I call this room *the death chamber*," she replied.

For the second time in a minute, this girl, whose name I still didn't know, had startled me. She should be making movies, she already frightened me, I thought. Here, at Barnard, in the safest big city in America.

"Why do you call it that?" I asked, unable to keep a tremor from my usually confident tone.

The girl's gaze turned toward the corner of the room. She stared for several moments before raising her arm and pointing to my bed.

"That's where I found their bodies," she said.

Chapter 4

Anyone saying "bodies" will get my full attention. Even saying "body" will do it. Call me squeamish but at the few funerals that I've attended, of elderly teachers and teenage drivers, I've passed up the opportunity to view the body. I've read that funeral directors wonderfully restore an appearance but would rather remember the deceased as I knew them. So this girl's statement drew me up straight. I sat on the bed and pointed for her to sit in the desk chair.

Then I asked my burning questions: "What's your name?" "What happened here?"

Before seating herself, the girl stared at the chair, as if she had never seen such an object before. I waited and, when she didn't immediately speak, I asked if she wanted water or juice. When she didn't reply, I got two juice packs from my stash and handed one to her. She took it without a word, unwrapped the straw and pushed it through the foil closure. I waited while she sipped.

"My name is Kimberly. I must seem pretty weird," she said, after regaining her bearing.

She did, but tact insisted that I smile and remain silent.

"It was a shock. Seeing their bodies," she said.

The sight of *one* body would have stunned me, I thought, as I remained silent with an idiotic smile plastered to my face. Like my lawyer-dad says, when a person's story is rolling, let it roll.

"But they *must have* cleaned this room before you moved in," Kimberly said quickly.

That's a relief, I thought, and unwillingly glanced toward the red carpet stain peeking from under the bed.

"What happened here?" I asked.

"What do you mean?"

Kimberly's replies are disproving the notion that Barnard students are smart, I thought.

"How many bodies were there? How did they die?" I asked.

I tried keeping calm though the deaths had occurred in the room where we sat. This became harder the longer we spoke.

"Just two."

Just two? Does Brooks Hall have its own morgue? I asked myself.

"How did they die?" I again asked.

I controlled my snowballing impatience as my tolerance drained away.

"No one knows," Kimberly replied.

Her tone was matter-of-fact, as if we were discussing the merits of lipsticks rather than the cause of deaths. Kimberly suddenly became paler. She looked down as if she were ashamed.

"It might have been me that killed them," she said, softly, as if talking to herself.

Chapter 5

I didn't immediately speak. Kimberly scared me. Not from the fear that she would attack me but because *she* seemed terrified. Her slight smile didn't change my conclusion.

"It would have been clearer to say that it was what I told them that might have gotten them killed," she explained.

I nodded understanding and felt relief. Kimberly leaned back and tried to relax in the rigid desk chair.

"I'm not brave. My leaving the light on all night drives roommates crazy. That's why I looked into this room. I wanted to see if I could comfortably live here after what happened. You see, I'm terrified of...*Hangman.*"

I've gotten terrified of you, I thought, though maintaining a calm, sympathetic look plastered to my face.

"Hangman?" I merely asked.

Kimberly nodded.

"Just so. The fear came back because of what I saw. It began when I was twelve. It's why I keep the light on all night. You're only the second person to hear this."

I ordered myself not to ask but couldn't resist.

"Who was the first person that you told this to?"

"William, a Columbia student. He's dead."

Ejecting Kimberly from my room straightaway would have the smart thing to do. She wasn't a friend and I wasn't obliged to hear her story. But, to make one of my bad puns, I was deadly curious. Wouldn't you have been?

Still, I first wanted us out of this room. Though the scent from its recent painting still lingered, the room, and maybe it was only because of Kimberly's presence, seemed to reek of horror. We should be away, out in the sunshine or in a well-lit diner and not here. Which is what I suggested.

"Let's get out of here," I said.

But this was not the *"Get away, Kimberly!"* that my survival instinct had kept insisting.

Chapter 6

The diner that I led us to was three blocks away. Another one was closer but since I had invited Kimberly, I would pay. This restaurant was cheaper and my spending money came from my babysitting and I was currently unemployed. The family that I worked for had recently moved to France.

My initial sense that Kimberly was tall was true. I'm 5'10" and she was several inches taller. But while I walk straight, she slouched as if she were ashamed of her height or was trying to hide. People stared at her when we entered the restaurant. *She* was afraid but something about her concerned others too.

I ordered my usual snack, a toasted whole-wheat bagel and orange juice, and Kimberly ordered the same. Her gaunt body told me that she didn't concern herself with food. She was a cheap date and I needn't have worried about the cost.

"Why do you leave the lights on all night?" I asked, after the waiter took our orders and left.

"I'm afraid to sleep. Not always but when *the thought* enters my mind and I never know when it will. It's of a hanging man, *a Hangman*. I try not to think about it. When I see something looking like a noose in a magazine, I must quickly throw it out to stop the picture from invading my thoughts," she replied.

Kimberly had given me an explanation but I still didn't understand. As every kid knows, *Hangman* is a children's game in which the figure of a hanging man is added to when a mistake is made, one line/limb at a time. Despite its name, the game has nothing to do with death.

I summarized what Kimberly told me.

"OK. Something happened when you were twelve and ever since you've been afraid. What happened? How were you involved in these deaths? Who were the students that died?" I asked.

Kimberly took a small packet of crackers from the metal container on the table. She opened it and chewed each cracker slowly, one after another. When she finished, the waiter had returned and this prompted another delay. Finally, Kimberly spoke.

"Do you remember I told you that William was the first person to hear my story and he is now dead?" Kimberly asked, and I nodded.

"Riley's body was next to his," Kimberly said.

Though her voice was calm, my heart seemed to skip a beat.

Chapter 7

Though I hate to admit it, Kimberly's story had freaked me out. What can one say after being told that two people died after hearing the story that you are about to hear? It was during this spell of nervousness that *Jingle Bells* played.

My biological mother had placed this ringtone on my iPhone when she bought it for me and I never changed it. I felt that doing so would hurt her if she found out. Realistically, I knew that it wouldn't matter but adoptees get such strange feelings.

Though Christmas was months away, I considered this sound a minor miracle. I needed a break from Kimberly.

"We're getting married!" was the breathlessly delivered fact from Missy, my former roommate.

My mood caused my sour reaction.

"Do I know the boy?"

Missy laughed and ignored my comment. My friends are used to my weird humor.

"The wedding is this Friday and you're coming!" she insisted.

This news *was* a surprise. While I certainly knew *who* she was marrying, I couldn't conceive of their wedding being this week. Weddings take planning. I had spoken with her two days earlier and she said nothing about getting married.

"That's in four days. I don't understand," I said, in what I believed would be my understatement of the year.

"*Yes,*" Missy replied, letting a long silence heighten the suspense. This annoyed me but brides-to-be have rights.

"OK, slow down a bit. Why are you marrying Artur so quickly? Weddings require arrangements and, well you know..."

The fear aroused by Kimberly's story instantly vanished. Missy's love life was complicated. After a lengthy affair with her high school counselor, she had discovered that she was pregnant soon after arriving at Barnard. Thankfully, her new boyfriend, Artur, loved her and her baby daughter unreservedly.

Artur was a brilliant student at Columbia College and planned to become a doctor. But there was a problem, and it wasn't small. Missy is the daughter of a Mormon bishop and Artur is an atheist like his father, a Russian diplomat.

His lack of religion never bothered me but it would disturb Missy's father. OK, probably not as much as when he learned that his picture-perfect, former Homecoming Queen, unmarried daughter was pregnant but still...

While not wanting to burst her bubble of happiness, I felt the need for more information before offering my help though this was a formality: I don't desert my friends.

Chapter 8

"Artur is a fabulous guy and I wish you every happiness but why are you getting married *now*? You both have three more years of college and he plans to be a doctor. Shouldn't you wait until after graduation?" I asked.

I said this even though knowing that giving sensible advice would be a waste of time. The intention to marry quickly isn't made lightly by those who don't drink. And, like most Mormons, Missy didn't touch alcohol and I hadn't seen Artur with a drink since their relationship became serious.

"There are two reasons," Missy explained, calmly. "The first is that Artur's father heard a rumor of his promotion to a position in Moscow. Once we're married, Artur will be the husband of an American citizen and can remain in America."

That makes sense, I thought.

"What's the second reason?" I asked.

"I'm pregnant."

This is becoming a habit, I thought unkindly, feeling jealousy. It would be years before I found myself in Missy's enviable position and babysitting doesn't substitute for the real thing.

"That's wonderful!" I gushed, knowing that this was what Missy wanted to hear.

"It wasn't planned," she added.

"No, I don't imagine that it was," I said.

I knew from my babysitting experience that parenting two children is far more work than caring for one.

"Where will the wedding be?" I asked.

"The Municipal Building, at 10AM this Friday. Artur's parents will feel at home. 'It'll be like the weddings in Russia,' he said."

"Are your parents coming?"

"They're in Europe but all my brothers except for Odis will be there. He's tied up with the lawyers."

Odis was helping the government's prosecution of an international criminal conspiracy.

"What did your father say when you told him?" I asked

"I think he's finally gotten used to me. Just that 'things will happen,'" she replied, with a laugh.

"I have to go. Justin is yelling for me," Missy added, before hanging up.

She and her daughter lived with the single-parent obstetrician who had delivered Missy's baby. Missy cared for the doctor's son, seven-year-old Justin, in exchange for room and board.

I sat silently, thinking.

"What?" Kimberly asked, sensing that I had received big news.

"Missy, my roommate last year, is pregnant and getting married," I said.

"That's wonderful! Where is the wedding? Will it be big?"

"It'll be at City Hall and not big at all," I replied.

"Huh?"

"There's a religion problem. Missy is Mormon like me and her fiancée isn't," I said.

"Nowadays, many couples have different religions. What's the issue?" Kimberly objected.

Here I go again, having to explain my religion to people who know us only as polygamists from the TV series, *Big Love,* I thought.

"The problem is that Missy's father is a bishop and Mormons are expected to have a temple marriage which is our special ceremony. To qualify for this, they must be church members in good standing. Which means that they've been a member for at least a year, have tithed ten percent of their income, and don't use tobacco, alcohol, or drugs.

"The couple must also pass a worthiness interview with a Church leader who asks how religious they've been and their sexual behavior. Missy won't get points for having an out-of-wedlock child and being pregnant," I said.

"Oh," Kimberly said.

"Yes, oh," I repeated.

Chapter 9

The screech of a car horn returned my thinking to Kimberly. She was now chewing her bagel and seemed calmer. I nibbled my bagel and thought. While Kimberly's childhood had aroused my curiosity, my life was hard enough. I didn't need more trouble but did want information. What did Kimberly tell the students that she believed had caused their death? And if it was murder, why hadn't I heard about it?

A double murder at any college would be headline news and for more than one day. But there had been nothing. I made a mental note to check past, online editions of the student newspaper, the *Columbia Daily Spectator*, when I returned to my room: *the death chamber!*

I caught myself, and faced Kimberly.

"Tell me," I said, forcefully.

"What?"

"What happened in my room? For a start, who died?"

"They were a First Year girl and her boyfriend. He lived in a Columbia dorm and was visiting."

"*OK*," I said slowly, feeling pleased that we were getting somewhere.

"Who found their bodies?"

"I did. When I smelled something in the room."

I don't ordinarily waste food but dropped my half-eaten bagel onto the plate after she said this. I read enough detective novels to know what caused the odor.

Kimberly paused again. After a few moments of silence, I encouraged her.

"Well?" I asked.

"Yes."

Could Kimberly be smart but socially dumb? I wondered. She certainly seemed this way. It was as if her words were detached from her feelings so though she might excel on written tests, she would fail at social tasks. I had read about geniuses with these weaknesses. Asperger's Syndrome they called it.

Maybe Kimberly could tolerate socializing only briefly, I thought. I would ask her a few more questions and save my others for another time.

It was unlikely that two teenage friends would suddenly die of natural causes but these things can happen. They could have caught the same disease while on a trip, and there had surely been an autopsy. I tried to contain my exasperation.

"Kimberly, why was there no publicity and how come there are no rumors of these deaths?" I asked, hoping that my directness would penetrate her emotional bubble.

Now, Kimberly looked thoughtful. She had finished her bagel and put down her juice.

"I've wondered about that too. What I concluded was that the event was so disturbing. it had to be hushed up. After girls were murdered at a sorority house in Florida, their college practically shut-down. No school wants the reputation of being unsafe. It could take years to recover. Better to try pretending that it never happened. The dorm adviser didn't tell you?"

"Nope."

"That's my point," Kimberly said.

Chapter 10

Erika, one of my best friends, once shared something that her shrink had said: that if you're lost, it's best to go back to where you started and begin again.

Kimberly must be very smart, I told myself. Being hopeless at relating, only if she were exceptionally bright would she have been admitted to Barnard. I knew that Barnard officials were pitiless. They tried to expel Missy for being pregnant while living in Brooks Hall and might have succeeded were it not for support from her lawyer and friends.

I had judged, from Kimberly's last comment, that she wasn't naïve. But apart from this conclusion and her fragile appearance, I still didn't feel that I knew her.

My father, who is a lawyer, said that truly mysterious people seem ordinary. Kimberly didn't, so I began my investigation of who she really was by asking the common, non-threatening question that all students ask.

"What's your major?"

Kimberly's eyes lit up, like those of a girl in love, and her reply couldn't have been more unexpected. For Kimberly loved what most students hate, and her choice of this isolating subject explained her. She knew that people had difficulty relating to her but just couldn't get the people stuff right.

"I'm a math major," Kimberly replied, with a broad smile, as if I we had now entered *her* world.

"Math?" I asked.

I wasn't sure what to say next so I asked another common question.

"When did you choose math?"

Kimberly's joyous expression remained fixed to her face. Do mathematicians have the biggest orgasms, I asked myself, jokingly.

"After I discovered the Conway-Kochen theorem. I was twelve. It's all about free will," Kimberly burst forth.

My dumb expression produced her explanation, which was as clear as any that I had gotten from any teacher about anything. Now, I didn't doubt it: Kimberly very definitely *was* some kind of genius.

"At its heart, the Conway-Kochen theorem is a statement about quantum mechanics. Do you know what that is?"

"A little, I said, nodding hesitantly.

What I knew, from high school physics, is that quantum mechanics is a group of scientific laws describing the interaction of atomic particles. These concepts have given rise to important practical applications including the transistor and the MRI.

My nod seemed a go-ahead for Kimberly's lengthy explanation of this fundamental branch of physics. Over

the next months, accommodating to the Conway-
Kochen's notion of free will would devour my life.

Chapter 11

Kimberly spoke slowly, as is she were a teacher confronting a not very bright student.

"The Conway-Kochen Theorem, which is also called the Free Will Theorem, is a mathematical formulation about quantum mechanics. Speaking simply, if people have free will, then so do atomic particles with their behavior being only partially controlled by what happened in the past. The proof of the theorem relies on three axioms: Min, Spin, and Twin."

When she completed her explanation, the above was all that I understood. Matters like "quantum entanglement" were way above me. But I had continued smiling and nodded with apparent understanding at what seemed appropriate moments. I didn't want to seem too dumb.

"That's really something. Who thought it up," I asked, when Kimberly concluded her lecture.

"A genius mathematician at Princeton. When he had heart trouble and was going broke, he tried to kill himself with pills. After recovering, he wore a t-shirt imprinted with the big letters, 'SUICIDE.' He believed this would help others feel less awkward when they met him."

"That is one strange guy," I said, with emotion.

"Maybe, but he's been married three times and I've never had a boyfriend last for more than one date. What would you call me?" Kimberly asked, and her eyes teared up.

Her confession didn't surprise me though it wasn't something to be ashamed of. But a popular belief is that all teenagers have a great love life. Probably not with the partner that they'll wind up marrying but to gain skill with relationships. Dating has its pitfalls, like with learning anything new.

I felt sad for Kimberly. Her situation wouldn't be easy to fix since dating wasn't her only problem. Being odd, she might never have had a friend and learned how to relate to them either. Now is the time for her to start. Kimberly needed a friend and I would be her friend, I decided.

But my goal hadn't been entirely unselfish since I needed a friend too. My past roommate, Missy, lived off campus and was consumed by her toddler, her pregnancy, and her upcoming marriage. We had been joined at the hip during our first year at Barnard and I hadn't made another friend. My other friends and my boyfriend lived in Greenwich.

My decision was a no-brainer. Both Kimberly and I were lonely and needed someone. I would teach her dating skills and she would help me with math. We would have an untroubled friendship that would benefit us both.

That was my intention but, as they say, man proposes and God disposes. I hadn't bothered about fate though this is a definite no-brainer with every decision.

Chapter 12

We had left the coffee shop and were strolling along Broadway. People stared at Kimberly.

"I get stared at a lot. Everyone thinks I look weird," Kimberly said.

Whenever this happened, she had immediately looked down. I noticed that she did this often, even when she was ignored. Her walk seemed very body-conscious. It was not a natural walk for a girl so beautiful for it was a denial of the unself-conscious pride that she should have had.

"No, they're admiring you because you're beautiful," I said quickly, in my most sincere tone. "You dress beautifully too," I added.

My statements weren't lies. Apart from being very tall, all of Kimberly's features were average or nearly so, and this made her beautiful. Her nose was straight and of average length, her eyes and mouth weren't unusual, and her other features were unobtrusive. While fashion sometimes defines beauty in different terms, as being anorexically gaunt, its basic elements are never far from average.

Some men might quibble with Kimberly's small breasts and butt, which I had too, but these are personal judgments. She could probably find work as a model if she were more self-confident, I thought.

Any modeling agency would also approve of her dress: a white crepe go-everywhere piece. Men stared at her face but women gawked at her clothes.

"That's a lovely dress," I couldn't help remarking.

"It's a Balenciaga, their Day-to-Night Dress, so you needn't change if you're going out. My mother chose it years ago, hoping against hope," Kimberly said, with a hang-dog expression.

I loved the dress but knew that its cost was far outside my league and likely always would be. The price of Balenciaga's dresses begins in the thousands. Kimberly's book bag was expensive too.

I felt jealous. Walking alongside her, I looked like a cleaning woman. That's what poverty does to you. The income from my babysitting went toward necessities. My clothing came from a Salvation Army store. My father's disability income didn't allow luxuries for our family of six.

My thinking returned to Kimberly. Telling a friend who hates themselves that they're wonderful won't work since they'll assume that you are lying. Change the subject and forget about giving her dating tips now, I told myself. Kimberly isn't ready to hear them. First, be her friend and let her learn what friendship is. Later, when boys come knocking, you can help her deal with dating issues. Then, she'll listen.

Many Barnard girls dressed well. More Madison Avenue exclusive than upper West Side trendy but never with French imports. Who really is Kimberly? I asked myself, and not for the first time.

But I knew that finding out wouldn't be easy. There must be a good reason why Kimberly didn't have a boyfriend and hadn't made friends. And it wasn't because of her makeup, which had caused me to wonder if she were colorblind.

Chapter 13

My difficulty in learning more about Kimberly shed light on her problem socializing. Not because of her appearance or height or brilliance but because she was nearly impossible to talk to.

When you asked Kimberly a question, the only certain thing was that her answer would be interesting. She didn't behave like this to be intentionally difficult, because she was angry and trying to give you a hard time. Instead, her speech reflected how her thinking operated, in an associative rather than a sensible manner. She would tell you what your question *reminded her of.*

One such exchange occurred as we passed a Cuban-American restaurant.

"Have you eaten here?" I asked.

It took a half-minute before Kimberly replied.

"The major inhabitants of Cuba, when the Spanish settlers came in the late 15th century, were Taino. *Havana* is a Taino word, as is *Cuba,* which may be translated as 'where fertile land is abundant, *cubao.*"

Getting to know Kimberly would be no easy matter. But considering how much I feared math, having her as my tutor would be worth it, I decided.

After strolling in silence for several more blocks, I suggested that we return to the dorm. Kimberly nodded agreement and I nodded that I understood.

I had begun fearing what her response to *any* of my statements would produce for she might say *anything*. Constructing our friendship will challenge us both, I predicted to myself.

An easy way of getting to know Kimberly will be to see her room, I thought, as we entered Brooks Hall.

"My room's still a mess. How about going to yours?" I asked.

My question seemed to shock her. It was as if no one had ever asked this and it took several moments for her to respond. When she did, the normalcy of her answer surprised me.

"OK," she answered.

Kimberly's double-room was similar to the one that I had shared with Missy the previous year. There were two twin size beds, two desks and chairs, two dressers, and two closets.

When we entered, I noticed that only one side of her room looked inhabited.

"Who is your roommate?" I asked, and immediately regretted my question.

"She lasted just a day. They're looking for another one for me," Kimberly replied, and her hang-dog expression returned.

But it was quickly replaced by an unusual, perceptive smile, one that distinguishes those who are both very beautiful and very rich, I had learned this from living in Greenwich. Kimberly's beauty is obvious. Is she rich too? I wondered.

Chapter 14

Kimberly's room didn't parade wealth but it would be hard to do this in Brooks Hall where many additions are forbidden: cooking appliances and extra furniture, even extension cords. On the wall hung a flag that I didn't recognize. Quirky teenagers had gotten involved with terrorists and I instantly feared that Kimberly might be one of them.

"What's that?" I asked, pointing to the flag.

"Huh?"

"The flag."

"A flag."

"Yes, but what flag is it? From where?" I asked, restraining my annoyance.

"Brazil, of course."

Our relationship was improving and I felt pleased. This answer had been direct, not associative, and I hoped for more.

"Why do you hang a Brazilian flag?" I asked.

"Aren't I obviously Brazilian?" came Kimberly's puzzling reply.

This wasn't obvious to me, I thought. But I let her answer pass for I had learned another fact: Kimberly was from Brazil.

"My father is Brazilian. He *was* Brazilian. My mother was American," she added.

Now we're getting somewhere even if her past-tense phrasing had added more mystery, I thought.

Like most Americans my knowledge of Brazil is sketchy. I know it's in South America and the people there love soccer but that's about it.

While speaking, we had settled in the usual positions that friends take in a dorm room: she sat up in bed while I sat facing her in a desk chair.

"You said '*was*.' Did your father become an American citizen?" I asked, this being the most tactful question.

This silence was prolonged. What I said had touched a nerve though it seemed innocent enough. When Kimberly finally spoke, her reply added to the puzzle of who she was.

"He's dead."

"I'm sorry. It must have been painful," I said, with feeling.

I didn't think that I could tolerate my father dying. His past Emergency Room visits, caused by Lyme disease, had left me with frightening memories.

Now, Kimberly looked at me directly. Her smile was knowing, like that of a clever child who feels pleased at having gotten away with something. It disappeared quickly from her face but her words chilled me.

"No, his death was for the best," she said.

Chapter 15

I pulled back from Kimberly. A new friendship can only tolerate limited intimacy and I felt that ours had reached that point. Kimberly's weird smile when revealing her father's death indicated that I had entered touchy grounds. But I didn't want to leave her abruptly lest she feel that I too considered her weird. So I extended an invitation which she could accept or not.

"I have to sort out my room and buy books. How about meeting for lunch at one?" I asked.

Kimberly didn't say anything immediately. This might also have been the first time in her life that she had gained an invitation, or she might have felt that what she revealed had pushed me away. But I had learned that difficult people can turn out to be great friends once you get to know them.

Kimberly finally nodded, and I quickly picked up on it.

"*Great!* I'll be back at one. We can eat in the Dining Hall," I said.

Another nod came after a briefer hesitation, and I left before she could change her mind.

The Dining Hall is located in the basement of Hewitt Hall and reached by a tunnel. I had suggested that we eat here for two reasons. The first was to save money. My Platinum Meal Plan was included in my scholarship though, judging by her costly clothes, money couldn't be an issue for Kimberly.

My second reason was to reassure her. Kimberly was obviously a loner and staying within the known school surroundings would be comfortable. Here, she wouldn't have to endure the maelstrom of the streets or one of the few cheap, always crowded restaurants that I could afford. My being vegetarian limited the choice of these, and the Dining Hall had vegetarian selections. Not as many as I would have liked but, as the saying goes, beggars can't be choosers.

Chapter 16

Most students wait until the first day of class to buy textbooks. I get mine early though I probably shouldn't. Leafing through them makes me worry about what I'll have to learn and this usually seems worse than it is.

Unlike in high school, colleges permit students to select the classes that they want. But there are limits of choice and probably every school has classes which are worthless. This happens when the instructor emphasizes their personal views and not the serious literature. I placed two of my required classes in this category: *Ethics and Values,* and *Social Analysis*. I chose them now, wanting to get them out of the way.

For the rest of my schedule I added *Introduction to Psychology*, and *Calculus 1*. In high school, when needing help in math, I relied on my boyfriend, Randy. Like Kimberly, he is a math genius. I hoped for Kimberly to be my tutor here.

After registering for the classes, I bought the textbooks but didn't skim them as I usually did. This would have made me nervous and I felt edgy enough. Instead, I returned to my room and considered my soon-to-be lunch with Kimberly.

The more of our conversation that I remembered, the more I realized that even eating with her would be difficult since her way of relating was so strange. She answered most questions with unconnected information, whatever entered her mind at that moment. So if seeking a fact, I need begin a long, circuitous route of inquiry.

And although Kimberly disliked speaking about herself, she would also tune out when I volunteered something personal about myself. What kind of friendship can that be? I asked myself

Still, I reminded myself, there *is* more to Kimberly than these. She obviously cares about her appearance since she dressed beautifully and applied makeup carefully even if it wasn't my style.

Had she always been like this or had some event caused her to behave as she does? I wondered. Her behavior certainly pushed people away. Could this be deliberate? Her odd smile and response when speaking of her father's had been more than a little strange.

The first man in a girl's life is her father. Did their bad relationship warp Kimberly's desire for a lover or even a friend? And how much emotional scarring can be repaired through later friendship? I didn't know this answer either.

Could this be why I signed up for the psychology class? Hoping that what I learn there will help me to understand Kimberly, and to find out why I had become obsessed with her? Along with this thought came an image floating in my mind. I couldn't grasp it but sensed that it would return.

Chapter 17

Perhaps from her desire to be less formally dressed in the casual student lunchroom, Kimberly had changed into a classic white blouse with lace-up neckline and simple black trousers. I noted that their cost could feed a family for months. I told her the classes that I had signed up for.

"What are you taking?" I asked, as we walked through the tunnel to the Dining Hall.

Though this was the least threatening question that I could think of, there was still a long silence before Kimberly answered. She faced downward as we walked, stooping as if being ashamed of her height. The voices of passing students seemed to disturb her. When she spoke, it was barely above a whisper.

"*Honors Math B, Physics–Electricity and Magnetism*, and two computer classes at Columbia."

Barnard College is part of Columbia University and is across the street. All graduate level classes are held there. I thought of saying that studying there would be a great way to meet eligible boys but didn't. Learning to be a friend comes before learning to be a lover, I reminded myself. Moreover, I wasn't confident about my ability to help Kimberly cope with a torrid affair, and felt increasingly nervous too.

I hadn't been able to relax since learning about the deaths that occurred in my room. I knew, from TV crime shows, that there are businesses specializing in disinfecting a room after a death. While feeling confident that the school had hired the right people, a lingering fear embraced my mind. If there was doubt about how the students died, how good could the cleaning have been?

What if an undetectable biological agent had been used to murder them? What if they had returned from abroad carrying a fatal disease? This event was continually in the news.

"What?" Kimberly asked suddenly, and I almost jumped.

I had been holding my fork aloft, halfway to my mouth with a piece of baked soy chicken on it.

"You looked funny," she added, helpfully.

Either Kimberly is becoming sensitive to people's reactions or she has always been, I told myself.

"Well, I'm glad to have gotten a single room but can't stop thinking about the students who died in it. I know it's silly since their deaths were probably caused by something ordinary, like from a bug that they picked up from somewhere far away," I said.

Kimberly's peculiar smile appeared, as it had when speaking of her father being dead.

"No, they were murdered. But I don't think that *you* need worry," Kimberly said.

Chapter 18

Kimberly's bizarre reply caused me to stop asking questions. But it didn't end my thinking about her weird, knowing smile. It took minutes for me to relax, after I realized that it likely hadn't meant the same for her that it would for another person.

Kimberly had problems and her reactions to people were screwed up. Her comment and smile might merely indicate her belief that the deaths were suspicious, or be another instance of her odd behavior. For all I knew she would smile if told that I had lost my scholarship, maybe even upon learning that I had been murdered.

I hated thinking this of anyone but it was probably true. Teaching her friendship will be my Good Deed for this semester, I told myself, not unkindly.

Kimberly had stopped eating and was staring at a couple. Two tables away, a boy and girl were talking excitedly.

"How is sex with your boyfriend?" Kimberly asked me suddenly.

Her unexpected question had shocked me, the more so because her tone had been the sort that one uses when asking something impersonal, like where a dress was bought. I reminded myself that Kimberly is tone deaf where people are concerned.

"That's a pretty personal question," I replied.

"Is it?"

She hadn't realized this, and I explained.

"Well, I don't even tell my best friend, Erica, about that and she doesn't talk about things with her boyfriend either. We had a girl's group in the babysitting business we ran and spoke about sex there: how much sex is too much, orgasm, oral and anal sex, things like that. But that was for support, not to share details though some came out. Why do you ask?"

Kimberly's eyes had been steady as I spoke but they now lost focus, as if she were peering within herself rather than facing me. When did speak, her voice seemed to come from a distance, like what one hears in a thriller movie before the horror appears.

"There's a violence to sex. I wondered if your boyfriend likes hurting you and if you enjoy being hurt" she said, with the same odd smile.

"Mormons are uptight about teens having sex and we haven't sex yet. But if we did, and he deliberately hurt me, I'd hurt him badly and wouldn't see him again," I replied, in as calm a tone as I could muster.

Her question angered me for men had hurt me in the past. The past is a ghost that haunts and never abandons us.

Kimberly looked pleased after I spoke. She took my hand and held it.

"*Yes, yes,*" she whispered, almost breathing these words.

Margaret at Barnard/Part Two: Deliverance

We didn't speak anymore during lunch.

Chapter 19

While Kimberly was an interesting puzzle, I had other things going on in my life too. When deciding what classes to take, I had assumed that the Calculus class would require most of my time and that I would breeze through the others: Ethics and Values, Social Analysis, and Introduction to Psychology.

But it turned out that vast readings were demanded in these classes and that I found the math class easiest. The class's tutoring sessions were great and Kimberly clearly explained whatever difficulties remained. Despite her social problems, she could be a great math teacher, I thought.

Kimberly attracted attention. Jealous girls made snide remarks about her clothes and boys wanted inside them. She used me as a buffer against both sexes, clinging to me as if we were twinned. I often found her sitting on a roll-up red yoga mat outside my door, awaiting my return.

I didn't mind for I found her touching. Kimberly had a childlike mind within a grown woman's elegance, as if some early experience had both prematurely stunted and aged her.

Boys sensed her sex appeal and I sensed that she wasn't a virgin but that was where these conclusions remained. Kimberly hadn't spoken further of her life so I knew nothing more about her. She tuned out when I spoke of my family and it became a forbidden subject when we met.

The gatherings that we attended were Kimberly's, and weren't the typical social. These were informal meetings of Columbia University computer science students. They met every Thursday evening for what they but few others would consider a party. There, each presented their latest computer project to exclamations of encouragement and joy.

Kimberly and I were the only girls present. Here, she starred, not because of her beauty but for her creativity. She seemed comfortable there, possibly because the boys appeared to have little interest in dating. None ever "came on" to her or to me.

Apart from this "socializing," we did the usual. We studied in the library, ate in the Dining Hall, and watched movies and more movies.

My older sister, Melody, had attended New York University's Film School. She originally intended to become a movie scholar and critic but, at my father's suggestion, had applied to law school. Her new career goal was entertainment law. Using this skill, she could meet the film industry's movers and shakers.

Thanks to her influence, I had seen many movie classics and enjoyed introducing others to them. This would be a "safe" activity for Kimberly, I thought. While seated in a dark movie house, she could avoid the stress that dealing with people aroused for her.

The theater that we most often attended was the small Paris Theatre on West 58th Street. It is the longest continually operating art cinema in the United States.

When I learned that Alfred Hitchcock's renowned movie, *Psycho,* would be shown, I excitedly exclaimed to Kimberly, "We *must* see it! You'll love it."

I had loved it and was sure that she would too. But the love that she discovered that night had nothing to do with the movie.

Chapter 20

Psycho is an ancient black-and-white movie. It is in the genre of horror films like *Scream* though there had been earlier ones: *Dracula,* and *Frankenstein.*

Psycho goes like this. Marion meets with Sam, her out-of-town lover. They want to marry but don't have enough money since Sam owes money and has alimony payments.

While working as a secretary at a real estate office, Marion has the opportunity to steal $40,000 in cash. When her boss leaves for the weekend, she takes the money and leaves town. She hopes to vanish and live happily ever after with Sam. On her second night on the run, a rainstorm pops up. Unable to see clearly, she stops at the lighted sign of the Bates Motel and that's where it happens.

I'll tell you only one more thing, to not to spoil your enjoyment if you decide to see *Psycho*: the bathroom scene. Marion is taking a shower when a knife repeatedly slashes her. Unlike present thrillers, nothing gory is shown but the sight of the blood dripping down the drain is enough.

While awaiting the start of the movie, Kimberly and I shared popcorn and Hershey Chocolate Kisses. This happy moment reminded me of my childhood in Greenwich, during the years before my father became ill. Kimberly faced the aisle in the half-lit theater.

Her hand had just reached into the bag of popcorn on my lap when it suddenly froze. I didn't initially notice since I had been busily eating Kisses and texting Randy. When I looked up, her upset was obvious. Her face was twisted with fear and her fist lay clenched in the bag.

She stared toward a small group of people that was walking down the aisle. They seated themselves in the second and third rows, center stage. A tall caped man in their midst seemed to hold sway. He spoke energetically to them.

Kimberly gripped my hand and moved her head until her mouth lay against my ear.

"We must leave as soon as the movie comes on. The Devil is here," she whispered.

Chapter 21

Though Kimberly's demand was weird, I didn't hesitate and simply nodded. I was used to her odd behavior, and knew fear when I heard it. The word "devil" can mean many things but none of them is good.

Was the tall man in the theater ("the devil") truly evil and known to Kimberly? Or had his caped appearance merely symbolized all of her fears like in a nightmare? I was never to learn.

It had been a special showing of the movie so there were no teasers of upcoming films. After the usual screen request to turn off cell phones and refrain from talking, *Psycho* began.

When viewers' eyes were glued to the screen, as Marion left the real estate office with the stolen cash, we rose quietly and slipped from the theater.

Once outside, Kimberly again gripped my hand. She pulled me down the street, walking at an almost running pace. Upon turning the corner at Sixth Avenue, she crashed into a man who was standing there.

He gripped her shoulders to keep her from falling. She tried to speak but couldn't, being unable to excuse herself and walk on like a normal person. Collisions like this aren't unusual on the crowded Manhattan streets.

Every breath seemed to have become an effort for Kimberly. The sight of "the Devil," and the sudden appearance of this stranger, had caused her system to shut down. She must have felt terrified, and very alone.

But the stranger had sensed her feeling of helplessness since this was part of his job. He was in his mid-twenties, casually dressed in a sport shirt, jeans, and sport jacket. Kimberly and I are tall but he was taller, about six foot four inches. He towered over us.

"I'm a police officer. Is something wrong? Can I help?" he asked, in a calming tone.

Then, as if being aware that his clothes disputed his words, he withdrew a wallet from his jacket and flipped it open it. Within, lay a badge and identity card.

I quickly gave a logical even if unlikely explanation. I feared that, being hysterical, Kimberly would babble something that would cause her to be taken to a mental hospital for evaluation. That's what most police officers would do when coming across a person who frantically declares that they are fleeing "the devil."

"We were watching an old movie, *Psycho*, at the theatre around the corner. My friend panicked," I said.

"Was it during the shower scene?" the policeman asked, with a smile.

"Exactly," I replied, returning his smile.

Kimberly had stopped hyperventilating but still clung to the policeman. He made no move to disengage while speaking to her.

"It's human nature. You suffer a crisis and are afraid. Then it passes and you're OK," he said softly.

Kimberly looked up and nodded. As they stared into each other's eyes, I sensed the beginning of a love affair. An auto horn sounded from close by.

"That's my partner," the policeman explained, sheepishly.

He took a card from his pocket and handed it to her.

"My card has my cell number on it. Call me if you're frightened again, or need a friendly voice," he said.

What happened next astonished me and seemed to surprise him.

"Thank you," Kimberly said, in a husky voice.

Then she hugged him, kissed his cheek, opened her jacket, and slipped the card beneath her bra.

And I was going to teach her about men! We had better leave before something else happens, I thought. I told the policeman our names.

"We're students at Barnard, in the Brooks Hall dorm. We have to get back but feel free to visit," I said, trying to be helpful to both.

The policeman nodded, and looked thoughtful.

I grabbed Kimberly's arm and hustled us away. When I looked back at the policeman, he wasn't moving though his partner's car horn blared.

Kimberly had only murmured "devil" when I asked what was going on so I stopped asking. Her anxiety didn't end when we reached the subway platform. There, she continually scanned the waiting travelers. Her usual hang-dog expression was gone. Now she was watchful and wary.

I didn't understand what had happened that night but was sure of one thing: that Kimberly would see the policeman again.

Upon awakening the next morning, I wondered if Kimberly regretted that I had seen how she handled the policeman's card. Though being far from naïve, I shivered when remembering the scene.

Chapter 22

Kimberly's seductive behavior with the policeman was my second thought upon awakening. This came after staring at the blood-red carpet stain, which had become my daily preoccupation. Could this be otherwise for anyone living in my room?

How can two students die at a Barnard College dormitory without arousing publicity? I wondered. While school officials would want to keep this matter quiet, this is not easily done in today's world of cellphone video.

But when I casually raised this event with other students, they seemed not to know of it. Why not? Ambulances and police would have created enough commotion to be heard even within the thick, hundred-year-old walls of Brooks Hall.

Rumors should have been widespread amongst last year's students, most of whom had returned. Decent, reasonably priced housing is not easily obtained in crowded Manhattan.

These thoughts became interrupted by the "crisis" texts that had been sent by my fifteen-year-old sister, Melanie. The last was dated 11:46PM on the previous day. I had gone to sleep an hour earlier and shut off my phone.

I instantly phoned her to leave a message, expecting that she would be at school. Even if her crises weren't as big as mine, they deserved a fast response. I was nineteen and understood other teenagers.

I had just made a mental note to phone her again when she picked up on the third ring, sounding sleepy. It was a little after eight. Why wasn't she at school? I wondered, and worry set in. Was she ill? Had our father's Lyme disease relapsed and our mother didn't want to worry me?

"What?" she asked angrily.

"I'm sorry, it sounds like I woke you. I turned off my phone last night and just got your text," I explained.

"I texted you four times!" she blasted at me.

Sisterly anger and logical thinking don't often go together.

"Yes, I know and I'm sorry. What's up?"

"What's up? What's up?" Melanie asked, in only a slightly lower tone.

She's giving me great practice at being a mother, I thought.

"Yes, I'm sorry. What's up?" I repeated.

There was silence while Melanie calmed herself.

"Douglas, is up."

"Yes?" I asked.

Douglas is the teenage son of a Greenwich neighbor. Our families had often socialized though less in recent years. People and their interests change.

"Well, I do like him but he wants to be more than friends and I don't like him *that* way. How can I get him to back off without ruining our friendship?"

This *is* a problem. I thought for several moments.

"OK," I began slowly. "Tell him that he needs to give you space, and show him what you're thinking. Flirt with someone when he's around but not in a mean way. He'll back off when he realizes that being pushy isn't working. And if he backs off on his own, he'll feel comfortable staying friends with you."

There was silence while my advice sank in.

"Oh, you're the *greatest*," Melanie gushed.

"I love you too but why aren't you at school?" I asked, as my anxiety returned.

"There's teacher training this morning. School starts at 12:00," she said, before abruptly hanging up.

Melanie's "crisis" was over, and she still loved me.

Chapter 23

Kimberly was her usual self that morning. It was as if the odd events of the previous evening had never occurred. I was curious about them but didn't ask. "Let a person tell their story when they're ready," my lawyer-father had advised, and I sensed that Kimberly wasn't ready. Besides, asking Kimberly a direct question was a losing proposition. She would tell you what was on her mind, not explain what was on your's.

Kimberly's concern that morning was her computer science instructor. As I understood her, he was being *too* friendly. He hovered around her work, invaded her personal space, and invited her to visit his office for individual help–which she very definitely didn't need.

I immediately got the picture: he wanted *her* help for an extracurricular activity. Kimberly didn't know what to do.

"While explaining something, he put his arm about me and I didn't know what to do," she said.

Distress had caused her to speak more clearly than she usually did.

I considered what Kimberly might do. She could complain to the administration but her teacher would undoubtedly say that his behavior had been misinterpreted. He had merely tried to support a student who had a problem communicating. The teacher would be praised and Kimberly would be shunned by the other faculty.

Another possibility was for Kimberly to say, "Please, I don't like to be touched," Or she could slug him and take her chance in court. Each of these ideas had drawbacks. I had a brainstorm when seeing that Kimberly's fingers were bare.

"Wear an engagement ring and spread the word that your fiancée is a cop," I suggested.

"Huh?"

"We'll buy you a ring after breakfast," I said.

That's what we did. The ring was gold color with a phony diamond and cost $8.99 in a 106th Street bodega.

While the ring solved that problem, it created a new one when the real policeman that we had met came calling.

I was in Kimberly's room when we learned from the front desk that he had arrived.

"Did you phone him?" I asked.

Kimberly shook her head.

"Do you like him?" I asked.

This might seem a ridiculous question to ask of a girl who had behaved seductively but Kimberly wasn't an ordinary girl. She gave me a blank look and I gave up.

"OK, take off the ring and invite him up," I said.

This she understood, and did.

Chapter 24

Edward was the policeman's name and he was as handsome as when we had met. Now, his clothes were just as casual but smarter: cashmere shirt jacket, black jeans, and Italian lace-ups. He carried a small, obviously expensive leather briefcase. I wondered if it held his gun, and also if he had family money. He couldn't afford what he wore on a policeman's salary.

I smiled, he smiled, and I left. I know when I'm not wanted. My friends do the same when Randy comes calling.

"I'll be back at noon. We have a wedding to attend," I said.

Kimberly looked puzzled before nodding agreement. She's forgotten that Missy's wedding is at City Hall at 1PM, I told myself.

I spent the next two hours doing the readings for three of my classes. I would save the calculus assignment for later, when Kimberly was available to ask questions.

At 11:30 I changed out of shirt and jeans and put on my standard church-going dress. It would be acceptable at a wedding though not getting a glance compared to what I expected Kimberly to wear.

I knocked on Kimberly's door at noon. Edward was gone and I could see that they hadn't wasted time talking. Kimberly was dressed, if you could call it that, in a negligee so sheer that her pubic hair was visible in the sunlight streaming into the room. Still, her makeup was already on: violet lips, brows, and nails.

"The wedding is in an hour. We have to go!" I said, with a tinge of annoyance.

My tone got through to her.

"Ready in 10," she said.

"I'll wait downstairs."

I left without waiting for a response.

I'm going in exactly fifteen minutes, with her or alone, I vowed to myself. Kimberly strode off the elevator twelve minutes later.

Her dress was light gray with piped silver detailing. It had cap sleeves, a V-neckline, and a structured silhouette that accentuated her hourglass figure. Her shoes were metallic color, crafted in clear plastic, with a sharp pointed toe and towering stiletto heel. Her clutch had a gold glitter finish, chain strap, and printed logo ("JIMMY CHOO").

Her ring wasn't our $8.99 purchase. This one had an intricate pattern and was set with diamonds.

No one will pay attention to the bride, I told myself, but my only comment was, "Ready?"

Chapter 25

After leaving Brooks Hall, I stopped at the corner to hail a taxi but Kimberly stopped me.

"It'll be faster by subway. I've been there," she said, leading us in the direction of the entrance to the subway at 116th Street.

I wondered why she had been so far downtown but the rush of a wedding day wasn't the time to ask. Kimberly was turning out to be very different than I had believed her to be. Apparently, her social problems didn't interfere with her ability to travel, or to attract men.

Had I lacked a boyfriend, my first date with a man would have involved going for a walk or seeing a movie, not an invitation to bed. But people usually underestimate others until they know them well, I reassured myself.

We took the 7th Avenue Subway to Times Square, changed to the Shuttle going across 42nd Street, and then took the Lexington Avenue Subway south to the City Hall station. We got there five minutes late but it didn't matter. When you think of a wedding you picture one couple. Here were at least thirty couples, dressed in a variety of costumes.

Missy and Artur were in the middle of the pack. They were surrounded by Missy's brothers, Artur's parents, and Charlotte and her son, Tristan, with whom Missy was living.

I indicated toward Kimberly, who stood beside me.

"This is Kimberly, my class mate," I said.

The adults smiled and Kimberly tried to smile but didn't quite make it. Like I said, she has problems.

We all went into the building and Artur took a ticket from a kiosk inside the Manhattan marriage bureau. The ticket number was D462. We waited to be served at New York City's deli of matrimony.

Those who had arrived earliest were seated on a long couch, holding hands until they were called. When our ticket number was announced, we entered the clerk's office.

Missy was tearful throughout the ninety-second ceremony. When it was over, she and Artur kissed passionately until being reminded that other couples were waiting. Upon leaving the building, we crossed Worth Street into the small park to collect ourselves.

Many couples stood in the park. All were friendly, having shared the same rite. Being together seemed to reduce their tension by proving that they had not done something unique.

The wedding ceremony cost $25 and our spontaneous park celebration didn't cost much more: $30 for a fake bouquet and $5 for each paper plate of syrup-soaked pancakes. The real party would be later, at a yacht rented by Artur's father. It would be attended by many of his diplomat colleagues. To get there, we traveled by taxi.

Chapter 26

The yacht was something from another century with its twenties style teak decks and mahogany trim. A glassed-in observatory enclosed cushioned seating and conversation-friendly tables.

Much of the buffet-style food was edible for vegetarians: fruits, vegetables with dips, and pasta. There were lobster tails, chicken, and steak for the others. Something for everyone, I thought.

For dessert there was ice cream, brownies and, of course, wedding cake. There was a bar for those who weren't hungry.

After introductions and well-wishing, the revelers separated into groups separated by age. Missy, her brothers, Artur, Kimberly and I munched and gazed at the skyline. Charlotte spoke with the guests that had been invited by Ivan, Artur's father, and Tristan trailed beside her.

Kimberly was silent and ate little, possibly feeling stuffed by her earlier love-making. Or was she? I wondered. I didn't know. Her seductive behavior upon first meeting Edward had been so expert that she might have had a dozen lovers before him. And maybe another that day, I thought, as I noticed hungry male eyes undressing her.

The conversation noise rose and I left the observatory to lean at the railing. Emotion overcame me as I stared at the rebuilt World Trade Center towers. I had seen pictures of their destruction: ashen-covered workers, and the posted "missing" photos of those who were never to be found. A soft voice interrupted my troubled reverie.

"Another pointless human tragedy," the man said, reading my thoughts.

"I knew your father," he added, a moment later.

I turned toward him but didn't immediately reply. It took a moment for me to regain my bearings.

While having an adoptive father in Greenwich, two other men also consider me their daughter. One lives in London and the other lives in Berlin.

My biological mother had affairs with both men around the time that I was conceived, and the truth of my parentage isn't known. A DNA test would provide the answer but it will never be done. The findings would disrupt several lives. Best to let sleeping dogs lay, as they say, or perhaps to "let sleeping dogs lie," to make another of my awful puns.

My London father is a retired British spy. He co-manages a security business with my other possible father who is a retired Russian general. Admittedly, this sounds confused but it does work. Both men respect each other and I love them both.

With this complication in the back of my mind I made my usual safe reaction: "Hmm." I expected to quickly figure out which of my fathers this stranger referred to.

"Yes, we were comrades in Afghanistan. He saved my life."

Chapter 27

"I should have said that I *know* your father since *knew* implies that he is dead. Even after living here many years, I still have problems with English grammar," the man said.

"I understood what you meant," I replied.

But I still didn't know which of my fathers he referred to. My English father had been stationed in Southeast Asia and my Russian father, who is thirty years older, had fought in Afghanistan during the Russian invasion. Now, both ignored politics.

Things became clear when this man introduced himself. Piotr was Russia's Consul General in Manhattan. He could only be speaking of Vladimir, my Russian father.

"Has he spoken of me?" Piotr asked.

"No, he doesn't speak of his military days. He said that he prefers to speak of the future," I replied.

"Very wise, for those of us who can forget," Piotr said.

He motioned toward two chairs on the deck. There, he told me his story.

"Four of us, including your father, were moving toward an Afghan village for what was supposed to be a candid meeting with a group of elders. Dozens of enemy fighters attacked us and two of our soldiers were killed, I was wounded, only half-conscious, and your father's neck was bleeding. But he carried me up the hill and kept the enemy away until our helicopters arrived. He is a great man," Piotr said.

He leaned forward and kissed my hand. The Russians are an emotional people. After rising from his seat, he handed me a business card.

"If I can ever be of service," he said softly, before leaving.

I had once asked Vladimir about the scar on his neck but he brushed off my question.

I returned to the observation deck as the yacht moved toward port. Kimberly stood close beside a tall man. He was speaking intently and I feared the worst. I went near and addressed Kimberly.

"We're all going to Constance's apartment. Are you coming?" I asked Kimberly, before remarking to the man, "We're students."

I hoped for him to consider Kimberly too young despite her grown-up appearance.

Upon hearing my words, Kimberly seemed to catch herself, as if she were coming out of a reverie. She turned toward me, nodded, and left the man without saying a word. Having two new lovers in one day might be too much for even Kimberly's superior mind to digest.

Chapter 28

Travelling by taxi to Charlotte's apartment took longer than going from City Hall to the yacht. She lives in what was historically called the *good area* of Central Park West. In the past, crime increased dramatically north of 96th Street. But this changed after recent gentrification and apartments and brownstones there now sell for astronomical prices.

Charlotte and her son, Tristan, live in a three-bedroom apartment in a building with a doorman. While a rarity outside Manhattan, his presence is considered important for safety. But considering their low wage, the belief that any doorman would risk their life to protect a tenant seems laughable. Still, his presence, the building's video surveillance system, and the three locks on Charlotte's door permit her to feel safe.

Missy and I laid out a light spread of cheese, crackers, water, and juice, and that was enough. No one was hungry after the pancakes in the park and the buffet on the yacht. We just wanted to sit around and talk.

I had worried about Kimberly since socializing isn't her strength but things turned out well. Tristan is, literally, a genius, and he sensed a kindred element in Kimberly. He invited her to see his Raspberry Pi computer creations and they spent the rest of the afternoon in his room.

This had initially made me nervous considering Kimberly's weirdness so I discreetly checked on them, using the excuse of offering juice and ice cream. They sat on the floor which was strewn with small parts and printed instructions. Kimberly was speaking slowly and Tristan was engrossed. Just two geniuses together.

Kimberly just made another male conquest and without taking off her clothes, I told myself. Then I felt guilty, concluding that this thought reflected too much jealousy and too little kindness.

When I returned to the living room, all were watching Missy lift the lid off a large white box that contained Charlotte's wedding present. We all laughed at what was inside. It was a typical baby shower present, and practical too: a "diaper cake."

This consists of diapers rolled into the shape of a cake with a small stuffed animal on top, to give an expectant mother a moment of merriment before the pain of childbirth. It takes time to make but you can buy them at Toys R Us. This one was 3-Tier with pink mums and pink and chocolate dots.

Then something occurred to me. Charlotte is an OB-GYN, on the staff of both Lenox Hill Hospital and Columbia University Medical School. Being associated with the University, she would be the ideal person to ask, I thought. Which is what I did when there was a pause in the conversation.

"Charlotte, do you know what two students died from in the Brooks Hall dormitory last term?" I asked.

My question got everyone's attention.

Chapter 29

Everyone became silent and stared at me. Charlotte put down her glass.

"*Two* students died? I never heard about it," she said slowly.

"I didn't either but I now live in the room where it happened. Kimberly calls it *the death chamber*," I said, and the silence returned.

"*The death chamber*," Ivan mused.

Missy looked upset. Death is the worst topic to raise in the presence of a pregnant woman but I felt that I had no choice. The issue preyed on my mind.

"What do the others at Brooks say about it?" Ivan asked.

"Nothing, and it's not because I haven't asked. If people die in a dorm there *must be* commotion from the police and Emergency Medical Services doing their job but none of the students from last term seems to know anything. Some might, but none are saying. Dead bodies aren't a favored topic of conversation," I said.

"How did you find out?" Ivan asked.

"Kimberly told me when she came to my room to introduce herself," I replied.

"What else did she say?" Ivan asked.

I didn't want to tell that Kimberly had entered my room uninvited after imagining an odd odor. Or that she had said, "I call it the death chamber because that's where I found their bodies." Learning this would have made them consider her weird, and she had a big enough problem socializing.

Unfortunately, I then blurted something else that she had said that morning. "When I pointed to the blood-red stain on the carpet, Kimberly said that the deaths weren't accidental but that I needn't worry."

Kimberly and Tristan chose that moment to return. He was a growing boy and hungry. To end that topic of conversation, I fled to the kitchen with him. There, I very slowly made peanut butter and jelly sandwiches. Upon our return to the living room, I found the others looking intently at Kimberly and feared what she had said. It didn't take long for me to learn.

"Kimberly has interesting ideas. We think that you should hear them," Ivan said.

Chapter 30

Tristan seated himself on the sofa beside Kimberly and I sat on a club chair opposite them. I waited for her to expand on Ivan's statement but she remained silent, looking like an exquisitely dressed runway model.

Though I sensed what was happening, I didn't understand it. Kimberly was turning out to be even more complex than I had assumed. Her emotional limitations weren't black and white. In some arenas and with some people she related normally while in others she froze. Now, she sat frozen.

Charlotte is a sensitive doctor. Recognizing Kimberly's awkwardness, Charlotte helped by repeating what Kimberly had said.

"Rumors of two student deaths would certainly spread immediately so either it never happened or there are sound reasons why the news is being kept silent.

"But Kimberly said that she saw the bodies–and I believe her–so there is no doubt that the deaths occurred. What happened was real and not a nightmare that she's been carrying around.

"The death of any young person is unexpected and all are investigated. Yet Kimberly wasn't questioned or even offered the crisis counseling that one would expect for a student who had experienced such a traumatic event.

"Margaret said that there was no fuss in the dormitory so the whole thing must have been cleared quietly by the police and the EMS. But they wouldn't do this on their own so college and government officials must be involved. Why? We don't know.

"One possibility is that the students were believed to have been infected with a deadly disease. Yet this couldn't be known without an autopsy and lengthy lab work and why would it be kept secret?

"Infections happen everywhere. The college wouldn't be held accountable unless it was something like Legionnaires Disease caused by the Brooks Hall water tower being contaminated. But this test also takes time and the officials reacted immediately.

"Based on these factors, Kimberly concluded that the students' deaths involved their activities and are unrelated to you, that the cause of their deaths is known and not communicable, and that their parents were informed and wanted everything kept secret.

"Ask yourself, if you suddenly died, wouldn't your parents storm the school come hell or high water?" Charlotte concluded.

"Your room is safe, Margaret. You are safe," Ivan agreed.

His eyes softened with understanding as they turned from me to Kimberly. She looked up, sensing that she was being studied. Her eyes looked wary and very old.

Ivan and Kimberly had never met before that day but they seemed to recognize each other as alike. This, though she was a college student and he was a far older diplomat. He was also a trained killer.

Chapter 31

The party broke up after another hour. We could have taken the bus or subway to the dorm but Kimberly wanted to walk. I love to walk and readily agreed. I needed time to think and hoped that Kimberly was in the mood to provide answers though not about her sexual behavior.

I regard a person's sex life as being *their* business and never ask about it. If a girl recounts details of her glorious night, I smile but say nothing. For me, talking about sex holds as much interest as talking about Christmas.

Plus, I've always felt that "being promiscuous" refers to anyone who has more sex than you. Which was just about every college student since I was still a virgin. Edward might have been Kimberly's first lover or her tenth. So be it.

Ivan's knowing glance at Kimberly had reminded me of how little I knew about her, not even whether she had brothers or sisters. Walking the one-and-one-half miles back to the dorm would give me the opportunity to find out.

From the moment that we left the apartment house, Kimberly had been picking up her usual stares. She was unmindful of this and I understood. Beautiful women get them all the time. It's simply another part of who they are, like having two arms and two legs.

We turned left at the corner of 95th Street and Central Park West. From there we would walk toward Broadway and then north toward Brooks Hall, a mile away.

I began my investigation with the most stress-free question that I could think of.

"Where does your family live?" I asked.

Kimberly looked up but didn't reply. I repeated my question half-way down the block.

"Do they live in the United States now?" I asked, remembering Brazil's flag on her wall.

"In that house," Kimberly said, pointing to a four-story brownstone in the middle of the block.

Now, many people live in America live in houses. Even my low-income family does though ours is owned by an old family trust. But to live in a private house on the Upper West Side of Manhattan requires *serious* wealth. Their prices start in the millions of dollars but I wasn't about to ask Kimberly that. I asked something else.

"Do you think they would like to see us?"

Chapter 32

I was more interested in meeting Kimberly's mother than with whether she wanted to see us but I didn't say that. I relied on the inertia of habit, having often suggested going to a new friend's home. I like to know about who I'm becoming involved with.

Some Barnard girls hated their parents and never went home. For all I knew, Kimberly might be one of them.

She didn't reply. Instead, she led us up the steps of the house, removed a keyring from her purse, and opened the door onto a tomblike silence. This door also had three locks. That seemed the minimum for the Manhattan homes that I had visited.

When I return home, I automatically call out to let people know that I've arrived. Kimberly didn't say anything and I heard nothing in the house. Well, family customs differ, I told myself.

But apparently the house wasn't empty since I heard a sound from far down the hall. Moments later, a middle-aged woman in a white maid's dress came into view. She jumped in fright upon seeing us before a broad smile creased her face. She walked toward us and opened her arms. Kimberly allowed herself to be embraced though her arms remained at her side.

"Kimmie, it's so good to see you. Julia asks for you all the time," the woman said.

She looked toward me and I introduced myself.

"I'm Margaret, a student at Barnard. I live in the same dorm as Kimberly," I said, extending my hand.

"I'm Gabriela, Kimberly's nursemaid when she was a child. Now, I help out. I'm pleased to meet you," she said, with a welcoming smile.

"Will you be staying for dinner?" she asked Kimberly.

Kimberly nodded agreement without expression though I sensed that she would like to be anywhere else. But she also seemed to recognize that Gabriela wouldn't take "no" for an answer.

"Oh, that's wonderful. I'll make your's and Julia's favorites: moqueca and brigadeiros," Gabriela gushed, as if wanting her excessively animated expression to substitute for Kimberly's blankness.

"Moqueca is a fish stew and brigadeiros is a chocolate truffle," Gabriela explained.

That's good information but I'm more interested in who Julia is, I thought. Which is what I asked Kimberly as soon as Gabriela had returned to the kitchen.

"Who's Julia?"

Kimberly looked annoyed by my question and I didn't think that she would answer but after several moments she did.

"She's my daughter," she said, with the same blank face that I had seen so often.

Chapter 33

I have good self-control and didn't respond quickly to Kimberly's astonishing fact: that a girl who I had initially concluded was a social misfit and a virgin was a mother. Wow! I thought, as I tried to think of something common-sense to say. Failing this, I asked, "When is dinner?"

Kimberly seemed less tense as she replied to this question.

"It's always at six."

"Can I see your room?" I asked.

This was another "safe" question and Kimberly nodded.

Though the house was decorated in the Victorian style, sound-insulating windows must have been installed since the City's pervasive traffic noise was absent. Its interior reminded me of the homes that I had seen during my summer in London.

When I remarked on this, Kimberly provided another fact in her longest statement thus far: "My mother's ancestors were English. She patterned our house after theirs. It's the *Downton Abbey* look."

The father of my best friend, Erika, is a multi-billionaire. Their huge house in Greenwich was furnished by a famed decorator in the modern style. It has all the toys and luxurious fixtures that the super-wealthy expect but their furniture was nothing like this.

These furnishings were massive and of heavily sculptured wood. A club chair sat on a pedestal, enclosed by a seven-foot high chest containing a bar with stools. Wood ceiling beams were exposed and old-fashioned lighting fixtures hung from the walls.

Kimberly's bedroom was just as elaborate with one-of-a-kind design touches on the ceiling and carpeting. Her twin-size bed had a large headboard and footboard. There was an antique-inspired, multi-shelved, multi-drawer armoire with fanciful scenes painted on its side that served double duty as a desk. Much of the furniture, if not original, could pass for antique.

If my family lived so close to campus, I certainly wouldn't be living in Brooks Hall, I thought. But Kimberly had already shut down. I had asked too many questions and now wasn't the time for another. So I merely said, "It's a beautiful home. If I lived here, I would never want to leave it."

Kimberly didn't speak. Instead, as we sat on elegant chairs in her bedroom, she began crying.

Chapter 34

A person usually has only one feature that can't go unnoticed. With Kimberly, it was her eyes. Even with her frozen, blank face, her eyes revealed what she felt and I read long, deep sadness. Keeping a smile on Kimberly's face would be an all-consuming task and I wondered if any man would ever take it on.

I wanted to help her but knew that asking the obvious questions wasn't the way. She would tell me everything when she was ready, and I would be there for her. So, after she composed herself, I said, "I've known pain too," and left it at that.

I looked about the room until finding a non-threatening item to comment on. There were so many that it was hard to choose the best. Should I ask about the painting of a Victorian lady above her bed, the beaded-handled, flower and dog printed, antique handbag hanging from her bed's footboard, or the framed vintage Valentine's Day card on her night table ("On you my soul always joyed to dwell, all seemed to fade before affection's spell."). I chose the latter.

"It's a lovely card. Where did you find it?" I asked, pointing to it.

"It was a present," she said, briefly.

Her tone told me that she didn't want to talk about anything.

"I need a nap," Kimberly said, getting up from the chair.

"I've never seen a house so completely Victorian. Is it all right if I look around?" I asked.

Kimberly nodded, and I left as she was taking off her shoes. Dinner wouldn't be for another hour and in that time I could see a lot. But I didn't feel comfortable looking around with only her permission. I felt that I should inform Gabriela, which would give me the opportunity to question her. Gabriela was talkative and, having been her Kimberly's nursemaid, knew of her past.

How old was Kimberly's daughter? Who was the child's father? Why wasn't Kimberly living in this gorgeous house rather than our bleak dorm? But rather than ask these questions directly, I hoped to learn these answers by chance.

Though lacking Kimberly's intellect, I knew that I had better instincts. Despite the obvious wealth, something was very wrong in this family and the presence of a teenage mother was the least of it. My other friends, Hillary and Missy, were also teenage mothers and they behaved nothing like Kimberly.

Though feeling sad for Kimberly I also warned myself that it can be hard to tell those situations where it is best to use your heart from those where it is best to use your head.

Chapter 35

After leaving Kimberly, I walked slowly down the corridor. Her bedroom was on the third floor of a four-story building. It had many rooms and I wondered at the size of her family. The presence of a maid in wealthy families is common but the existence of Kimberly's daughter had been a shock. What others await me? I wondered.

I had never been in a house that was so *decorated*. Though Erika's home had been furnished by an interior designer, it possessed a lived-in quality that was absent here.

This house had elegance. Wherever one looked, a special piece caught the eye. The wallpaper's shimmering inks gave a dramatic glow to the walls. In the hallway, beneath antique globes, lay heavily carved tables containing seashell trinket boxes and Limoge porcelain vases. The scent from lavender-filled sachets intoxicated me as I walked toward the stairs.

The silence of the house was beginning to unnerve me. Once, when a child and alone in my house, I had frantically run from my room down the stairs and outside, fearing the monster that followed. It did exist, but only in my mind.

I stood at the top of the stairs and listened. A noise came from above, on the top floor. I considered investigating but, despite what my mother says, I'm cautious and particularly when confronting the unknown. So I walked downstairs to speak with Gabriela and to learn more.

Gabriela was busily engaged in the kitchen, preparing the evening meal. Her face brightened at my approach.

"Kimberly is taking a nap. I'm a lousy cook but I can help with the washing up," I said.

I was being honest and not modest. A melted cheese sandwich is about my limit of my cooking ability.

"Oh, I'm sure that's not true. Put on an apron," was Gabriela's tactful reply.

I did, and stood watching. Gabriela put fish, diced tomatoes, onions, rice, and coriander into a large pot. Annatto seeds are added to give a natural red coloring to the moqueca, a fish stew, she explained.

"You can help with the brigadeiros," she said.

Brigadeiros–chocolate truffles–are made by simmering condensed milk with cocoa power, then whisking the mixture in butter and shaping it into balls that are rolled in chocolate sprinkles. After the shaping and rolling, I did the tasting. This sweet would give anyone a sugar high.

"Taste the quindim. It's made of just sugar, coconut, and eggs," Gabriela said, handing me a small, yellow cupcake on a plate.

With every bite, I felt weight adding to my hips.

"Everything is delicious!" I exclaimed, with total honesty.

"*Hello,*" a voice drawled from the doorway.

The woman's accent seemed neither English nor American but a combination of both. Though a stranger, I instantly knew who the child beside her was.

Chapter 36

Every local newspaper runs mother/daughter photo contests of girls who bear a striking resemblance to their parent. On a scale of one to ten, Kimberly and Julia would be a ten.

I was so taken by their similarity that I stood tongue-tied until Gabriella introduced me to the woman.

"Margaret is Kimberly's friend from Barnard. They're staying for dinner," she said, to relieve the awkward silence.

The woman beamed a radiant smile, walked closer, and extended her hand.

"I'm Elizabeth, Kimberly's mother, and Julia is her sister. We're very pleased to have you and hope that you'll come often," she said.

I again became tongue-tied but now it was by what I had just heard. Elizabeth had described Julia as being Kimberly's sister. Is Julia her sister or her daughter? I asked myself. Could I have been confused by what Kimberly said? But this couldn't be since there are no two ways to interpret the statement, 'She's my daughter.'"

I held my tongue, fearing the minefield that asking questions could arouse.

"Thank you, Mrs. Rosilias" I said.

"We're not formal here. Call me Elizabeth. I'm sure that we'll become good friends. We'd best wash up for dinner. Come Julia," she said.

As they left the room, Julia turned back. Her look of interest seemed older than her years.

When their footsteps could no longer be heard, I asked Gabriella, "How old is Julia?"

"Nearly six, and she's such so smart! Everyone in the family is," Gabriella replied proudly.

As my fingers worked the ingredients of the brigadeiros, I did the simple math. Julia being nearly six-years-old must have made Kimberly twelve-years-old or barely thirteen when she conceived. This is one strange family indeed.

I left the kitchen a half-hour later and returned to Kimberly's bedroom. I knocked and opened the door. Kimberly awoke immediately with a start and I apologized.

"It's alright, I was half-awake," she said, stretching.

I sat on a club chair facing the bed.

"I met Elizabeth downstairs. Your mother is nice," I said, casually.

"She's *not* my mother and she's *not* nice," Kimberly said, angrily.

Chapter 37

I spoke, but only after regaining control of myself. Speaking impulsively is always a mistake, my father often tells his daughters. You are less likely to achieve your goal when you are not in control.

"Kimberly, you're a great girl. I'm proud to have you as my friend and hope that you consider me your friend. But what you've told me about your family is driving me crazy. You told me that Julia is your daughter. Elizabeth says that *she's* her mother and is your mother too, which you deny. Which is it?" I asked, calmly.

"I need a cigarette," Kimberly said, sitting up in bed, but not reaching for anything.

"Do you smoke?" I asked.

This was another surprise for I had never seen her smoke. What comes next? I wondered.

"I stopped when I became pregnant. Tobacco, not pot," she replied.

I waited silently through the silence that followed, sensing that a terrible story was coming.

"I *do* value you. You're my only friend," Kimberly began.

I waited, and remained silent.

"Julia *is* my child. She's been told that I'm her sister to avoid...*difficulties*. I'll tell her the truth when I'm ready to perform as her mother.

"Elizabeth is my step-mother. Both my parents are dead and she is my father's second wife. He died in a freak accident two months after their marriage. She was much younger than him. She may have been involved in his death."

Kimberly's story was shocking but anyone who reads the news knows that such things do happen, though almost never to anyone that they know.

"Why would she want him dead?" I asked.

"For his money. Statistically, it's the commonest reason for murders. But he tricked her. He was much smarter than her, smarter than any of us," Kimberly said.

"How so?" I asked.

"*Well*," Kimberly said, smiling and drawing out this word. "My father had told her that he made a new will after their marriage, inferring that *she* would be his principal beneficiary. He did make a new will but it designated me as the sole heir with my daughter being secondary."

One doesn't kill for a just a few dollars, I thought.

"Is much money involved?" I asked.

"My father owned media companies and mines and industries in Brazil. I'll come into my inheritance when I'm twenty-three. According to my lawyer, who is also my uncle and legal guardian and I trust absolutely, I am the ninth richest person in America," Kimberly said.

Kimberly's voice was firm and her gaze was steady. That was when I first sensed her core of strength. Unlike her emotions, it had not been burned away by her suffering.

Chapter 38

The large dining room had been created from two smaller rooms. It contained a fireplace, a large Georgian-style pedestal table, and more chairs than were needed for our group of six.

The newcomer to the table was Eric, a man of about thirty who described himself as being the live-in chauffeur/handyman. After noting his shared glances with Elizabeth, I wondered what other services he provided.

I was still wearing my Sunday church-going best. Kimberly had offered me anything of hers but I refused. Her clothes are expensive and I didn't want to accustom myself to an extravagance that I could never afford. Moreover, even if I become financially successful beyond my dreams, French and Italian imports will be at the bottom of my list of purchases.

Because black was the fashion that evening, my dark-colored dress fit in. Kimberly had changed into a black, long- sleeve, silk, midi dress by Valentino. It had a hidden back-zip closure, two-tone pleats, and swingy skirt.

Elizabeth wore an Oscar de la Renta black strapless silk gown. Julia's dress came from Oscar de la Renta too. It had a black top and red/multi-colored, floral print skirt.

Eric wore a black suit, a pale blue shirt, and a Guardsman tie. He was far more formally dressed than any of the household staff at Erika's estate but, as I said, his duties might be special.

Kimberly sat at the head of table, Elizabeth sat at the other end, and Eric sat facing Julia and Gabriela. I sat beside Julia, feeling that she needed support close by.

Meals at my home are a noisy affair with everyone telling a story or raising an opinion and getting an argument. Here, the conversation was minimal. Elizabeth praised Kimberly's dress, Kimberly praised Elizabeth's dress, and both applauded what Julia wore. No one spoke of their day's events or worries. The food was praised, the "exemplary" wine was passed from Eric to Elizabeth, and that was it. It was like a gathering of zombies.

Two summers before I had dined with an equally strange family in London. There, the father turned out to be a crazed killer. I hoped for better here.

I turned toward Julia. She would have the smallest agenda of anyone.

"What grade are you in?" I asked.

Elizabeth replied before Julia could say anything.

"Mrs. Frazier, her tutor, meets with Julia daily. The public schools in our neighborhood are..."

I nodded with understanding though, considering the wealth of the neighborhood, I would expect the local schools to be good. These parents would storm City Hall if they weren't.

After dessert, when Gabriela had left the room, Kimberly rose and placed her hand on Julia's arm.

"Come, we'll read together," she said, and I went with them.

I heard Elizabeth and Eric whisper as we left the room.

Chapter 39

It was evident that Julia spent much time in Kimberly's room for she immediately chose a book on the night table that I hadn't noticed. It was a chapter book, a children's edition of the classic novel, *Swiss Family Robinson*. Julia lay on the bed and Kimberly held her. They took turns reading one page at a time. It was how my mother had taught her children to read.

I sat nearby and watched. Julia was a good reader. As she became engaged, a child's normal animation arose. The story tells of a family that became shipwrecked on a desert island. Deserted by the crew, they must fend for themselves in a land of hidden dangers. This isn't much different from what Kimberly and her daughter seem to have experienced, I thought.

Julia grew sleepy, and pleaded for Kimberly to stay. Kimberly looked at me and I nodded. We had no reason to return to Brooks Hall that night.

"Julia has scary dreams and likes to sleep with me. You can use the bedroom beside this one," Kimberly said. "Take underwear from my dresser. There's a guest robe in the bathroom, and a laptop you can use on the desk. The Wi-Fi password is beside it," she added.

"It sounds like home to me," I replied, with a smile.

Julia snuggled and Kimberly kissed her forehead. As I searched through the dresser for underwear, I heard Kimberly croon an old English lullaby:

"Hush-a-bye, don't you cry.

Go to sleep little baby.

When you wake, you shall have,

All the pretty little horses."

I gathered the underwear and my bag and left the room, closing the door softly. Tears filled my eyes. They might have been for Kimberly and Julia, or for all the pain in the world.

My bedroom was styled like the rest of house: dark wood furniture accented with floral carvings, oval-back chairs, a marble-topped night table, intensely colored fabrics and wall coverings, and upholstery and drapes decorated with long fringes. The thick duvet and swamp of pillows caused me to imagine myself a princess.

I opened the laptop to check my Facebook page but decided not to. My mind felt foggy. There had been too many activities and surprises that day.

I stripped off my clothes and got into bed, not bothering to brush my teeth. Despite my exhaustion, I couldn't sleep for a question rattled in my mind. Who was Julia's father?

Chapter 40

We had breakfast before leaving in the morning. At the front door, Julia clung to Kimberly as if she were losing the brightness in her life, Kimberly's eyes became tearful, and I felt for both of them.

While waiting for the bus on Broadway, I suggested something that had occurred to me in the shower that morning. Despite its luxury, Julia needed breaks from her dark home. Charlotte's son, Tristan, and my sister, Claudine, were about her age. They could become her friends, I told Kimberly.

The bus had just arrived and I didn't get her response until after we were seated. Despite her blank face, I could almost see the gears working in her brain. For some reason, my commonplace idea was tricky.

"Charlotte is a doctor and lives close so I don't see a problem. My dad is a well-known lawyer and Greenwich is certainly safe. Traveling there is a short train ride that Julia would love," I wheedled.

"It's not those things. It's that I can't make this decision. I'll have to check with my uncle. He's our legal guardian. But it's a good idea. I'll call him today," she promised.

Julia told me of their conversation later.

"My uncle agreed that it would be a good idea but feels that he must first check the families. He said this shouldn't take more than a few days. He wanted to know if we would be visiting other homes in Greenwich."

I thought for a moment.

"Well, maybe my friend, Erika's. She has a young nephew living with them who is the right age. You can check her out too. I'll give you her address," I said.

"I'm sorry. My uncle is cautious because our family's past has been...*challenging*," Kimberly said, with a look of discomfort.

"That's OK. Any parent would want to know who their kids are meeting, and your wealth makes you a prime kidnapping target. Erika has the same problem. Having a bodyguard made her dating tough until she met her fiancée, Clarence. The bodyguard scared boys away," I said, in a sympathetic tone.

"I don't have that problem," Kimberly said.

No, you certainly don't, I thought, and was tactful enough not to say it.

Chapter 41

That evening, while Kimberly helped me with calculus, the issue of kidnapping returned. It had apparently been on Kimberly's mind while we worked on my homework.

"We left Brazil because of the crime. After the country's economic downturn, kidnapping became an almost accepted industry. The police deal with it using *death squads,* and the wealthy live in gated communities. Was Erika ever threatened?" she asked.

I considered how much to reveal since Kimberly had enough worries. But she deserved to know the facts and these had become public knowledge. Moreover, Kimberly would likely learn them if she and Erika became friends. So I told her.

"Erika's mother and sister were raped and murdered by a business rival of her father. After that, her father hired bodyguards. Their estate probably has better security than the White House.

"Later, an attempt was made on Erika's life. I threw her down as the killer began shooting. A guard was killed," I said.

Kimberly's face had remained expressionless as she stared at me. After a few moments, she resumed tutoring without missing a beat.

Two days later, Kimberly's uncle told her that Charlotte and Erika were approved for visiting and that play dates with Justin would be OK.

Charlotte was curious about Julia and I told her the truth: that Julia was Kimberly's child but had been told they were sisters.

"I've come across this in the free clinic where I volunteer but never with my middle-class patients. Is her family poor?" she asked.

"Her father was a Brazilian tycoon. She's an heiress," I replied.

"*Curious*," Charlotte said, slowly. "I'll keep her secret though kids are smart and hear everything. Julia probably already knows the truth."

"But so long as it remains unspoken, it's not real," I said, and Charlotte agreed.

Neither Kimberly nor I had classes on Monday. It was planned that Tristan would meet with Julia at Kimberly's house after he returned from school that day. Elizabeth decided to spend that afternoon shopping.

Chapter 42

Julia's fidgeting and thumb sucking revealed her nervousness. She had never had a playdate or friend. Like her mother, Julia sporadically appeared adult or childlike. Now, she clung to her doll, a large Minnie Mouse. Kimberly's security blanket was her laptop.

Kimberly had scripted the playdate. The children would play in one corner of the library while the adults watched and talked amongst themselves. Kimberly vetoed my suggestion that the children play in Julia's room.

"I don't want her alone with a boy!" Kimberly asserted, with passion.

To worry how a very young boy and girl would play together, Kimberly must have had troubling childhood experiences, I thought.

The library in Erika's house and that of my London grandmother is on the main floor so I expected that it would be the same in Kimberly's house. But here it was on the second floor, next to Kimberly's dressing room which was adjacent to her bedroom. Curtains hung from the dressing room's ceiling for when privacy was desired.

"City houses are elbowed in on lots of twenty-five by one-hundred feet so architects must make the best of it," Kimberly explained.

Kimberly's knowledge of this unusual fact caused me to change my judgment of her once again. When we first met, I had placed her in the category of socially awkward nerd, and maybe financially strapped like me. But within weeks I had discovered that she was wealthy, a mother, culturally sophisticated, and expert at seducing men. How could I have been so wrong?

Well, maybe I hadn't been a complete idiot, I reassured myself. We are all a mystery to others though dropping clues every so often which may or may not be noticed.

The library was a cozy room with a bay-window and alcove for books. It had an open timber ceiling, a parquet floor covered with rugs, and a marble mantel and fireplace.

The room contained a large solid table, a desk with many drawers, and low, wooden bookcases. Strips of cloth were tacked to the edge of each shelf to prevent dust from accumulating.

"The architect also wanted to create an English billiard-room but my uncle vetoed this," Kimberly said.

This was a new fact. Why had her uncle made this decision rather than her parents? When had she moved to the United States? I didn't yet know.

The aroma of furniture polish was overcome by the fragrance of the snacks that Gabriela had lain on the table. Kids are always hungry and, strange though this food would be to Tristan, I didn't doubt that he would love it: brigadeiros (chocolate truffles), pão de queijo (cheese bread), and Açai smoothie.

"The Açai smoothie is made from a hard purple berry. It's the choice of surfers in Rio de Janeiro," Kimberly informed me, as I tasted it.

The stage was set. The playdate would soon begin.

Chapter 43

Because Kimberly has a scientific bent, it was only natural that she had tried to organize the play date.

"First, we'll introduce each child to the other. Then, they'll snack and figure out what they want to do," Kimberly said.

It didn't work out that way. In the rush to arrive at Kimberly's house on time, Tristan's normal routine had been interrupted. This consisted of his snacking before checking out the latest online news about his beloved Raspberry Pi. This is a cheap computer module with which millions of children have learned coding and more.

Charlotte hadn't told him of the playdate and he arrived in a foul mood. At these times his normal reaction to any request is a loud "no!" I knew this from babysitting him for nearly a year.

But his mood could also change on a dime as it did when Julia, noting his anger, became frightened and tearful. Instantly, Tristan became a perfect gentleman. He smiled, told her his name, and asked if she wanted to play his video game. She didn't reply and her thumb remained in her mouth. He then sat on the floor and she hesitantly sat beside him.

Tristan told her that he had built the game using his Raspberry Pi. She said that she had been using Mathematica on hers and that was it. For these two child geniuses, this was an exchange of love.

I asked Kimberly what Mathematica was.

"It's a twenty-five-year-old computational programming tool that can be used on Raspberry Pi. It's been bundled on it along with Raspbian and NOOBS since last year," she explained, glibly.

"Oh," I replied.

I had understood little of her explanation but left it at that.

Charlotte turned toward Kimberly.

"They get along well. You have a beautiful child," Charlotte said.

"Thank you," Kimberly replied, as a look of pride spread over her face.

"They should get together more often," Kimberly said, and Charlotte nodded agreement.

I relaxed and felt angelic. My suggestion of a play date now seemed to be changing Julia, and Kimberly too. She was becoming a *real* parent. I wondered how much longer she would be comfortable living apart from her daughter. Later that afternoon, I learned the reason for their separation.

Chapter 44

Adults can't speak freely when children are underfoot for kids learn everything. If you don't believe it, ask any child. Nowadays, parents are lucky if cellphone video of their sex life doesn't wind up on YouTube.

"Gabriela can watch the kids. Why don't we go to another room," I suggested.

Kimberly hesitantly agreed after Charlotte supported this idea.

"We can go to my room," Kimberly said, nervously.

Kimberly told Gabriela where we would be and insisted that she be informed of "anything." Gabriela smiled, and agreed. Having been Kimberly's nursemaid, she was used to her ways.

In her room, Kimberly courteously suggested that Charlotte recline on the chaise lounge. Our chairs were well-cushioned and, with the hassocks, were comfortable too.

After moments of silence, Kimberly rose to bring us snacks from the kitchen. Upon reaching the door, she wavered and looked as if she were about to faint. Rushing to Kimberly's side, Charlotte caught her and lowered her gently to the ground.

After Charlotte loosened Kimberly's collar, I saw a discolored patch of skin above her breast, as if a scar had been removed by skin graft. Charlotte raised Kimberly's legs above her heart level with pillows, and checked her airway to be sure that it was clear.

Kimberly opened her eyes a few moments later. She wanted to get up but Charlotte insisted that she lay for a while.

"Who is your doctor?" Charlotte asked.

"I don't have one."

"When did you last see a doctor?"

"Years ago. Doctors make me nervous," Kimberly replied.

"*OK*," Charlotte said slowly. "Then let me tell you about fainting, which is medically called *syncope*. It is a sudden loss of consciousness and posture caused by a lowered flow of blood to the brain. Most episodes are brief with complete consciousness being quickly recovered.

"Fainting is common and can be caused by something as ordinary as hunger. It can also result from low blood sugar or anemia or irregular heartbeat. Have you fainted before?"

Kimberly didn't immediately answer, and Charlotte repeated her question.

"I fainted twice before," Kimberly said, finally.

Her voice had a haunted tone, as if it were coming from far off.

"When was that?" Charlotte asked, with an expression of concern.

Kimberly looked away, as if being unable to answer while facing someone.

"Once, when *it* happened, and then later," she said, in a barely audible voice.

Chapter 45

Charlotte wanted to call the Emergency Medical Services but Kimberly refused.

"What do you think happened?" she asked.

"Being a doctor who hasn't examined you, I shouldn't express an opinion," Charlotte replied.

"Our kids will be best friends and I promise not to sue you. I feel OK now. What's your best guess?" Kimberly asked.

She had regained color and now lay in bed.

"I can't say for sure. As I said, fainting can be caused by several things but at your age it's generally not serious. When did you last eat?"

"Yesterday evening. I got involved in a project and worked all night and today. Then it was a rush to get here," Kimberly replied.

"Your fainting may have been caused by that but you should be examined. By the way, did you girls get a flu shot?" Charlotte asked.

"In early September," I replied.

"Never. I'm afraid of needles," Kimberly replied.

"You're like Randy," I burst out.

Both of them stared at me.

"My boyfriend, Randy, is terrified by the sight of blood, or getting an injection. His father is a doctor and wants him to become one. To cure him of his fear, he insisted that Randy witness the birth of his sister. I caught him as he fainted and he wound up in the bed next to his mother. It was the hospital's laugh of the week."

My story eased the tension in the room.

Kimberly turned toward Charlotte.

"Can you be my doctor?" she asked.

"I'm certified in Internal Medicine and OB/GYN but do mostly the latter now. I could refer you to an excellent colleague. His patients rave about him," Charlotte said.

"I won't see a man. I want you," Kimberly said.

Her insistence reminded me of how a child gets when there is no changing their mind. Charlotte seemed to recognize this and that more than stubbornness lay beneath it. Kimberly had secrets and must be cautious who she revealed them to.

"OK. My private office is three blocks away. I'll see you at six-thirty tonight, after taking Tristan home. I'll need your insurance data to get authorization," Charlotte said, handing her a business card.

"I have the college's insurance but you can send the bill to my guardian. He pays all my bills," Kimberly said.

Charlotte looked hesitant. Knowing of Kimberly's speedy need for a doctor and her problem communicating, I felt it important to add my two cents.

"Don't worry about being paid. Kimberly is an heiress and one of the richest people in America," I said.

Chapter 46

Money relieves many worries and paying bills will never be one of Kimberly's. The cost of the dress she wore would have paid Charlotte's fee many times over.

I believe that a doctor's examination is best undergone alone, and returned to campus. Moreover, Kimberly had secrets like the scar on her breast. She might discuss this with her doctor but only if it were the two of them.

The playdate had been successful. Julia liked Tristan, Tristan liked Julia, and their mothers bonded as well as Kimberly could with anyone. I couldn't have hoped for more.

After the emotion filled events of the past week–Missy's wedding, learning the surprising fact about Vladimir, the discovery that Kimberly was both a mother and super-rich, the fright caused by her fainting–I looked forward to the dullness of college life as a welcome retreat.

Back at campus, I studied for the rest of the day before leaving the dorm. I sat on a bench on the Columbia University campus, envying the strolling couples walking arm-in-arm. One could have been Randy and me. He had wanted to attend Columbia College but his father, who would pay his tuition, had insisted that he attend Yale and there was no sensible argument against that.

The quadrangle where I was sitting began emptying as the sun set. I became cold and walked back to the dorm. I was so lost in my thoughts that it took me time to notice the commotion. Police cars and fire trucks crowded the street and students stood staring. People exiting the 116th subway station added to the crowd.

Those trying to leave the campus were rudely pushed back by police officers. The relationship between students and police has never been friendly.

"What's happening?" I asked the girl next to me. "I don't know. I just came out for coffee," was her unhelpful reply. A coffee shop is directly across the street.

Suddenly, from down the street, came a muffled roar that seemed the shocked expression of many people. Murmured words of what happened gradually spread through the crowd.

"*What?*" I called out loudly.

"I think they're dead," a male voice answered.

Chapter 47

It has been said that unpleasant facts create welcome opportunities but I couldn't see any from this situation. The only good point was that I probably didn't know the deceased well. Missy no longer lived on campus and Kimberly was downtown. My life at Barnard had been so stressed that I hadn't made other friends.

I waited for answers to the obvious questions but none came. When we were finally permitted to approach Brooks Hall, I saw a stretcher moving toward an ambulance. It's carrying the body, I thought.

Several years before, during my summer vacation in London, there had been a terrorist bombing. People huddled afterward. No one wanted to be alone. It was like this at Brooks Hall that evening.

The girl's name was Emily but no one seemed to know her well. She had transferred from a Florida college this year. She had bought meals for others at local restaurants and always seemed to have money. Her BMW convertible was parked at a local garage. A girl from a wealthy family whose life ended in tragedy, I summarized to myself.

"How did she die?" I asked, hesitantly, being unable to forget the bodies that had lain in my room.

"Suicide. She took the screen off a window and jumped," a student said.

Though knowing that it was unfair, I couldn't help blaming the Barnard administration for her death. If Brooks Hall were air-conditioned, the windows would have been sealed and she couldn't have been able to jump. But then she might have driven to the George Washington Bridge and thrown herself off it, I told myself, after regaining a clearer mind.

Like with thoughts of ghosts, any event that people don't readily understand, from a sudden crash on a quiet day to the midnight creak of a floorboard, causes alarm to an already nervous mind as mine was that evening.

This had been the *third* student death in Brooks Hall over the past year. If the building wasn't haunted, which I didn't believe for a moment, *something* was going on. Barnard didn't recruit suicidal students.

I remained huddled with others in the TV lounge until after the 11PM local news. We hungered for information but the program was notably uninformative. It provided fewer facts than we already knew.

"A twenty-year-old Barnard College student, whose name is being withheld pending notification of her family, was found dead outside her college dormitory. The police have provided no information about the cause of her death and college officials have refused comment."

There was the usual video of passersby expressing shock, and of the building where the tragedy occurred.

The trembling girl next to me seemed particularly shaken.

"She was so happy this morning. Her fiancée graduated from West Point last June and she was planning their wedding. Why would she kill herself?"

Why indeed? I wondered, shaking my head.

Chapter 48

The TV station was switched to Turner Classic Movies as soon as the news ended. No one protested. Watching a romantic film with a happy ending might help us sleep.

Unfortunately, a classic gangster movie, *White Heat*, was showing. It's a 1949 production and now considered one of the best movies ever made.

When the film's Oscar nominated writer, Virginia Kellogg, was mentioned, there were cheers in the lounge. It had been a bad night and we girls needed something to cheer about.

White Heat tells the story of a crazed gang leader, Cody Jarrett. His father died in an insane asylum and his mother, a real bitch, is his only confidante. In one scene, he sits on her lap while she feeds him whiskey and makes a toast, "Top of the world." These turn out to be his final words before his death.

Despite our gloom, the room remained quiet as the movie played. It is that good! The film begins with Cody and his gang causing four deaths while robbing a mail train. To avoid the death penalty, he pleads guilty to having committed a lesser crime at the same time, gaining a false alibi and brief prison sentence.

While in prison, he learns of the death of his mother at the hands of his treacherous wife. Cody breaks out of prison together with a police undercover agent whose task it is to identify "The Trader," the fence who launders stolen money for Cody.

I won't tell more since you may decide to see it. A critic commented, after the film ended, that the movie portrayed the age-old good versus evil conflict. Here, a gangster meets an early violent death because he has sinned against society.

The critic said that a gangster survives continual threat and heavy odds because of his cunning and energy. He is a badass whose motto is "Do it first, do it yourself, and keep on doing it." His nation is not the U.S.A. but the streets.

Though depraved, the movie gangster has basic American traits: Puritanism, with its sense of strictness of behavior; Social Darwinism's struggle for survival; and the Horatio Alger battle to gain wealth despite their poor upbringing, the critic concluded.

These ideas gave me a thought: Me–against the world! None of us is as sane as we pretend.

Chapter 49

I didn't see Kimberly until two days later. Her medical exam took far longer than she or Charlotte had expected. There were abnormal findings and these had to be checked with equipment that Charlotte's office lacked.

Kimberly's body had an admirable model-like slimness. Which would be OK except that when she became involved in a project she virtually stopped eating. Her weight got dangerously low at these times. Her periods had also stopped.

Charlotte found that Kimberly had an imbalance of electrolytes: the minerals such as sodium, potassium, and calcium that maintain the balance of fluids in the body. She also had abnormal heart rhythms. These symptoms are dangerous and can lead to sudden death.

Kimberly was admitted to Lenox Hill Hospital and remained there the following day. After being medically cleared for discharge, it was feared that she was anorectic so the hospital referred her to a dietician. They also insisted that she schedule an appointment with a therapist but Kimberly refused. Like I said, she is a very private person.

Her uncle, who is also her guardian, was called. He took charge and her appointment with a shrink was made. Finding one was not easy since Kimberly insisted that her treatment be conducted in Portuguese, the language of Brazil.

While this made no sense since Kimberly speaks better English than I do, her reason for this strange request made perfect sense: "I was in a bitchen mood that day," she said.

As luck would have it, there was such a psychoanalyst available. He was an American who had lived in Brazil with his Brazilian wife. They had recently retired to Manhattan to be close by their daughter who lives here with her family.

Kimberly's demand was met, and she received good medical news too. She was basically healthy but had to eat better. Her period was expected to return after she began eating better.

"So you're OK," I said.

"Not really. Just as OK as I'll ever be," Kimberly replied.

I said nothing, having often thought that of myself.

The next day, I watched what Kimberly chose in the cafeteria. Her dietician wouldn't have objected: turkey and Swiss on whole wheat, a spinach salad with broccoli on the side, milk, an apple, and a banana. She topped this off with four pills: Calcium with Vitamin D, Vitamin C, a multi-vitamin, and a garlic pill.

"Garlic is very healthy. I added it to what the dietician ordered," she said.

I couldn't argue. Garlic is considered to have many health benefits. My father, who suffers from Lyme disease, had been prescribed it years before.

"Did you learn more about the girl's death?" Kimberly asked.

"I haven't heard a word. It's like it never happened," I replied.

"With three student deaths in a year, Brooks Hall will soon be considered more dangerous than Afghanistan. But that's not why I'm leaving," she said.

Chapter 50

Besides being my calculus tutor, Kimberly was my only friend at Barnard. I immediately became nervous and my face must have showed it.

"I'm not leaving *totally*," she said quickly. "During the playdate, I saw how important Charlotte is to Justin and realized how much Julia needs me. My session with the shrink helped too. I felt freer afterward though I didn't say much. Most of the time, he told me stories. It's hard for me to talk," Kimberly said.

Her doctor had sensed this and that is why he told her stories, I thought. My knowledge of therapy came mostly from Erika, who had been in therapy for years. My baby sister, Claudine, was on her second therapist, her first having been murdered. Learning a patient's secrets can be dangerous.

"What are your plans?" I asked.

Kimberly finished taking the last of her pills before answering.

"For the rest of this term, I'll stay at Brooks from Monday through Thursday and spend the rest of the week at home with Julia. Elizabeth won't like it. We never got along though she doesn't look much older than me. She was my father's trophy wife. Men can be dumb.

"According to my father's will, she has a lifetime allowance and is permitted to live in the family home until she marries. Maybe she and Eric will run off. It's about time for my luck to turn," Kimberly said.

I wondered about her last sentence but said nothing.

"I'm still sticking with my project to get you an 'A' in calculus," Kimberly said, with a smile.

I smiled too, and thought how greatly one therapy session had changed her. During the last several minutes she had smiled more often than she ordinarily did in an entire day or even longer.

"Have you told Julia yet?" I asked.

"No, I plan to tell her and my uncle this afternoon. He also thinks that my father's marriage to Elizabeth was a big mistake. Can you come with me?" she asked.

"Absolutely," I replied quickly.

"*After* you do your calculus homework," Kimberly added, with a grin.

"You're *not* my mother," I said sternly, but matched her smile.

Chapter 51

Kimberly's uncle had anglicized his name to Richard when he moved to America. "He likes to fit in," Kimberly explained, as we traveled to meet him.

Richard's apartment was a duplex penthouse in an apartment house that covered a full-block on Central Park West between 61st and 62nd Streets. Kimberly had described its features to me as we traveled there by bus: multi-directional views; a kitchen with top-of-the-line appliances; bathrooms with deluxe fixtures and finishes.

There was also a 24-hour doorman, a private dining room and library, a movie screening room, a health club, a lounge, a pool, and an individual wine cellar.

"It's OK but the building is huge with over two-hundred apartments. There's too much traffic, and it lacks a roof deck. Far from perfect," Kimberly further informed me, as the bus stopped.

I didn't reply. I try not to advertise my family's poverty. Our large house in Greenwich is owned by an old family trust. If not for that, we might be living in a camper.

"He's divorced and will want Julia and me to live with him but it wouldn't work out. I'm not easy to live with and he often has a girlfriend over when he's not traveling. It wouldn't be good for Julia either. She's been through enough changes, and we both love our house," Kimberly said.

I again kept silent. What she said sounded sensible but the decision wasn't mine.

The building where her uncle lived *was* impressive. It consisted of two towers joined by a lavish lobby. There was a large motor court so the rich residents need not be seen when entering or exiting the building. Having traveled there by bus, we walked toward the doorman and I momentarily feared that we wouldn't be admitted. Thinking like this is what poverty does to you.

"Many foreigners live here. One is a Russian billionaire who spent a year in prison after being accused of murdering a fellow businessman. But he was acquitted," Kimberly added reassuringly, as we rode the elevator.

Vladimir might know him, I thought.

Richard was casually dressed in a sport jacket, open collar shirt, and double pleated pants. He embraced Kimberly and kissed me on both cheeks. "I already feel I know you from what Kimberly has told me," he said, with a welcoming smile.

"She's very kind," I replied.

My proper London grandmother had spent an entire summer drilling tact into me.

"Come. I've ordered Brazilian food. Kimberly said you're vegetarian but there'll be something for everyone," he reassured me, as he led us toward the dining room.

Chapter 52

The food was definitely Brazilian. Meat is Brazil's favorite dish but there was also much for me to choose from. The meal was served buffet style, eat what you like, and I did. For those with food allergies, the restaurant had been thoughtful enough to enclose cards describing the ingredients in each dish. This is helpful for vegetarians like me.

I chose the Goat Cheese Salad (roasted beets, cashew nuts and onions on a bed of arugula, endive and radicchio drizzled with balsamic vinaigrette). Then, Sopa de Feijao Preto (black bean soup topped with green onions) and Hamburger Vegetariano (grilled vegetarian burger with tomatoes onions, arugula and tofu, with sweet potato fries).

The food was very good and I followed up with Moqueca de Peixe (white fish sautéed with peppers, onions, tomatoes, fish broth, coconut milk and palm oil, finished with cilantro and served over pirao, rice and beans).

I drank mineral water, and watched my figure by ignoring the desserts: brigadeiro (chocolate truffles) that I had munched at Kimberly's home, rice pudding, and flan (custard).

Kimberly chose the Stroganoff (beef sautéed with mushrooms and onions in brandy cream sauce), rice, and French fries. She had side orders of Fried Banana and Yucca Rings. I wondered what her dietician would say.

I spoke little, being an outsider to the purpose of the meeting. Kimberly seemed to have a problem raising her issue and Richard took up the slack in the conversation.

"I'll be traveling to Brazil next month," he said.

We both looked up from our food.

"I want your grandmother to move here," Richard said, facing Kimberly.

"Why?" she asked.

"The country is in another crisis," Richard replied, before turning to me.

"All national groups have peculiarities. Brazilian's is their fussiness. They take more showers than anyone else. Their neighborhoods are spotless, and even the shantytowns are free from litter. But they don't respect laws. An old saying is that in Brazil the law *doesn't take*, *não pegou*. It's a chronic problem.

"Some laws don't take because they're unworkable or out-of-date. Others, because there is a shortage of money and the political will to enforce it.

"Brazil has among the worst performing currencies in the world and its credit rating was just slashed to junk. The country is in the worst recession in a quarter century and there's a huge political crisis. The Speaker of the lower House of Congress has been charged with corruption. President Rousseff is clutching onto power by her fingernails."

"How will this affect our family?" Kimberly asked.

"Financially, it won't. Your father converted his assets into American properties and securities before his death. He was a shrewd man, bless his soul. It's your grandmother that I'm worried about. Crime is the only growth industry in Brazil and I want her here where it's safer. I've been trying to convince her to come but I may have to kidnap her."

"She's a stubborn woman," Kimberly said, with a concerned look.

"She's like you," Richard said, with a small smile. "Now, what brings you here on this lovely day?"

Chapter 53

Kimberly looked steadily at her uncle. *Now* was the moment for her to tell.

"I've decided to move back home. I'm ready to be a real mother to Julia," she said.

Her voice had initially been hesitant but become firmer as she spoke.

"That's *wonderful*, and I'm pleased that you're seeing the doctor too. I'm your godfather and worry about you. You can live with me. There's plenty of room here."

"No, and it's not because we don't love you. Julia is used to our house and she has already had too much change in her life," Kimberly replied.

Richard sipped his coffee before speaking again.

"I read about the student's death at your dorm. Did you know her? What happened?" he asked.

Kimberly looked at me.

"None of us knows much. I heard that she had transferred from a Florida college and planned to marry a West Point graduate," I said.

Richard took several more sips of coffee before speaking again. He looked thoughtful.

"I've considered hiring a bodyguard for your security. It wouldn't have worked while you were living at the dormitory but you'll be moving out," Richard said.

"Margaret's father owns a security company," Kimberly said, wanting to participate in a decision that concerned her.

Richard looked at me and I gave my best marketing spiel.

"It's a multi-nation company that my father in London manages with two partners: one is a former CIA official and the other is a retired general in Russia's Presidential Security Service. They provide security for government officials and wealthy families.

"My friend, Erika, has been protected by them for years. This began after her mother and sister were murdered by her father's business enemy.

"The guards are former soldiers, mostly Russian but there are Americans and British too. You won't find better," I concluded.

"Give me their number. I should have done this years ago. I'll never forgive myself if anything happened," Richard said, handing me a sheet of paper.

I looked up Vladimir's number on my IPhone and wrote it.

I turned toward Kimberly.

"You and Julia can spend a weekend in Greenwich. My sister, Claudine, is a little older than Julia. They could play and you can ask Erika's opinion of her bodyguards.

Her young nephew lives with her and he could be another friend for Julia," I said.

"It would be a good idea to get Erika's judgment," Richard said.

I felt pleased as we left the apartment for I had done two good deeds: helping Kimberly, *and* my dad's business.

Chapter 54

"You'll love Erika," I said, as we walked to the bus stop.

"Hmm," Kimberly remarked.

The light of the past hours was extinguished from her eyes. She was back to being her isolated self again.

Her therapy appointment hasn't changed her that much, I thought. After initially speaking freely, she had returned to her usual personality. But I shouldn't have expected more. Real personality change takes time and one therapy session isn't much, I told myself.

I chatted away about nothing important to help Kimberly relax. Getting away from Manhattan will be good for her, I thought.

"Greenwich is gorgeous this time of year. Why don't we go this weekend?" I asked.

My question had caught Kimberly by surprise and it took her time to adjust. It required a minute before she replied, "OK."

I babbled on.

"We needn't bother with a hired car since the train ride from Grand Central is under an hour. Erika can pick us up at the station and we can talk over lunch. Their cook is fabulous. Then we'll go over my house and I'll introduce Julia to Claudine."

I had spoken in a rush, wanting to get the details settled. Kimberly felt comfortable when matters were fixed. Making decisions was hard for her.

Kimberly's agreement with my plan came quickly, and I didn't speak again. Our friendship had now developed to the point that we were comfortable with silence.

We were a block from the bus stop before she spoke again. She looked thoughtful, and then nodded down the block.

"There's someplace that I want to see," Kimberly said.

She left me without another word and I followed.

It was a small hole-in-the-wall store, one that was easily passed. The neighborhood was expensive but the crude sign in the window had been made by hand. It read, *African Market.*

But the clerk behind the counter befit the prosperity of the neighborhood. He wore a three-piece suit, his white shirt was starched and immaculate, and his tie was sharply knotted. He stood straighter as we approached the counter.

"How can I serve you?" he asked, in an even, well-modulated tone.

"I need Yoruba herbs," Kimberly said.

"Do you follow the Santeria faith?" he asked softly.

"Yes. I wish Eucalyptus, Hawthorn, Bloodroot, and Motherwort," Kimberly demanded.

The man blinked. He looked startled.

"You are certain of the Orisha (spirit) that you seek?"

Kimberly nodded.

The man went into an adjoining room. He returned a few minutes later carrying small paper bags that he handed to Kimberly.

"The cost is sixty dollars," he said.

Kimberly removed a wallet from her purse and handed him a five-hundred-dollar bill.

"I have no change," the man said.

"Use the change to help the poor. Poverty is slavery," Kimberly said. It is an ancient Yoruba proverb.

"May Ogun bless you and bring you justice," the man said, before bowing deeply.

We left the store and walked toward the bus stop. Kimberly didn't explain this odd encounter but she didn't have to. Years before, a Santeria priestess in Greenwich, Mother Marie, had provided information that cured me of what was believed to be an incurable illness. Thereafter, though being raised Mormon, I became a follower of the Santeria faith. "The Gods are not jealous," Mother Marie had told me.

The herbs that Kimberly purchased are associated with the Orisha, Ogun. He can strengthen the heart and muscles, is the spirit of divine justice on earth, and is known for his keen insight into the human mind. He is also the liberator–or executioner–in the world.

Chapter 55

I was surprised but not shocked. The Santeria faith originated in Africa and was brought to the New World by slaves. Here, its practices were hidden within Christian beliefs. Its followers are now found throughout the world including the United States.

Santeria is an ancient religion in which certain spirits are associated with particular human difficulties. This is little different from that of Roman Catholicism where aid is sought from specific saints.

I hadn't expected to find a Barnard student who practiced this faith. Because some of its rituals, as animal sacrifice, have long been absent from more established religions, identifying with the Santeria faith is not often publicized. It has become popularly associated with sticking pins in dolls depicting an enemy and zombie movies.

I knew that Kimberly felt herself weird and wanted her to know that I understood. So I told her about Mother Marie and how I too became a follower of the Santeria faith.

"When I was a child it was believed that I had ADD. I couldn't concentrate or sit still and my grades dropped from 'A' to 'F'. I was sick and nobody knew why.

"At Johns Hopkins Hospital in Baltimore, which might be the best hospital in America, I was diagnosed as having Sanfilippo Disease. Because I lacked an enzyme, my cells couldn't properly break down sugars. This condition leads to problems with behavior and attention, and these children usually die in their early teens.

"My parents didn't tell me this but I looked up the diagnosis online and learned the truth. They tried to be cheerful but looked worse than me.

"My father is a lawyer. He had once helped a man without charging a fee. The man told his mother and she came to thank my father.

"The woman, Mother Marie, is a retired French teacher and she offered to tutor me without charge until the school could arrange for my home instruction.

"Mother Marie is an *iyalorisha*, a Santeria priestess. She prayed to her personal spirit for guidance with my illness and it worked. That night she had a dream which revealed the medicine that I needed. It was an ordinary food: soybeans. Each day that she visited she brought me a bag of dried soybeans. They're sold in every health food store.

"Within weeks, I was better. When I returned to the Hospital for a follow-up, they first thought that they must have made a wrong diagnosis since my illness was supposed to be incurable.

"I told them about eating soybeans but not about Mother Marie of course. They began researching it as a cure for Sanfilippo Disease. Someone might have gotten a prize from this but I never checked. I was happy to be alive.

"When I came home, Mother Marie held a ceremony during which I was spiritually married to the

Orisha, Babaluaiye. He has made me strong and will protect me."

I opened the top button of my shirt and lifted a small gold locket two inches square. It was inscribed with an ancient language and held a lock of my hair and a bit of ash to symbolize Babaluaiye's great enjoyment: smoking cigars.

My concluding words were brief.

"I understand," I said.

Kimberly isn't a touchy feely person so I was surprised when she took my hand. She spoke in barely above a whisper.

"We are sisters and linked for life," she said.

Chapter 56

Saturday morning was a good time to travel to Greenwich. Our homework was done, Julia's home schooling week was over, and Kimberly's therapy appointments were on Fridays and she was more relaxed afterward.

Erika sometimes tells me what her therapist says but Kimberly never did. I knew only that his office was in a high-rise apartment building on East 85th Street. Diagonally across from it, on Madison Avenue, is a bakeshop where she regularly bought pastries. These were a welcome change from the commercial productions at the campus cafeteria.

Along with Kimberly and Julia came the usual mothering supplies: bottles of water and small bags of Cheerios and raisins. They would be staying for the weekend and had a change of clothes in one suitcase. Whatever else they needed could be found at my home, which I wanted them to consider their home too.

Kimberly would share my room and Julia would share Claudine's room. That was the plan but, as they say, man proposes and God disposes.

One of my mother's passions is to increase the number of Mormons through conversion. She considers my friends to be her candidates but, that weekend, this seemed not to be in God's plan either.

What did happen was that after Erika picked us up to deliver us for a meet-and-greet at my house, the three of us went to her house for lunch.

Being a forty-million-dollar mansion with twenty-two rooms and thirteen bathrooms, it clearly made better sense for Kimberly and Julia to stay at Erika's home for the weekend. There, they could each have their own bedroom. My mother understood, and was tactful enough not to show her hurt feelings.

I've seen Erika's house often enough to know when something is different. Though her house is big, the addition was noticeable.

"What's that?" I asked, pointing toward it.

"My father's latest addition. He said that he's always been a car guy and wanted to have a really cool garage. He's a workaholic. Hopefully, this'll make a change."

"How can a garage be cool?" I asked.

"You'll see," Erika replied, and I did.

When we entered, her father was admiring his latest toy. The garage contained a revolving turntable on which lay his newest car, a Bentley. The turntable rotated 180 degrees so that the driver need never back out through the titanium-and-wood garage door. The garage also contained a laser system with a beam that guided the driver onto the turntable.

"It's for safety though when too much wine flowed, a guest sent the car spinning," Erika's father said, almost apologetically.

He joined us for lunch. It included the treats that I love but my family, being on Food Stamps, couldn't afford: salmon and caviar. For dessert there were *pupcakes,* cupcakes with the face of a puppy, and *owls,* cupcakes with the face of an owl, from Greenwich's St. Moritz Bakery. I remembered them from when I was a child. They're always a big hit with kids.

I had intended to raise the question of security, for Erika to give her favorable opinion of my father's business. But when Erika's father ("Hamilton, call me Harry") learned that Kimberley was Brazilian, his anger boiled over and he barely contained himself.

He said that the value of the Brazilian companies that he owned had plummeted despite the nation being basically wealthy. He blamed Brazil's problems on its gargantuan tax code and "absurd method of collecting taxes."

"Thousands of government entities produce a dizzying array of taxes that prize complexity and punish the poor and middle class. Wealthy Brazilians find loopholes to avoid paying taxes, and the system is designed to confound people.

"One tax expert–he is both a lawyer and an accountant–spent so many years writing a book on the system's absurdities that he suffered three heart attacks and two divorces. His mission is to put dignity into the tax system. America should follow that lead," Harry said, stopping to catch his breath.

"But I'm being a poor host by monopolizing the conversation. You're young and have other worries," he said, apologetically.

"No, my father would have agreed with you. He converted our family's assets into American securities and properties before he died. Brazil has 'too many boom and bust periods,' he once told me," Kimberly said.

Harry's eyes brightened.

"What's your last name?" he asked, and Kimberly told him.

"Your father was a *wonderful* man. He changed my life," Harry said softly, reaching to touch Kimberly's hand.

Chapter 57

Kimberly was not an emotional person but she teared up when Harry mentioned her father. My eyes did too after Julia spoke.

"I didn't know grandpa. What was he like?" she asked, in her childlike voice.

Erika's father leaned back in his chair and there were moments of silence before he spoke.

"He was the person that I'd like others to consider me. I met him when my life was in a bad way. I'd been on the wrong side of a squabble at Columbia University and was forced from my job teaching math. Academic politics are the worst since the rewards are so minor.

"My wife, a doctor, was a stay-at-home mother. I had encouraged this decision when I was working but now we were broke. Living in Manhattan is expensive, and teaching jobs weren't available in the middle of the year. Then I had a lucky break. A person's life can change on a dime.

"I was sitting on a bench in Central Park regretting my fate when a neighbor stopped to say 'hello.' He was strolling with your father, we all went for coffee, and I poured out my problems. Your father sent me to the manager of a hedge fund. They had begun using algorithms to make financial trades and I wrote a paper about it a year before. We spoke for a few minutes, he offered me a job, and my money worries were over.

"A few years later we began our own hedge fund though it is terrifying to create something from nothing. And all began with a chance meeting..." Erika's father mused.

"But that's not what you asked: you wanted to know what he was like. I'm not sure that I can give you an honest answer since I liked him so much and still follow his proverbs: 'A compromise decision during a crisis is often wrong. One must go either left or right.' 'The primary rule of meetings is to never surprise anyone.' 'Success is not necessarily the result of good brain work.' 'When things go very wrong in a business, an unpractical person is needed since a practical person is one who is accustomed to doing things the usual way.' 'Friendship is a pact that no quarrel will break.' I've never found reason to dispute his advice.

"Your father was the essence of goodness. He was kind and generous and humble and I still miss him. If I can ever be of help, I would be in your debt if you would ask.

"I heard about the death at Barnard. Your wealth places you in Erika's situation. What arrangements have been made for your security?" Harry asked.

Upon hearing these words, I felt like kissing him. Harry had done my sales job for me.

Chapter 58

"I was thinking the same. Maybe Erika can share her experience with Abram," I said quickly, and turned toward Erika.

Abram is Erika's bodyguard. She complains about his watchfulness but doesn't feel comfortable unless he's around. Her therapy has helped her but therapy can do only so much.

We all looked at Erika. A moment before, while her father spoke, her face had reflected deep interest. She was learning something important about him. Now, at the reminder of her vulnerability, I saw the change in her face and so did her father and Kimberly.

"Abram is *wonderful*," Erika said. "It's thanks to him that I can live freely and fully. I am a survivor. I became terrified after my mother and sister were murdered and the attempt on my life. Terror destroys people. When you live with terror the only thing that matters is to survive one more day.

"I walked with my head down, hoping not to be noticed. I feared that if I were seen I would be killed too. I tried not to feel anything and my worst characteristics surfaced. I was no longer kind or thoughtful or generous. My mood would suddenly change from 'I'm the smartest, prettiest girl in the world' to 'I want to kill myself.' I felt like I was sitting on a bridge set with explosives that would go off at any moment.

"Abram taught me to live again. While protecting me, he taught me to fight and to shoot. Now, though the terror is gone, I still want him close by me."

Julia sensed the gloomy atmosphere and looked troubled. Erika picked up on this and quickly changed the subject, regretting what she had said in the presence of a child. Her comments weren't matters for their ears. Children have their own terrors, from having to survive in an adult world.

"What would you like to do after lunch?" Erika asked Julia.

Julia said nothing.

"Do you like to read?" Erika persisted.

"Yes," Julia answered.

"Why don't we go to the library? They have a wonderful children's section. After that, we can go shopping and buy you something pretty," Erika said.

Julia's response was a small smile.

"Then that's settled," Erika said, firmly.

I said nothing. I had learned years before that nothing relaxed Erika more than planning an activity, and that she was far better at this than me.

Chapter 59

The Greenwich Library on West Putnam Avenue has a snack bar downstairs, Elton's Café. After Julia chose a brownie and milk and logged into the Library's Wi-Fi network with her iPhone, we let her do her thing. Abram sat with her and she taught him to play her latest video game. From one table over it sounded like he often needed her help.

Erika chose her usual coffee. She had stopped off at Starbucks every morning throughout high school for her early morning "fix." Kimberly and I chose water and the three of us shared two brownies. It was our way of dieting, not that any of us needed it.

The three of us made an odd group. Erika and Kimberly were super-wealthy and I was Food Stamp poor. They're considered beautiful while I'm described as pretty.

The day before, I had told Erika that Kimberly was "different, like most geniuses," and Erika got my point. It had taken her time to get used to my boyfriend, Randy, who, like Kimberly, can be accurately described as "socially challenged."

Thus, Erika made no demands of Kimberly. Instead, so we need not sit in silence, Erika rattled on about fashion. She assumed that this topic must interest expensively dressed Kimberly.

"Just before fall is the best time to get stylish winter fashions," Erika began.

I fixed a feigned look of interest to my face. It had been many years since my clothes were bought at other than a Salvation Army store or rummage sale. But Kimberly looked genuinely interested.

"Before everyone is back from the beach, I'm already trying on coats at Bergdorf's. I shop in Manhattan once a month," Erika said.

"Where else do you shop?" Kimberly asked, with increased interest.

"Lord & Taylor, and Barney's," Erika replied.

"I get my basics there but they're *so* American. I prefer Oscar de la Renta and Akris. I got this coat there," Kimberly said.

She indicated her double-faced, speckled short coat with wide notched lapels. I couldn't help smiling at her one-up-man-ship, which was followed by Erika's immediate response. Erika *loves* shopping.

"The current fashion is more classic and less trend-driven. I picked up high-waisted, wide-leg trousers and easy to dress-up-or-down knee boots from Chloé. Also, a printed, window-pane plaid Marni dress.

"You'd look stunning in the Gucci coat that I saw. It was a herringbone pea coat with leather-covered buttons and red piping. It won't look dated next year and is *made* for layering."

Kimberly nodded and then shut up. She had reached her limit of socializing. But their meeting had been a success. Each had taken the other's measure and been found acceptable. Both considered me a sister, and I was glad that they were now friends.

Chapter 60

A child will play for only so long and Abram is never at his best with children. An armed attacker won't intimidate him but kids do.

So after twenty minutes, Erika decided to release him from his torment and we returned to her house, to hang out for a few hours until my dinner time. My friends know that arriving home in time for dinner is a Godly commandment to be sternly enforced by my mother.

Julia was sleepy. She lay in her mother's arms as we spoke in Erika's bedroom. Kimberly reclined on the chaise lounge, I sprawled over large pillows on the floor, and Erika sat up in bed. It was like being back in high school.

Erika turned toward Kimberly.

"Living in New York must be very different from life in Brazil. How do you like it here?" Erika asked.

I didn't expect Kimberly to answer since talking about feelings wasn't her style. But she did.

"All big cities are the same. The wealthy have always lived apart from the day-to-day troubles of the poor," Kimberly said.

"Have you traveled much?" Erika asked.

"Occasionally with my father, on his business trips."

"It's sad that he died so young," Erika said, in a more questioning than noting tone.

Kimberly had been gazing down at sleeping Julia. Now she looked sharply at Erika and her eyes blazed.

"Yes, he died in a car accident."

"Traffic can be dangerous," Erika said, sympathetically.

"That was the inquest's verdict but it wasn't an accident. He was murdered," Kimberly replied.

Erika and I stared at Kimberly. I turned toward her.

"Do you want to talk about it or would you rather we shut up," I asked.

"His death was big in Brazil but didn't merit a line elsewhere," Kimberly shrugged. "A truck hit his car on the driver's side. He never had a chance."

"Why couldn't it have been an accident?" I asked.

"Because the truck was stolen and had been wiped of fingerprints. A witness said that it had been waiting at the corner. My father always drove the same route at the same time to his office. No, the killer waited for him and was never caught."

"Why would someone want to murder your father?" Erika asked.

She had more than a casual interest. Her father's business rival had arranged for her mother and sister to be raped and murdered. He had tried to kill her too, to make her father suffer more.

There were moments of silence before Kimberly replied. No one would have expected the explanation that followed.

"Because he paid to have someone killed that they loved," she said, in a matter-of-fact tone.

I asked the expected question.

"Who was that person?"

Kimberly looked wrapped up in her thoughts as she gazed at Julia. At my words, she abruptly turned toward me, as if only now becoming aware of my existence.

"He was Julia's father," she said, in a hoarse voice.

Chapter 61

Most people aren't capable killing unless it's a matter of self-defense, a question of them or me. But the act that Kimberly stated was deliberate, not one that occurred during battle.

What had so enraged her father and his enemy that they engaged in murder? I couldn't imagine though everyone has their hot-buttons. I felt that this event was too painful to ask about but Erika didn't hesitant.

"What went on? Was it some kind of Brazilian feud like with America's Hatfields vs. the McCoys?" she asked.

A combined look of anger and weariness passed over Kimberly's face.

"No, it wasn't anything like that. I was raped. My family is Catholic so abortion wasn't an option but vengeance was. The rapist was arrested, my father paid for him to be murdered in jail, and his dad then contracted for my father's murder. That's why we fled Brazil. That's also why I resisted being Julia's mother."

"Does she resemble her father?" Erika asked, softly.

"No, thankfully she looks like me and not him."

I had a sudden intuition.

"Did you know him?" I asked.

"He lived down the road from us," Kimberly said, with a sigh.

He must have come from another wealthy family, I thought.

"Kimberly, if you'd rather, just tell us to shut up. We can all join Julia and nap," I said.

"No, it's all right. I've relived these events countless times in my mind and now with my therapist. It's like reading a book with an unchanging plot that you've often read."

We waited silently and she told us, a little at a time. It was a terrible story.

"The rapist's name was Bolade. It's from the Yoruba meaning 'honor will come,' and maybe someday it would have. I had gone to his house, to walk my father home from a business meeting. They lived a short distance away and it was early in the afternoon so my mother let me go. I liked being seen with my father. He was an important person.

"Bolade opened the door. He had probably been looking out the window and saw me coming. He was six years older than me. Our families were close and I viewed him as an older brother though rarely saw him. He had a drug problem and been expelled from several boarding schools.

"He offered to show me his antique record collection and gave me a Guaraná Antarctica, a guaraná flavored soda. It tastes like raspberry flavored ginger ale. I soon realized my mistake but only months later did I learn how big a mistake it had been."

Chapter 62

Kimberly hunched over and sobbed, softly so as to not awaken Julia.

I rose from the floor pillows, went to her side and touched her shoulder. She looked up.

"I'm alright. I *want* you to know," she said.

"I was excited that Bolade wanted to spend time with me. He was nearly a grownup and I was still a kid. And he was polite, leading me by the elbow as we went to his room.

"It was really two rooms: a sitting room with chairs and bookshelves and TV and stereo, and a separate bedroom. I drank the soda as he chose the records. I considered this my first step toward what teenagers dream of: going to parties and clubs, maybe even a rave.

"A few times, while selecting the records, he said, 'I'll be through in just a minute.' I later realized that he was waiting until I finished drinking my soda, the soda that he had drugged.

"The change happened so fast that I didn't realize anything until the drug took hold. If I'd been older, at a club, I might have watched my drink. But would you have done this at a relative's home, which was what Bolade nearly was to me? Of course not. I never should have felt guilty but couldn't help it because of what happened."

Kimberly stopped speaking. She again stared at Julia. I waited for her to continue and, when she didn't, I spoke though knowing that I shouldn't. My lawyer-dad often says that when a person's story is flowing, let it flow.

"What happened?" I asked.

My face remained fixed on Kimberly's. She smiled her weird smile that wasn't a real smile.

"I was murdered," she said.

A heavy silence filled the room before Kimberly continued.

"I began feeling dizzy and *really* tired. It was like I couldn't keep my eyes open to save the world. I couldn't hold my head up, and felt like I was floating. My body seemed gone and sounds seemed far away. I had no feelings as I watched Bolade scan the record covers. He occasionally glanced at me, checking to see whether the drug had taken hold. He had probably drugged other girls before.

"If I had drunk alcohol I would have assumed that my sensations were due to the drinking but I drank only soda.

"The next few hours were hazy, memories of laying on a bed followed by blank spots before falling asleep. My father had returned without me and told my mother that he hadn't seen me. They called Bolade's house and were told that I hadn't felt well upon arriving and lay down. After being driven home, I went to my room and slept.

"I vomited and had diarrhea when I awoke. I was sick for three days, feeling exhausted and sleeping most of the time. My mother thought that it was from the flu which was going around. It didn't occur to me that I might have been raped until I couldn't find the panties that I had worn that day. It was a present from my mother after my first period: a silk muslin from Guia La Bruna."

Chapter 63

Kimberly looked haggard beneath her beauty. Sharing her story had worn her out. I looked at Erika and we nodded agreement: Kimberly needed a break. Erika and I sometimes have identical thoughts, as if we are real sisters. She spoke first.

"Why not put Julia to sleep and we'll go downstairs. The chairs are more comfortable there," Erika said.

Without replying, Kimberly somberly picked Julia up and followed Erika to the bedroom that Julia would use that weekend.

Though Andrei was the only child living in Erika's home, there were always young visitors: his friends, and the children of her father's business associates who visit. Some remain for weeks, helping to fill the loneliness that had consumed Harry's life after his wife's murder. *This,* none of his girlfriends seemed able to relieve.

The room that Erika chose for Julia suited a child her age. The radiator was shielded with a cloud-shaped screen to protect from harm. There was a roll of drawing paper on the wall and a large blackboard to save scribbles. There were stuffed animals and child-sized table and chairs.

The sturdy pine bed held drawers for storage below. It also had a safety railing since the bed was higher than average. A canopy above the bed kept off draughts and encouraged a feeling of security. There was even a small tent for the hiding that children love, and a large, electrified doll house containing the expected figures and furniture. The room was every child's dream except for one glaring exception: there was no television.

"My mother had a thing about having a TV in the bedroom," Erika explained, when I remarked on its absence.

Kimberly tucked the sleepy Julia into bed and kissed her. We waited silently, watching her for a minute. Julia murmured, and instantly fell into a deep sleep. Erika set the baby monitor and we left the room. "You can watch her on the TV downstairs," Erika said, in a reassuring tone.

Erika's house has both smaller and larger living rooms. She led us to the cozier one. It was a relaxed, stylish place in which the emphasis was on softness, harmony, and homeliness. Matching floral patterns in the curtains and furnishings gave the room a fresh, country feel which was heightened by the numerous plants. Family photos added character to the room.

We sprawled on thick, comfortable sofas. I sat with Erika on one while Kimberly sat on a smaller sofa opposite us. She positioned herself to be able to watch Julia on the TV monitor. Over the past weeks she had changed from a detached to a fiercely protective mother.

Erika offer of snacks was refused. I hungered only for the rest of Kimberly's story. To lower the atmosphere and reduce her distress, Erika began speaking of the love that they both shared: shopping for clothes.

"I wear the same brand underwear. Guia La Bruna is expensive but well worth it," Erika said.

Expensive? Consider a hundred dollars for their panty-bra set. Curiosity had later forced me to check its price on the Internet. They do cost far more than my Walmart underwear but was it worth it? Men have little concern with their girlfriend's underwear apart from getting it off.

Chapter 64

"Embroidery is coming back this season," Erika continued, in a calm and soothing but stilted tone, as if she were reading from an ad.

"Several collections were marked by a rainbow of flora and fauna and abstract motifs. Rocha, the newest fashion darling, has created edgy traditionals in nude tulle dresses embroidered with flowers. They're made of chunky cotton-blend yarn, not slender silk."

Kimberly shook her head, as to say that she knew what Erika was doing but didn't need her support. I chimed in.

"Kimberly, I don't understand something. A few minutes ago you said that you were murdered but you're obviously not dead. What did you mean?"

Kimberly nodded at my obvious question.

"Yes, but there was a time that everyone was sure that I had been sentenced to death. It was this that drove my father crazy and made him a murderer."

We waited during the lengthy silence that followed. Finally, Kimberly resumed her story.

"The symptoms that my mother had thought indicated flu–headache, diarrhea, nausea, fever, feeling worn out and achy–didn't go away. They got worse and one was weird: a red rash that didn't itch.

"We've always been a healthy family and my mother credited this to keeping doctors away. They see something that means nothing and do a risky test which confirms that it is nothing while the worry destroys you. Or they're not sure and order more tests.

"My mother believed in the power of folk herbs and had a reputation as a healer. Some people considered her a saint; others called her a witch."

"That's an awful thing to say," Erika burst out.

I sensed where Kimberly's explanation was leading and said nothing.

"No, for she was a witch," Kimberly said, with her first real smile that day.

"My mother was a Santeria priestess. This faith has different names in different countries. In Brazil it is called Candomblé Queto. The religion was brought to the Americas by slaves from Africa. Here, it was criminalized and went underground, being hidden by combining its practices with those of the Catholic religion. Rituals relating to Orichás–Santeria saints–were performed on Catholic saint days.

"Becoming a Santeria priest or priestess is a long process and my mother was one of the few in Rio. First comes a cleansing ritual during which the initiator's Padrino, their godfather so to speak, cleanses the head with special herbs and water. Then follows an intensive week-long initiation in which rituals and the rules of moral behavior are learned.

"During another ceremony the *elekes* is acquired. This is a beaded necklace symbolizing the five most powerful Orichás: Eleguá, Obatalá, Yemayá, Changó, and Ochún. The initiate then reviews their life with a priest before receiving objects which represent the spirit warriors that will protect them."

Erika looked awestruck but, being a follower of the Santeria faith, I already knew what Kimberly described. Still, her next words stunned me.

"Next week, I undergo my final ritual. I will become an Iyawo, a Bride of the Orichá, and be *born again* into the Santeria faith."

When I got over my surprise, I asked, in a matter-of-fact tone, "This is all very interesting but how were you murdered?"

Chapter 65

Kimberly's round-about explanation made me realize that her way of explaining hadn't changed. She still spoke in her usual associative fashion, telling what immediately came to mind rather than answering a question directly.

That her mother was a Santeria priestess was striking news and possibly central in her mind. But how could it possibly relate to Kimberly having been murdered? Yet, maybe I am wrong, I told myself. I *was* wrong but not about that.

Kimberly made her wry crooked smile. It tended to signal that a surprising fact was coming.

"Both my parents had recently gotten the flu so that I was sick with it too was a reasonable conclusion which I accepted. I was healthy and had always recovered quickly. It would be the same with this, I believed, even as the symptoms remained and grew worse.

"I felt tired all the time, lost weight, and had night sweats. I had loved to run but now had shortness of breath. And new, strange symptoms occurred: swollen nodes in my neck; purplish spots on my skin that didn't go away; long-lasting diarrhea; and easily bruising.

"My parents worried, and took me to my life-long pediatrician. He listened closely, without his usual smile, and referred me to a specialist in infectious diseases.

There are tropical infections caused by insect bites that are virtually unknown in the U.S.A. I recently read of an airline traveler from Dubai, a world financial center, who was bitten by a spider while traveling on their national airline. He nearly died and was saved only by having much of his leg amputated. This, just from sitting on an airplane!"

Kimberly paused in her story as her throat grew hoarse.

"I need something to drink, some juice," she said.

In my house, one of us would have gotten up and gone to the kitchen. Here, Erika phoned the cook and asked for juice and crackers. As we waited, I became anxious. My father's disabling Lyme disease and my childhood brush with mortality make me nervous when illness is discussed. It is as if I feel that I could become ill simply from listening. I know this is a crazy thought but have been unable to rid myself of it.

The refreshments arrived and Kimberly continued her story.

Chapter 66

"I wasn't really worried. Kids believe that their parents can deal with anything but I could see that they weren't so sure. Being referred by a beloved pediatrician to an unknown specialist didn't sound like good news and it wasn't.

"What I'm saying will sound like a textbook but they're terms that I became as familiar with as with brands of cosmetics. I told the doctor my symptoms and he ordered many tests. Some were the usual and others were for all kind of infectious diseases.

"I had a urinalysis and blood count and blood chemistry profile including liver and kidney functions. I had tests for hepatitis and tuberculosis and sexually transmitted diseases. But it was the two that my parents had never heard of that gave the answer: a CD4 count and a viral load test. Do you know what they diagnose?"

Erika shook her head. I knew but shrunk from answering.

"You had AIDS," I said softly.

Kimberly nodded.

"That was why I said that I had been murdered. AIDS had been Bolade's gift to me," she said, sheepishly.

No one spoke for a while. Being infected with the AIDS virus was long considered a death sentence. But because of advances in drug treatment, the life expectancy of AIDS sufferers has increased dramatically.

Yet these women often give birth to children with AIDS. Did Julia have it? I wondered, but hesitated asking as Kimberly continued her story.

"I was an only child and my mother couldn't have more children. They went a bit crazy when the news hit them.

"I was given tests to see if I was sensitive to certain anti-viral medications and shouldn't be given them. Then I was prescribed NNRTIs, and PIs, Non-nucleoside reverse transcriptase inhibitors, and Protease inhibitors. They're miracle drugs but there hasn't been much research of their effect on developing teenagers. Most AIDS patients are adults.

"The drugs saved my life but changed it drastically. I had to remember to take them correctly, several times a day, and to eat at certain times a day. I needed regular blood counts and was at the doctor's office so often that I made friends there though most were much older.

"Our sharing of experiences helped me but the drugs' side effects were terrible: headaches and diarrhea and being tired all the time. Lab tests showed that my blood sugar levels had become abnormal and it was feared that I would develop diabetes."

Kimberly's face gained a look of horror and mine and Erika's exhibited shock. This was certainly *not* how we had expected the day's meet-and-greet to turn out.

"My parents frantically researched where the cutting-edge treatment was. We found my miracle in

Berlin. That was we learned that I was pregnant," Kimberly said.

Chapter 67

"I went a little crazy when telling my parents about Bolade. They didn't say anything but their looks were enough, and my mother cried. Their pure daughter had become dirty.

"I had been raped, had received a death sentence, and was pregnant. The doctors in Berlin advised an abortion. Getting it wouldn't have been a problem there. Any gynecologist would have done it.

"My mother gave offering to Obatalá, the Yoruba arch-divinity who aids children with illness. She had me take spiritual baths containing herbs. It was while trying to decide about an abortion that my miracle occurred. It was discovered that *I* was a miracle, another *Berlin patient*."

Erika and I exchanged glances. Kimberly's story was *some* story.

"We are who our genes insist that we are, whether healthy or not. It had been learned that some people, named *Berlin patients* after the first person that was discovered, have a genetic mutation making them highly resistant to the final, deadly HIV infection from the AIDS virus. This mutation, called Delta32, keeps a protein, CCR5, from rising to the surface of the immune system's T-cells. When CCR5 is on the surface of the cell, HIV can latch onto it and infect the cell; when it is absent, the cell's *door* is closed to HIV.

"Very few people have this genetic variation. It's believed to derive from ancestors who survived the massive bubonic plague in Europe centuries ago. Only 1% of Caucasians have it, and it's even rarer among Asians and Africans.

"My parents were tested too. Both have this mutated gene and had passed it on to me. I was lucky since if only one parent had it I could defend against HIV but still get it. When this was discovered, I could stop all medication. I was cured."

"But you had one big worry," I said, as Erika looked toward me and nodded.

"Yes, how my child would be," Kimberly replied.

"My parents decided that I shouldn't have an abortion. We had experienced too many thoughts of death. The image of a new life, despite how my child was conceived, filled them with hope. It would be a new path. Bolade's parents were accomplished like mine so our child should be highly intelligent too. The doctors had told us that intelligence has a large genetic component.

"We prayed that my child would be AIDS free and she is. She was tested regularly during her first four years to confirm this. She has been the healthiest baby imaginable."

At this, Kimberly broke down in loud sobs and we cried too.

Chapter 68

Hearing our cries, Oleg, one of the guards, ran into the room with his pistol drawn. Once inside, he stood motionless at the scene of three tearful girls.

"Everything's alright. We're just having a girl's moment," Erika said, and Oleg quickly left.

Kimberly wiped her eyes and sipped juice. Erika looked thoughtful as she snacked on a cracker. I stared at Kimberly and wondered again if I had been misjudging her.

Since we first met I had considered her *strange*, to put it kindly. Much of the time she would be socially awkward, unable to answer the most ordinary question. Yet at other times, like today, she would be fine.

I began wondering if Kimberly might be basically normal, or as normal as any teenager ever gets. Could her weird statements and behavior simply reflect too much stress? Did she have Post-Traumatic Stress Disorder? I had suffered this after my ordeal in Tokyo upon returning to America.

Kimberly had endured the violence of rape, the fear of death, and the extreme bodily changes of pregnancy. Both her parents were dead and her father had become a murderer. All this and the gaining of an uncaring stepmother too. It was surprising that she functioned at all!

Even Kimberly's promiscuity, her tendency to pick-up virtually any handsome man, could be reasonably explained. Her brush with death had been so long and deep that she now hungered for as much life as she could get, and for the love that the death of her parents had removed from it.

"Yes," I spoke aloud to myself. The others looked toward me but my thoughts were best left unsaid. I would later share them with Erika.

"This has been *some* afternoon. Let's go shopping," I said brightly, to raise the mood of the room.

Erika realized what I was doing and seconded my suggestion. She called Abram, her bodyguard, and told him that we were going out. Kimberly collected Julia and we were soon on our way.

Chapter 69

While driving into town, it was apparent that Julia was still sleepy. She yawned, closed her eyes, and leaned against her mother.

"Why not have Julia stay at my house. She could meet my sister and my mother would love to have her," I suggested.

This idea was as much for my mother's sake as for Julia's. My mother's feelings were hurt upon learning that Kimberly wouldn't be staying at our house that weekend. This visit would relieve the pain, and Claudine would love to meet Julia. They seemed alike.

"Wandering through a department store wouldn't be fun for her," Erika said.

Kimberly agreed, and Abram drove to our house first.

My mother was overjoyed to see us. She had always wanted a large family, the more than five kids of many Mormons in Utah. But after my youngest sister, Melanie, was born, this was medically impossible. Claudine was adopted when she was five. She is loved by us and is a real sister.

Like all mothers, mine instantly offered us food. We refused, but kids are always hungry. Claudine and Julia spent their first minutes together devouring my mother's peanut-butter cookies while checking each other out.

My other sister, Melanie, was experiencing a self-described "disaster." We dealt with it before leaving.

"How do you know when a relationship is over?" Melanie asked, in a worried tone.

"Tell us more. The facts are important," I said, sensing her distress.

"Well, Raymond and I have been going out for two months," Melanie began, before my mother interrupted.

"What?" she asked.

My mother is the nervous type. Mormons aren't supposed to have one-on-one dates until they're sixteen.

"*Oh, mom*, we just eat together in the cafeteria," Melanie reassured her.

My mother calmed down and left the dining room, sensing that her presence would disturb our attempt to help Melanie.

"Three days ago, Raymond began ignoring me. Whenever I tried talking to him, he said that he was in a rush and would run. I can't stop wondering what I might have done wrong. What should I do?" Melanie asked.

Melanie's pain was obvious and resolving her problem was what big sisters are for. The problem that she faced was one that almost everyone meets at some point in their life: when your intended decides to no longer be in your life.

"We've all been through that craziness. You have to tell yourself that it's not your fault. You're ready for a real relationship and are behaving like a grownup. He's not and isn't. You deserve better than how he's treating you. Ask yourself, if he's acting like this now, would you want him as a husband? I wouldn't," Kimberly said.

"It's not only that," Melanie continued, "I have to see him every day. What should I do then?"

Erika answered this question.

"OK, you may want to spin in your sneakers when you see him but trying to avoid him isn't the way to go and neither of you will be changing schools. Just smile or give him a quick wave. You'll soon become comfortable crossing paths with this jerk and it will be easier for you to move on."

"You might also write a list of why he was wrong for you, and find something exciting to do to remind yourself that there's plenty of fun to be had without him," I added.

Melanie's downcast expression turned into a grin. Her current crisis was over. She hugged each of us and quickly left the room, saying that she had to make a call. Is it to a new, prospective boyfriend? I wondered.

Chapter 70

Claudine and Julia got along well. I suggested that she remain at my house and Kimberly readily agreed. I had two reasons to make this suggestion: my mother would love to have her, and to avoid having Claudine along as we shopped.

Unlike what Erika had said, kids love to shop and most stores in Greenwich treat them like stars. But Erika and Kimberly have unlimited funds while my family is poor. Being smart and already aware of this painful fact, Claudine would inevitably feel the second-class status that I experience when strolling through wealthy Greenwich.

There's no fun in being poor. I had learned this aching lesson quickly after my father became ill and Social Security Disability payments became our livelihood. The annoyed faces of supermarket customers, when my mother paid slowly with Food Stamps, had fixed this belief.

Kids are sensitive and these lessons linger. I try to protect my younger sisters from being hurt. That is what older sisters and brothers attempt, knowing that growing up is hard enough.

Erika has an exhausting shopping routine. First, Richards, then Hermes, then Scoop NYC, with Saks Fifth Avenue being last. Each of these stores is close to one another on Greenwich Avenue, the main street of Greenwich.

Finding parking in Greenwich is always a pain. Because Richards' customers can park for free in the rear of the store, that is always Erika's first stop.

Though a billionaire's daughter, she obsesses about making small economies. I did her nails throughout high school though her father could easily afford its cost at any salon. As we walked, ever-watchful Abram remained a short, courteous distance behind. He knows his job.

Richards carries every major brand that you can imagine, is known for service, and is *expensive*. If you have a platinum credit card this is definitely the place for you. Obviously, it wasn't for me.

But I always enjoyed looking, and Erika continually offers to lend me (and give me!) whatever she buys so I never feel out of place. Nor did my cheap shirt and jeans arouse scorn from the staff. Some hedge fund owners were known to dress down on weekends and who could be sure that I wasn't a member of their clan?

A fashion show was ongoing when we arrived at the women's department on Richard's second floor. We spent a few minutes watching and nibbling the delicacies that had been laid. The display was looking forward to the spring runway shows in New York, Paris, London, and Milan.

Would the trend be neutral, buttery shades, like the relaxed but elegant trench coat, to gain serenity-amidst-the-storm? Would there be patriotic color combinations of red, white, and blue? Would the boundaries be pushed and the lines blurred between bedroom and boulevard with dreamy satin? You get the point.

"Let's start!" Erika ordered, after ten minutes of viewing and too many cookies.

Shopping for Erika is *serious* business.

Chapter 71

Orange might be the new black but that day both girls favored black. Kimberly's purchase was a Jenny Packham, a black neoprene, velvet beaded hem dress with deep V-neckline and V'd back. Erika chose a more modest creation by the same designer: a black multicolor bead and sequin with a gathered neckline and blouson bodice.

I noted their purchases with fascination, wondering where they would be worn. They didn't belong at any college party that I had attended. And, though being a dignified black, neither was suitable for Sunday church-going either.

But perhaps the dresses would be returned after consideration. Erika sometimes did this and Richard's never objected. Here, her yearly tab ran into the six figures with purchases for herself, her father, and friends. Regarding their prices: like they say about buying a yacht, if you need ask the cost, you can't afford it.

A smiling saleslady accompanied us to the door and, after leaving Richards, we turned toward Hermes. There, Erika bought perfumed body lotion, Un Jardin sur le Nil, and Kimberly purchased a watch. It was a slim steel watch set with diamonds. It had an opaline silvered dial, a quartz movement, and a sapphire blue, smooth, alligator leather strap. The price was a bargain at seven-thousand dollars, a mere two months' tuition at Barnard.

That day, Erika ended shopping after two stores instead of her usual four. Kimberly's story had taken its toll. After stowing the purchases in the SUV, we window-shopped at the Apple store until Erika steered us toward the Starbucks on Greenwich Avenue.

There, Erika ordered a Blonde Roast coffee with a Blueberry Yogurt Muffin and Honey. Kimberly ordered the same drink with a Cheese Danish. I ordered a Pumpkin Spice Crème: steamed milk with flavors of pumpkin, cinnamon, nutmeg and clove topped with whipped cream. Abram didn't order. He doesn't eat while on duty.

Saturday afternoon isn't a good time to be at Starbucks. It was packed with parents and kids, all having a great time or trying to pretend it. We occupied two tables. Erika and Kimberly sat at one table facing me while Abram sat at a neighboring table, scanning the room for threats. His table had three empty seats. Customers seeking seating would stare at the non-eating Abram but none dared to join him. Keeping a don't-mess-with-me look is part of his job description.

Kimberly looked more distracted than usual.

"I have the strangest feeling and am glad that I'm not alone. I know that today is Saturday but feel that it is a Monday. It's like something is seriously wrong, that I'm on the brink of a disaster, an echo from my past," she said, shaking her head.

Erika and I were silent. Neither of us could think of what to say except that this sort of conversation didn't fit at Starbucks.

We finished eating quickly. Along with the screaming kids, we weren't having a good time. Erika drove us to my house and left. Abram would return for Kimberly and Julia after dinner.

At the door, I turned toward Kimberly.

"I want you to meet someone. She lives close by, in a condo downtown. We can be there in a few minutes," I said.

Kimberly looked at me blankly. Her face had taken on the guarded look that I knew so well.

"She has helped me and can help you," I said softly.

Kimberly hesitated.

"She is an Iyalorisha. She will battle the ajogun, to regain your ayanmo," I said.

Kimberly's face relaxed for she understood. An *Iyalorisha* is a Santeria priestess, and a*jogun* are the destructive earthly and heavenly forces that try to keep us from our destiny (*ayanmo*).

"She's like my mother..." Kimberly murmured, and I nodded.

Kimberly's mother had been a Santeria priestess too.

Chapter 72

Based on what Kimberly had said in Starbucks, some people might conclude that she had gone crazy but I knew this wasn't the case. In her past she had experienced much fear. Her personal security antennae had grown overly-sensitive and now arisen. It insisted that she be cautious for danger approached.

Those who are completely alone, as Kimberly had been, are in a desperate situation. Humans are herd animals and removing a person from the herd is to cripple it. They become a part of nothing, a freak without a place.

If not losing their sanity, they become lost, a convulsing corpse. Alone, one is nothing. It is company that grants strength of mind and helps to keep fears in check.

One thinks of security as being normal but it is not. Only the presence of many forces keep the balance. When a lifetime is spent with one notion of order, responding to its change is no simple affair for everything must be learned anew.

Why am I so attuned to Kimberly's emotions? I asked myself, though the answer was obvious. I had known fear and pain, but had allies to help me too. I would be Kimberly's ally and mine would become hers, I vowed.

"Yes," I told myself aloud.

"What?" Kimberly asked, looking more uneasy.

"We're sisters. Mother Marie has helped me and will help you too," I said, in an even tone.

But it was an attending thought that went through my mind and one that I did not share: a decent intention can be a dangerous thing indeed.

We didn't speak any more as I led Kimberly to Mother Marie's condo. Greenwich has few apartments. It is mostly a town of big houses, bigger houses, and mansions.

This apartment house had been constructed sixty years earlier to house local government workers. Twenty years ago, when it lost its tax-advantaged status, it was turned into a condo and modernized in the Greenwich style. The original apartment owners are long dead and few of their heirs now live there.

My biological mother, Lena, lives in a two-bedroom apartment two floors up from Mother Marie. How can Mother Marie, a retired French teacher, afford such luxury? Well, her wealthy stockbroker son bought it for her, along with the classic Buick Roadmaster sedan in which he takes her for shopping. Mother Marie is in her eighties and healthy but doesn't like to drive.

I hadn't told Mother Marie that we were coming but knew her schedule. As a noted Santeria priestess, she held advising sessions on Saturday afternoon for members of the community. These were free and anyone could drop in. We might have to wait before seeing her.

The local community of Santeria followers is varied but not large. I had seen those who were undoubtedly poor and recognized others from their photo in the society column of the *Greenwich Times*. All sought benefit from the sacred messages of *Ifa*, the cosmic intelligence of Yoruba culture. This is granted to those who are considered deserving, by the angelic forces that exist to help with our endeavors.

Chapter 73

I rang the doorbell on the apartment and Mother Marie's son opened it. We hugged, and I introduced Kimberly and said that she required his mother's aid. He bowed, and led us to the foyer which was also a small waiting room. He offered us refreshments which we refused. Then he left us.

The tension in Kimberly's face disappeared as she scanned images of orishas on the walls: Obatalá, the Ruler of the White Cloth, the most even-tempered and intelligent of the orishas, who symbolizes ritual and ethical purity; Elegguá, the messenger divinity, who delivers sacrifices and offerings to the orisha from humans; Ogún, the essence of divine justice and truth on earth; Shangó, who grants protection against enemies, and others.

Kimberly's mother had been an Iyalorisha (priestess). Here, in Mother Marie's apartment, it was as if Kimberly had found a new home.

When the previous client left, Mother Marie entered and greeted me in the usual European fashion, with a kiss on both cheeks. She looked puzzled. A person customarily seeks her advice unaccompanied, and I quickly explained.

"Kimberly's mother was an Iyalorisha in Brazil but is now dead. Kimberly is troubled and seeks counsel from the Gods," I explained.

Kimberly looked into Mother Marie's eyes and spoke in an even, strong voice.

"It is to be that Ifa divination be continually performed so that the forces in one's life be understood and controlled," she said.

Both Mother Marie and I understood for what Kimberly had said was an ancient saying.

"Come," Mother Marie said, reaching out her hand which Kimberly took. Mother Marie led us to her study, the room in which offerings to the Gods were given and their advice was sought.

There, once seated, Mother Marie said to Kimberly, "You are troubled."

Kimberly nodded, and shared her past suffering: her rape, and feared deadly illness; her fear for her daughter's health; and the death of her parents.

Mother Marie listened, and spoke. "If we do not bear suffering that will fill a basket, we will not receive blessings that will fill a cup. We will pray, and seek guidance."

Mother Marie's prayer was to Obatalá, the arch-divinity of Yorubaland and molder of human form on Earth. Followers appeal to him for the avenging of wrongs.

Mother Marie placed eight small bowls of white rice on an altar covered with a white cloth. The color white and number eight are favored by Obatalá. Kimberly knew what to do. She touched her finger tips to her lips and to the shrine. Then she and Mother Marie kneeled, and Mother Marie spoke.

"Orisa'ala, the great one who owns the world,

And to whom the control of the world must be assigned,

Obatalá, Obatarisha, the orisha with authority

Who is as precious as pure honey.

The orisha with inexhaustible strength,

The inheritor of reputation

Whose great fame does not detract from his authority.

Obatalá save me!

One expects salvation from one's orisha,

"I do not know how to save myself."

Then, though the room remained silent, words rumbled in my head: "Ebo fin, Eru da. Dide, dide lalafia." ("The offerings are accepted. Evil forces depart. Arise, arise in peace.")

Despite this comforting response, questions jarred my mind. Why had Mother Marie chosen Obatalá to seek guidance? Though a Great Spirit, he had weaknesses while on Earth, having once languished in jail from being too proud to battle for his release. He had been imprisoned three times for doing the right thing at the wrong time.

What similarity did Mother Marie sense between Obatalá's and Kimberly's lives? Would the prophecy ceremony that followed tell us? I wondered.

Chapter 74

We make choices as we move through life. In the Santeria faith it is believed that everyone has a destiny that is forgotten at birth. During the ritual of divination, their destiny is re-discovered. It is learned how their fate is unfolding, and how to come in harmony with their preset fortune.

"Choosing a particular school, taking a certain job, and deciding whether to have children cuts off other opportunities. Divination, and communication with one's guardian spirit, can reveal whether a person's choices accord with their destiny. If not, divination teaches how they can return to the path chosen by their spirit so they can live in harmony with themselves, their family and community, and the world itself," Mother Marie had once told me.

These facts were already known by Kimberly. Since her mother had been a Santeria priestess, Kimberly had been steeped in that faith since birth.

"Cowrie-shell divination is called *merindinlogun* in Brazil," she said.

I knew of the ceremony but not that fact.

After the prayer, and our offering being accepted by Obatalá, Mother Marie brought out a bag containing holy seashells. She carefully selected sixteen for the divination, placing the remaining shells to the side with the natural "mouth" facing down. These are called *witnesses* and remain unused during the divination.

When the sixteen shells are cast on the mat, a numerical value is obtained from zero to sixteen by adding the values of the shells. The number corresponds to the *odu* (pattern) associated with a particular God, He or She then *speaks* to the priest.

This ritual is complicated and requires years of study to be skillfully used. For example, having one *mouth* up is associated with the God, Okana. It is a perilous odu when one feels only two things: the rage of the heart, and its desire to love.

Mother Marie threw the shells, and the results astonished us. How often in one toss do twelve out of sixteen objects turn out the same? A person getting results like these should play the lottery daily.

"It is *Ejila Shebora*," Mother Marie said, in a sober tone.

Kimberly nodded and turned toward me.

"*Twelve mouths on the mat* means that trouble is coming. *Big* trouble," she said, and I saw panic in her eyes.

Chapter 75

After the reading of the shells, a patakí (story) is told. This is intended to instruct the seeker and send them on the most beneficial course for their life. Choosing the correct patakí is difficult since prophesies based on the reading can vary greatly. I knew that choosing the best story when *twelve mouths on the mat* occurs would be particularly difficult since this result is rare.

The story that Mother Marie told us concerned Shangó, and I understood why. Shangó is more than a name. It is a word from an old Yoruba dialect and means *problems*, or, as Kimberly had said, "*Big* trouble."

"Though Shangó was a powerhouse who had unified the Yoruba nations, at one point his entire existence became one huge problem after another, to himself and those closest to him," Mother Marie said.

"Fog shrouded the battlefield and smoke and the rot of stench and decay burned Shangó's nose. Surrounded by the dead and the dying, a voice whispered to him: "My son, the wages of war are the bodies of your enemies and of your loyal men."

"But this had occurred in a nightmare, and Shangó awoke in a start. He was damp with sweat, his head throbbed, and his chest was tight with panic for this dream had tormented him for weeks.

"Seeking comfort, he turned on his side to reach for his wife but she was gone and he was alone. 'Even my wife has abandoned me,' he spoke aloud to himself. It was the lowest point of his life.

"Shangó sat on the edge of his bed and considered his life. His subjects had once cheered him but his greed for success had brought many battles and they now questioned their worth. His soldiers no longer wanted to die.

"Shangó had changed too. He had always had a hot temper and, as exhaustion warped his mind, he ignored his adviser's advice of caution and rest. He had behaved beyond reason, taking mistresses in foreign lands. His wife no longer wanted to wait and had left him.

"Feeling desperate, he sought out the diviner Mofá, who gave him the following advice: 'Do not fight so much. When you must war, do it for honor and treat your fallen enemies well. Follow the advice of your elders, do not argue, and be a good husband. But most importantly, do not fail to give ebó (offering) for even at your lowest point the Gods had not deserted you. There are no arms so strong that they can hold the sun, nor mouth so powerful that it can command the day.'

"Shangó did as the wise diviner, Mofá had instructed. In time, his life was renewed and he never suffered loss again.

"He had learned that life is not about war and conquest but about living and living well. He had discovered that fear serves no useful purpose in the quest for knowledge, and that knowledge frees us from spiritual slavery and is the beginning of spiritual evolution. After this, Shangó became a God who was not only feared but loved. He had committed himself to growth, not only to conquest."

Mother Marie paused before peering into Kimberly's eyes.

"It is these lessons that you must follow," Mother Marie said, and she rose from the chair.

Mother Marie could do no more.

Chapter 76

While walking home, I wondered what Mother Marie had told Kimberly as they embraced before we left.

"What did Mother Marie whisper?" I asked.

"That I must have faith, and an ancient Yoruba proverb: that 'truth, although seemingly slow and weak, overcomes falsehood in the end,'" Kimberly replied.

"What did she mean by that?"

"I have no idea."

We spoke no more until reaching my house. Divination is an important ritual and it had affected us deeply.

Kimberly's uncle had already contracted with Vladimir's company for her family's security and Oleg was assigned to handle this task temporarily. More staff was coming from Europe for the long-term arrangement.

Oleg was in his mid-forties, tall and sturdily built. I had known him for years. Though looking like a lawyer or a teacher, and with a ready smile, he had spent his life battling terrorists and gangsters in Russia.

When we arrived home, he was playing Chutes and Ladders with Julia and Claudine. They had drafted him and I watched as they played. His playing piece was a girl and I smiled as he moved it. He sensed our presence, looked into my eyes and returned my smile.

When the three of them had left, Claudine and I went to the dining room. I wasn't hungry but missing family meals is not an option with my mother.

Seeing the accustomed food made me feel at home: meat loaf for the others and vegetarian burger for me. My sister, Melanie, had baked Raspberry Linzer Tarts for dessert. She and my other sisters are gifted cooks. I don't even try more than melted cheese sandwiches. Thankfully, my boyfriend, Randy, doesn't mind my inadequacy.

"You will be joining us for church?" my mother asked, hesitantly.

This ordinarily was a demand and not a question. Her change of tone could have reflected my being older but more likely resulted from the mellowing influence of the Parenting Group that she had been attending at our church. The current minister was modern.

I worried about Kimberly, and wanted more face time with Erika. Our meetings had become infrequent since we began college at distant schools. But family is important too, and attending church would please my mother.

"*Of course I'm coming,*" I said, and my mother beamed.

Chapter 77

People of any faith aren't born enjoying religious services. If you doubt this, watch young kids at your congregation. Most adults attend services to gain a local community of like-minded people, and for the comforting rituals that religions provide to deal with birth and marriage and illness and death. Most people would probably be happiest with a ten-minute service followed by a social hour but no religion offers this.

Over the years I had become accustomed to the three hour Mormon service. Here, the singing of hymns is followed by prayers offered by members. Then the bread and water sacrament, and talks by assigned speakers. Religion groups, divided by age and sex, are held before or after the sacrament meeting.

I knew the routine. That Sunday morning we entered the church dressed in the expected plain clothes: a dress for women; a suit and tie for men. Families sit together and seating isn't assigned.

I had been attending this church since childhood and almost everyone was familiar. Smiles and greetings were automatically exchanged as we passed but, then and throughout the service, my thinking remained locked on Kimberly.

I trusted Mother Marie's intuition and knew firsthand the power of the Gods. They had saved my life, and returned my English father to me. Now Kimberly, who I considered my sister, was foretold danger. From who or what we didn't know but fate had marked her and we were afraid.

As if to reinforce the truth of the proverb that man proposes and God disposes, one of that morning's talks was on fear. The speaker was in her thirties. She had grown up in an abusive, alcoholic family where *both* her parents were drunks. She was the oldest of five children, and their care had fallen on her before she was a teenager.

During the frequent violent fights between her parents, she would take her brothers and sister to a large walk-in closet. There, seated in the dark with the sounds of parental battle reduced to a dull roar, she read stories to them by flashlight as they snacked on the cookies that she had brought. Terror had been changed into a party.

Child Protective Services became involved and the children were removed from the family. Then followed a series of foster homes ranging from uncaring to loving. That last couple was Mormon and this was how she discovered the Church.

After this biography, the woman turned to her topic of fear. She said that people share many fears ranging from snakes and public speaking to flying and dentists. She said that fear is a basic human emotion and is often dealt with in the Bible because God knows that all wrestle with fear at some time in their life.

The speaker said that fear arises when we must deal with difficulties, and that while these cause pain, they can also aid our personal growth. She said that we must maintain our faith in God, and that He has faith in us.

Though having heard similar thoughts many times, they hit the spot that day.

Chapter 78

After church, my family had brunch at home and the food wasn't special: Food Stamps don't allow for such purchases. But none of us minded since it was the intimacy that counted and not the food.

When you see someone often, you get accustomed to how they look. Thus, my mother's threadbare clothes had ceased to register with me, or that my younger sisters' clothes were hand-me-downs. It was how things had been in my family for many years.

Though believing that clothes don't make the person, it was hard for me not to feel badly for them in wealthy Greenwich. Our friends didn't care but not everyone behaved kindly. Worn clothes and purchasing with food stamps earns contemptuous looks and whispered comments here.

I wanted to brighten their lives, even if briefly. Christmas was coming and my presents would be special, I vowed. But this required money and I had little.

My babysitting job for Charlotte's son had ended. After that, I had brief jobs but none had "taken." The chemistry between us hadn't fit. Either our schedules couldn't mesh or the family demanded too much.

I considered myself a babysitter and refused to cook and clean and iron too. Some wealthy people are unnecessarily frugal. I intended to seek work from the Barnard Babysitting Service upon my return to campus.

Erika arranged for Oleg to drive us back to Manhattan. While I spoke with Kimberly, Julia lay sleeping in her arms.

"What do you plan on doing?" I asked, referring to Mother Marie's cryptic warning.

"Nothing, except try and keep calm. I have no idea what my trouble will be but can't think of anything worse than what I've already experienced. Can you?"

"No."

Still, I felt uneasy and wanted to do something concrete.

"Do you remember my phone number?" I asked.

Kimberly didn't so I wrote it down.

"Memorize it and call me if you need help. I'll be there for you and Vladimir will too. Day or night, you're never alone. You must remember that!"

Kimberly promised and I felt relieved. I had done all that I could and what will happen will happen. Her fate is in the hands of the Gods, I told myself.

In the night, as we drove back to Manhattan, an unpleasant thought entered my mind. A narrow cone of light had shot through our car creating a horror movie view. Some events are bigger than humans can bear, I told myself. I hoped that Kimberly's wouldn't be.

Chapter 79

After dropping off Julia at her home, we returned to Brooks Hall. Oleg opened the car door for us like a chauffeur, attracting stares.

Unlike Kimberly's impending disaster, most student worries are trivial. After entering the dormitory, I noticed a girl standing at the entrance to the lounge. She stared down at her body from right to left and then back again. This caught my attention.

"What's up with Darlene?" I asked, nodding toward her.

"Oh, *her*. She's afraid that her breasts don't match and continually checks them," Kimberly replied.

"No girl's breasts match. Mine don't," I said.

"Well, Darlene hasn't accepted this fact yet. She wants to be *perfect*. That should be my only worry," Kimberly said.

It can't be. Your breasts *are* perfect, I thought, and quickly dismissed the matter.

Considering what happened that weekend I feared that my sleep would be troubled but it wasn't. My last thought before falling asleep was to remind myself to check-in with the Barnard Babysitting Service the next morning.

"I was just about to call. You'll be *perfect!*" the Service's receptionist burst out after I introduced myself.

I began looking toward my breasts before catching myself and returning her smile.

"The mother is on Barnard's Board and it's a *wonderful* family. They live on the Upper East Side and have two *delightful* girls. The father works on Wall Street and the mother is a lawyer, a former state prosecutor. You'll *love* them, and they've offered 50% above our standard rate which means that you'll be paid 25% more."

That the Service should receive half my pay for simply making phone calls needled me but I kept an idiotic smile fixed to my face. Choose your battles wisely, my lawyer-father advises his daughters, and we try. I needed the money, the Service held the power, and arguing for more pay wasn't a battle that I would win.

"I'm ready to go," I said, brightly.

"*Great*! I'll call and set up an appointment. You can wait in our staff lounge, down the hall on your right. There's yogurt and milk in the refrigerator. We treat our employees *right*!"

I said nothing and broadened my stupid grin. The lounge was empty. I chose a strawberry-banana yoghurt, then sat and waited and waited. Making one phone call is taking a long time, I thought.

I began wondering why the interviewer had been so excited and the couple would pay more than the standard rate, which was already far from cheap. The cost of a full-time babysitter or a preschool in Manhattan costs more than housing in many American cities.

But this family's income would be well into the six figures and they might be concerned with buying loyalty, I mused. Many babysitters quit after earning enough for a desired purchase.

After finishing my second yoghurt and beginning on a raspberry-filled donut, the interviewer re-appeared and sat beside me.

"I'm sorry to have taken so long but Mrs. Krillbergh had to change her schedule and get back to me. She'll see you now and will pay your cab fare both ways. You'll *love* this family."

Despite my need for money, I began feeling uneasy. Families didn't usually offer benefits to babysitters apart from an occasional restaurant meal while on the job. Why were they willing to pay more, and to throw in taxi fare too?

"Have they had other babysitters?" I asked.

"The four that we sent haven't worked out. The longest lasted only two days but you know how unpredictable teenagers can be," came the hesitant reply.

"Your last employer, Charlotte, said that you were wonderful with her son and *absolutely* reliable. We do check-up on our workers," she added.

I rose to leave.

"I'll give it my best shot," I said, smiling despite my doubts.

Every family has a few skeletons in their closet but this family seemed to have an entire gallery of them, I thought, but didn't say.

Chapter 80

The Krillbergh apartment was on the 39th floor of a fifty-one story building on East 85th Street, a short walk from the Metropolitan Museum of Art and the Mayor's official residence. It is a neighborhood for the rich and politically connected. I didn't fit in on either count though, as a babysitter, I would be temporarily accepted.

Thus, even when wearing cheap clothes, I could stroll with my two expensively dressed wards without being hassled by the police. *If* I kept the job longer than the past babysitters, that is. I couldn't imagine what had so frightened them. Were the kids or their parents the monsters? Or both? I would soon find out.

The trip from Barnard to East 85th Street took a half-hour. The driver went south on Broadway to 96th Street, then crossing Central Park to the Upper East Side.

The Upper East Side and the Upper West Side neighborhoods of Manhattan are very different. While both areas are costly to live, you see far more poverty on the Upper West Side. There, homeless and obviously disturbed people abound but are largely absent to where I was going.

The building's uniformed doorman took one glance and barred my presence with an upraised hand. I smiled, told him that I had an appointment with Mrs. Krillbergh in apartment 3901, and he told me to check in with the desk clerk. Before releasing me, he called the lobby to say that I was on my way. The building's security impressed me.

The clerk in the lobby wore a black suit, white shirt, and black tie. He didn't smile or speak to me, and phoned the apartment before pointing me on my way. My clothes indicated that I wasn't worth talking to, that he would never get a Christmas present from me.

The elevator whisked me upstairs and a sign pointed me in the correct direction. I turned right and began walking.

The door of apartment 3901 was being held open by a tall woman in her thirties. I lack the clothing expertise of Erika and Kimberly but instantly saw that this woman's fashion fit the neighborhood. Shopping with Erika has given me an eye for such detail.

Mrs. Krillbergh's dressed-to-kill navy blue, wool crêpe jacket and pants had probably cost several thousand dollars, as much as my family's monthly income. The jacket had notched lapels, a one button front closure, and two pockets. The pants had two side slash pockets and an unfinished hem. Her red, swirl print scarf was silk, and expensive.

When I later complimented her suit, I was informed that it was a Giorgio Armani. "The scarf is by Pucci and also Italian," she added.

Mrs. Krillbergh's blond hair hit her collarbone and was carefully layered for the shape of her face. Her makeup was equally tasteful: rose blush across her forehead and cheeks, gold eye shadow, and nude-pink lipstick. She might be a prosperous lawyer *or* an expensive call girl, I told myself, and instantly wondered why my mind had erupted with such an out-of-the-box thought.

Mrs. Krillbergh stood silently, like a runway model, so I spoke first.

"I'm Margaret, the babysitter from Barnard," I said brightly.

"I was expecting you, come in," came her reply.

Her tone was exhausted and almost lifeless but it wasn't this that gained my attention. Her scarf had slipped when she turned to close the door and I saw a reddening bruise on the back of her neck. That could not be from an accident, I told myself. Someone had threatened her, or had tried to strangle her.

Chapter 81

We talked. This apartment was similar to others that I had seen in luxury Manhattan buildings. It had polished hardwood floors covered by rugs, color accents to create interesting optical effects, and floor-to-ceiling windows with stunning views.

The living room was designed to attract attention with its classy black and white color combination and bright red and yellow accents. Mrs. Krillbergh asked if I wanted coffee. I refused, adding that I was Mormon and didn't drink coffee.

"So are we, but we're not *that* religious," she said, smiling.

My being Mormon was probably another reason why I was considered "perfect" for this family, I told myself.

Mrs. Krillbergh leaned back on the sofa. She stretched, crossed her long legs, and got down to business.

"Tell me about yourself," she said, and I gave her my standard needful-babysitter-seeking-a-job pitch.

"I'm in my second year at Barnard. My family lives in Greenwich. My father is a lawyer and my mother worked as a teacher but is now a stay-at-home mom. I have an older sister who just graduated from New York University and two younger sisters.

"During high school, I and a friend began and operated a babysitting service much like Barnard's. I've worked for a number of families in Manhattan. The longest stint, for most of last year, was for a doctor's young son."

"That's impressive," Mrs. Krillbergh said.

I didn't respond. When interacting with wealthy people it's important to seem meek, like the silent, smooth servants in British TV dramas.

Mrs. Krillbergh paused for a moment, as if she weren't sure how to raise an issue.

"We're seeking a babysitter who will *stay*. Change is hard for a family and particularly on children. Why do you want to work? Coming from Greenwich and having a lawyer for a father indicates that your family has means."

I try to avoid revealing my family's poverty but didn't have a choice. Mrs. Krillbergh had made it clear that if I couldn't convince her *why* I needed a job, I wouldn't get it. So I bit the bullet and told her the facts.

"My father closed his law practice after catching Lyme disease. Since then my family has been supported by his Social Security Disability payments. Our house is owned by an old family trust. My family has long roots in Greenwich. A past relative was Chief Justice of the Connecticut Supreme Court. If I hadn't been awarded a full scholarship by Barnard, I wouldn't be able to attend. The babysitting money pays for my expenses," I said.

I left out that my family was getting Food Stamps. That would feel too humiliating to say though it's no shame.

Mrs. Krillbergh's face colored beneath her makeup.

"I'm sorry. I didn't expect for my question to be painful. I just wanted to be sure that you were serious. We've had bad luck with babysitters," Mrs. Krillbergh said.

"It's alright. We haven't always been poor but it's nothing to be ashamed of," I replied.

"Yes, there are far worse things in life," she said.

Mrs. Krillbergh's hand touched her neck. She meant for the gesture to seem casual but the mark that I had seen told me it wasn't.

I quickly looked away, feeling sure that she would not want me to see the tears in her eyes.

Chapter 82

"What are your children like?" I asked.

I wanted to change the subject and knew that parents love to talk about their kids.

"They're *darlings*," Mrs. Krillbergh said, after wiping her eyes with a tissue. "My allergies, it's the season," she explained.

I don't have allergies but knew from friends that these were most bothersome during the spring and summer, not near winter as it was now. But I said nothing. If you're talking you're not getting information, my lawyer-father often says.

"How old are they?" I asked, though having already gotten this information from the Babysitting Service.

"Kristina is seven and Alexandra is five. We kept them home from school so you could meet them. My husband took them to the playground in Carl Schurz Park. It's a few blocks away, 86th Street at the East River, close by the Mayor's residence, Gracie Mansion.

"There's a dog run so you have to hold tightly onto children. Some owners object to using a leash though it's against the law not to. The children will be back any minute. Are you sure that you wouldn't want something to drink?"

"Well, maybe some juice," I said.

Teenagers are always considered to be hungry and mothers become comfortable when feeding them. Doing this also serves to put teenagers in their needy role. After I took a sip from an apple juice box, Mrs. Krillbergh invited me to tour the apartment.

"There are four bedrooms: ours, one for each of the children, and one that's used as a home office. We added a bed there for visiting relatives. Both my husband and I work long, irregular hours. Would it be a problem if you stayed until we returned? If we're late, you could sleep in the bedroom. We need a babysitter with flexible hours. Of course we will pay for all of the hours that you are here," she said.

My answer was slow in coming. Not from reluctance but from calculating how much money I would earn. Mrs. Krillbergh raised her offer.

"We've agreed to pay 50% above the Service's standard rate and will add time-and-a-half for all hours worked after 8PM and double time on weekends," she added quickly.

"That would be fine. I could do homework while the children are sleeping," I said, with a smile.

I ordinarily refer to children as "kids" but have found that parents object to this common slang, feeling that it demeans their offspring. All cultures have peculiarities and the parenting must be the most individual, I had long before concluded.

The rooms were large with each being decorated in a different style. I murmured courteous expressions of delight.

"My husband had been a star-struck, only occasionally working actor. He suggested that I become a lawyer to support us. I had been working as an interior decorator and loved the work but it paid little and jobs were hard to come by. The career change lasted longer than the marriage," Mrs. Krillbergh said.

Then, as if recognizing that her statement was puzzling, she added, "He was my first husband. Bradley, the father of my children, is my second."

I fixed a smile of understanding to my face but wondered at her tone. While second marriages are common, her tone seemed to imply that she hoped for a third. Her bruised neck, tears, and quickly quitting babysitters are starting to make sense, I thought.

Chapter 83

Mrs. Krillbergh began her tour with the room that I would use if I had to sleep over. It was clear that this room was mostly used as a home-office. A swivel chair lay before a computer work center holding a desktop computer and a printer. Two file cabinets were alongside with additional storage being built into an alcove. There was also a modern version of the traditional roll-top desk with a pin-board fastened to the wall beside it.

The bed lay in a corner, almost as an after-thought. A walk-in closet held file boxes but a few clothes hangers too. A low chest of drawers, which doubled as a night table, was beside the bed.

A small bathroom was reached through a communicating door. There, a tiled partition wall divided the toilet and shower stalls. The washstand was of polished wood. Mirrored walls and cleverly designed storage made the most of the remaining area.

"It's like each room is a separate entity, detached from the others," I said.

"You have a good eye," Mrs. Krillbergh replied. "In interior design it's called the English arrangement. Each room is made independent and perfectly adapted to its purpose. Rooms have better space for furniture by reducing the number of communicating doors. This also allows for greater privacy.

"There's a limit to the construction permitted in a condo building but I pushed it. You can see that while there is no direct connection between the living-room and dining-room, they're brought into a conveniently close relationship by the arched doorways connecting them through the intervening hall."

Her face lit up as she spoke of this activity and I wondered if her current work as a lawyer provided as much joy.

"The living room is a place of cheer with three of its walls being windowed to admit abundant light. The windows were varied in size and shape to make each wall distinctive. A built-in bookcase to the right of the fireplace centers the inner wall.

"The dining-room is balanced by a door leading to the kitchen with the wall-space between providing an ideal location for the serving table.

"In the hall, the living room, and the dining room, the wood-trim is birch that was stained to the color of maple syrup. The walls of these rooms are sand finished plaster with hardwood floors installed throughout.

"The kitchen walls are painted and most equipment is built-in. Cabinets, shelves, and cupboards range around three walls. One wall is left free for the work-table.

"I designed the children's rooms with good lighting, comfortable flooring, and free-standing furniture which can be changed as they grow older," Mrs. Krillbergh said.

"You've done wonders. The other apartments that I've seen were obviously professionally decorated but seemed to lack the human touch," I said, with honest enthusiasm.

"Let me tell you the children's schedules," Mrs. Krillbergh said, smiling.

This was the first real–not practiced–smile that I had seen since we met.

I removed a small pad from my backpack to write what she would tell me but was unable to find a pen. I can be forgetful about such things.

Mrs. Krillbergh wore a small pen clipped to her jacket pocket.

"I have no pen," I said, and reached toward her's.

"*No,*" she burst out, in an alarmed tone, and instantly jumped back.

Then, catching herself, she spoke calmly.

"I'll get a pen from the office," she said.

Chapter 84

When still very young, I realized that things don't happen until they happen and it was the pen's *happening* that caused me to really think. That is not simply a pen but a video recorder too, I sensed. Mrs. Krillbergh's activity is being recorded and monitored, as if she were an imprisoned slave. There is *definitely* something wrong with this family, I concluded.

It hadn't been babysitter foolishness or nasty children or the bad-tempered demands of their parents that caused the previous babysitters to quit. I hadn't yet met the father or the children but already felt uneasy. The apartment and neighborhood were gorgeous and the pay was wonderful and needed. But the job felt risky and I didn't yet know why.

Still, there's a difference between a risk and a gamble. A risk is knowing the odds and taking them but a gamble is pure chance, closing your eyes and acting. It's sensible to take risks and, like everyone, I had been doing this all my life. But I never gambled. Either I lacked the temperament or a past experience had given me the correct lesson.

My family was prosperous before my father caught Lyme disease and stopped working. Once, while vacationing at a resort in Aruba, we passed rows of slot machines. They were colorful, I wanted to play, and my dad let me. "It'll teach her a lifelong lesson," he told my disapproving mother, and it did.

I won $100, kept playing, and quickly lost it all. I've never again had the urge to gamble, or thought that a babysitting job could be one. Though the other babysitters had left quickly, the worst that would happen is that I would quit too. My family would receive smaller Christmas gifts but this would matter far more to me than to them. Doesn't an old song say that you can't buy love?

Moments after these thoughts left my mind, Mrs. Krillbergh returned with a pen. I wrote the hours that I was expected to work and the children's school schedules. I was also told their parents' work and cell phone numbers and that of the children's pediatrician. I appeared to have been hired even before meeting the children or their father.

"They'll be returning soon. I wanted to meet you first, to be sure," Mrs. Krillbergh said, with her practiced smile.

I returned the smile. The intimacy that we had shared earlier was gone. It was now all business, as it should be.

I heard sounds, and then a voice from the hallway, "*Darling, we're home.*" The voice had an exaggerated, carnival-like, sing-song tone. The children and their father had arrived.

Chapter 85

The children's father wasn't what I expected. I was told by the Babysitting Service that he was a stockbroker and had created his image from there. He would wear the three-piece suit of executives in Greenwich. His starched, cuff-linked shirt would sport a regimental tie, a popular British import though out-of-place with a non-military crowd.

Mr. Krillbergh wasn't anything like this. Physically, he was a tall, lean figure crowned by a long, narrow head. His sharp nose leaned upward and his unkempt, gray hair flashed in the up-and-down motion of his stride. His clothes–green shirt, black jeans, red and black sneakers, herringbone sport jacket–were mismatched and too large. Either he ignores the advice of sales clerks or clothes aren't important to him and he's lost weight, I thought.

I had met others like him. Some, like my boyfriend, Randy, are geniuses and too involved with intellectual matters to be concerned with the ordinary. But others were lost. Crazy and homeless, they wander the City's streets.

I didn't draw an immediate conclusion. Mr. Krillbergh was certainly not homeless and he looked different, not lost.

He entered the room holding each of his daughters by a hand. Upon seeing me, he relinquished them and bounded toward me. I'm tall, five foot ten inches, but he was at least five inches taller. He smiled and held out his hand. I extended mine and he squeezed it. His grip was firm and almost painful but I said nothing. I was gathering facts.

"So *you're* our new babysitter," he said, as his face held a practiced smile.

"If that means I'm hired," I replied, being unsure what to say.

The children fidgeted as a heavy silence overlay us. Mrs. Krillbergh gave her husband a nervous look. He nodded, and she accepted her order.

"Margaret is *perfect*. I already showed her the room she could use and gave her the children's schedules," Mrs. Krillbergh said.

Both parents looked toward me. The decision was mine. I swallowed, smiled, said "yes," and joined this puzzling family.

A moment later, two pieces of advice from my father entered my mind: that impulsive actions can lead to trouble and unintended consequences; and that there is no greater folly in the universe than thinking that one is in control of things.

Chapter 86

While first impressions can be accurate, they are often incomplete. If you sense that you won't like someone at first glance, you probably won't though the reason for this will likely escape you. The unconscious mind is powerful and our instincts try to protect us without our conscious awareness.

So if you see a person that scares you, don't hesitate to cross the street. Most times, their angry look will only mean that they are having a bad day. But sometimes–*sometimes*–they *are* dangerous. Your innate reptilian survival instinct has picked up a signal, weighed it, and screams, *"Run!"*

I had gotten mixed signals from the Krillbergh parents: that they were odd but not dangerous, at least not to me. The wife, Jennifer, seemed cowed by Bradley, her husband. But it was obvious that both adored their children and, when with them, neither daughter had expressed concern. Still, how freely would children share their fears with a stranger, in the presence of their parents? I asked myself

My class times fit well with my babysitting duties. The Krillbergh's put their kids on the school bus in the morning and I met them in front of their apartment house in the afternoon. Then they snacked, did homework, played games, and awaited their parents' arrival.

If both parents worked late, I made supper for the children. My cooking skill is most charitably described as "limited" but the girls never complained. They loved pancakes, and macaroni and cheese, and peanut butter and jelly sandwiches.

Even from the start, Kristina, seven, and Alexandra, five, didn't give me trouble. I quickly became their big sister and confidante of their secrets, such as they were. Alexandra squealed when telling me her latest: that the video game she was playing had called her "Cutie," to which I responded, "Wow!"

Her sister's interests lay in a Princess puzzle that she put together repeatedly, and the simply written chapter books that she read.

One afternoon, Kristina needed a scissor for an art project that she was constructing, I searched for it in the kitchen and the home office without success.

"There's a big scissor in my parents' bedroom but they won't let me use it," Kristina said.

Your parents are careful, I thought approvingly, and went to get them. The parents' bedroom was obviously designed for the fabrics and wallpaper and even the lampshades matched. The dark colors were restful, and gave the room a sophisticated look. Their darkness seemed to sandwich the light colors in some mysterious way.

Above the king-size bed, wooden curtain rods were attached to the ceiling. From it hung a valence and curtains of ribbon-edged voile. It gave a feminine effect and I wondered at Mr. Krillbergh's opinion of it. But each to their own, I concluded, and dropped the thought.

Where would Mrs. Krillbergh hide the scissor? I asked myself. Probably in a drawer to keep prying children's hands away. I had learned that a file box or drawer present a psychological barrier for well-behaved children and Kristina and Alexandra were certainly that.

Atop a cupboard lay an antique lacquered wooden box imprinted with scenes of Oriental girls and closed with a simple hasp. Within, I found the scissor, and more: a short whip with thin, red-stained straps; four pairs of velvet-covered handcuffs; and a red ball gag to impose silence.

Their sight had a hypnotic effect. It reminded me of my experience in Tokyo from which I still have nightmares. I slowly replaced the torture gear, closed the box, and left the room. The Krillbergh's would not have wanted me to see this. I was calm when I rejoined the children.

"I'm sorry, but I couldn't find the scissor," I lied to Kristina.

Chapter 87

A ball gag is basically a ping-pong ball that is placed in a person's mouth and is held in place by a strap that fastens around their head. It is widely used in S&M sex play, and by sadistic killers with a different agenda. This gadget has become widely known through graphic TV shows and movies and can even be bought on Amazon.

I'm not into S&M and don't believe that any of my friends are. If so, they're not telling me. Voluntary adult sex play is one thing but the marks on Mrs. Krillbergh's neck indicated that this might not be the case with her. Still, this couple's sex life isn't my business. But if Bradley ever comes on to me, he'll be carried from the apartment on a stretcher, I promised myself.

It was hard to remain gloomy amidst the apartment's gorgeous furnishings and views. Jennifer had given me its keys so I could come and go at will. Because my small dorm room was suffocating and the bustling library was noisy, I began studying at the Krillbergh's apartment. Soon, I had become so familiar to the building's staff that they addressed me by name.

I had finished studying and felt that I needed a break. Being unable to afford the cost of cable hook-up, there is no TV in my dorm room. Thus, depending on what is on, watching TV can be a treat.

It happened an hour before the children arrived home. I was relaxing in the living room, immersed on the recliner, watching the fifty-two-inch TV that Bradley had proudly pointed out to me. I first checked Turner Classic Movies, but an ancient silent film was being shown. I switched to CNN and got an instant shock. Bradley's image was on the screen and he wasn't alone. Men held each of his arms and his hands were handcuffed. I walked close to the TV and stared.

My first thoughts came from the mark on Jennifer's neck and the torture gear: Bradley has been arrested for rape or murder or both, I told myself.

Chapter 88

My best friend, Erika, had a painful life After her mother and sister were murdered, she began seeing a therapist twice a week. They even take vacations in August.

Because of this, Erika is my go-to person about anything psychological. One of the many things that she told me, which her doctor had told her, is that the mind is efficient and tries to place thoughts and events within their proper place. This is usually helpful but can be wrong.

That is what happened when I saw Bradley on TV. My emotional shock caused me to tune out the announcer's words and assume that he had been arrested for a sexual or violent offense, which wasn't true. His perp-walk was caused by another crime. He was accused of stealing money, with a computer and not a gun.

I didn't understand from the announcer's description exactly what he had done and sensed from her tone that she didn't either. Jennifer explained it to me that night while the children slept, unaware of the catastrophe that had invaded their family.

Naturally enough, Jennifer looked drained upon arriving home. She had called me earlier to say that she would be late. She asked if I could stay at the apartment for a few days and I agreed.

Missing classes is OK at Barnard. I would get the notes from a classmate. Some students spend most of their time in local hangouts, coming for the first day of class, showing up for exams, and that's it.

I let Jennifer open the conversation as we sat in the living room.

"Bradley has...*difficulties*," Jennifer said.

I said nothing and nodded to indicate that I was paying attention.

"He's been...*arrested*."

I nodded again but now felt that I should say something.

"Things happen," I said.

This was a dumb thing to say but there may not be an accepted reaction for when someone tells you that their spouse had been arrested. Would it be sadness that they were caught?

Jennifer's brain seemed not to be working properly since she now stopped speaking. Our conversation was saved from further embarrassment by a piercing scream.

Chapter 89

Few sounds jar one more quickly than a child's scream. Jennifer and I walked quickly toward the bedrooms. The cry had come from Kristina's room. She sat-up, paralyzed in bed, as we rushed to her side.

"What's wrong, darling? Did you have a bad dream," Jennifer asked, after enfolding Kristina in her arms.

Kristina just nodded, being unable to speak. Jennifer patted her daughter's back and said nothing so I spoke up.

"Dreams can't hurt us. They're like mystery movies that our mind makes up. A scary dream tells us that we're afraid, of maybe having to do something new. Do you remember your dream?" I asked.

I had given this explanation to many children and it helped.

Kristina's eyes were wide with fear. I became aware of the odor of urine. She had wet herself.

"I was tied up, being hit," she said, hesitantly.

My thought went to the S&M tools that I discovered in her parents' bedroom. Had Kristina stumbled upon their sex play? I wondered.

"*All* dreams are our friends, even scary ones. They're just telling us that there are scary things going on inside us," I repeated. "Drinking juice helps. Would you like juice?" I asked.

Kristina nodded, latching on to my suggested cure. I had learned that food can almost magically improve a child's mood.

I looked toward Jennifer–she was the mother–and she nodded agreement. A minute later I returned with an apple juice box. This is always a safe choice with kids.

After taking several sips, Kristina looked toward her mother who was busy changing the wet sheet. Underneath, was a rubber pad. That night's bedwetting must not have been the first time, I thought.

Years before, after first confronting this problem while babysitting, I had looked it up on the Internet. Two unconscious motives were given for the behavior: that the child wants to return to being a baby, to begin their life over; and that they are expressing angry feelings, doing what pisses their parents, so to speak.

This had made good sense about the boy that I was then babysitting. His parents were more concerned with their social standing than him.

"Where's daddy?" Kristina asked.

"He's away on a business trip. He'll be gone for a few days," Jennifer replied.

It was a good answer but the children would soon learn the truth. Even keeping them from watching TV wouldn't help. In this wealthy neighborhood, children would inevitably overhear their parents speaking of Bradley's well-publicized financial crime.

When Kristina settled down, we left her room and Jennifer turned toward me.

"If he doesn't get out on bail, I don't know what I'll tell them," she said.

"We'll think of something," I replied.

Jennifer frowned.

"I'm worried for Bradley. Being in jail is so dangerous," she said.

"I know. I've been there," I burst out, causing Jennifer's astonished expression.

Chapter 90

While Jennifer's first reaction was surprise, her second was alarm and easily understood. *I permitted a criminal to be close to our children*, she must be telling herself. I knew that I would instantly lose this babysitting job if I didn't give a good explanation. Thankfully, mine was as good as it could be.

"I misspoke. What happened wasn't like it sounded," I said, apologetically.

Jennifer looked dubious, as anyone would be. How could a stay in jail be commendable?

"A murder plot was being planned by several students. The victim's identify wasn't known. I was invited to participate and told my father about it. He told a Greenwich detective, a family friend.

"I was asked to work undercover. To gain evidence after the girls' arrest, I spent time in jail with them. Afterward, the District Attorney wrote me a thank-you letter and offered me a job when I graduate college. I don't plan to take him up on it."

Jennifer visibly relaxed.

"That's *some* story," she said, letting out her breath.

"It wasn't my best experience but I learned about being jailed while there. I don't recommend its culture," I said.

I shouldn't have joked since Jennifer's worry was serious and real.

"We hope for Bradley to be out on bail but it'll take a few days. The charges have made him a hated figure to be made an example of. People are furious because no banker was jailed for the frauds that caused the 2008 financial crisis."

"I didn't understand the TV explanation. Exactly what is Bradley's crime?" I asked.

"He's been accused of everything, but mostly because he behaved like a world-class idiot. I'm a good lawyer and he should have taken my advice. It was the same advice that his lawyer gave him. *Damn all macho men!*" Jennifer burst out, with a look of disgust.

Chapter 91

"I need a drink," Jennifer said.

A minute later, she returned from the kitchen carrying a coffee cup half-full of a purple liquid. I doubted that it was grape juice. She sat down, took a gulp, placed the cup on the coffee table, leaned back and closed her eyes. Time passed during which I remained silent, sensing that she needed time to re-gain control. I was correct for her voice was firm when she spoke.

"Do you know what *LIBOR* is?" she asked.

"No, but the announcer said it several times," I replied.

"Yes," Jennifer said, and nodded. "Bradley's problems derive from the cursed LIBOR. It's an abbreviation for London Interbank Offered Rate."

Her anger boiled over as she spat the word. Then she caught herself and explained, so clearly that I felt sure she was an exceptional lawyer.

"*LIBOR* is the average interest rate that is calculated using the data given by major banks in London of their interest rates. A bank is supposed to tell the rates that they are paying, or expect to pay, for borrowing from other banks.

"Scandal arose when it was discovered that some banks were lying in order to profit from trades, or to make themselves appear more profitable than they were.

"The LIBOR also tells how healthy the economy is believed to be: a low rate means that bankers feel confident while a high rate indicates that they worry."

"I understand, but why was this lying so important that it became major news. Companies lie all the time and it's a one-day headline," I said.

"Because the LIBOR has a huge worldwide effect. Mortgages, student loans, and other financial products rely on it to determine their interest rate so its rigging affects millions of people. One example is that a high interest rate on a student loan can prevent a student from attending college."

"OK, I get it. But you said that Bradley's problems are caused by his having acted dumb. What is that all about?" I asked.

"Bradley thought that he was smarter than everyone else including his wife and his lawyer. Your father is a lawyer. Does he talk about his work?"

"Just in general terms, when he wasn't sick and had a large practice. Now he mostly reads law journals and writes articles for them. He takes on occasional cases that won't require lengthy court work," I replied.

"Did he ever tell you what a lawyer's best quality is?" Jennifer asked.

I thought for a moment.

"Well, if I had to choose from everything that he's said, it might be that the best lawyer is a world-class pest:

one who never gives up on anything unless they absolutely must."

"That's very good advice, and particularly to know *when* to give up," Jennifer said, with her first real smile that I had seen that day.

Chapter 92

"To understand Bradley's situation, you must see the government's position. There had been financial disaster. Fraud caused tremendous pain and nearly ruined the world's economy, requiring huge public sums to prevent this. People lost their homes and jobs and companies couldn't get loans to start or expand their business. And nothing happened to those who caused this mess!

"Now that's not quite true. A handful of small fish were jailed but none of their bosses. The public was furious, particularly after it was discovered that some of these frauds had been going on for years under the nose of government regulators.

"Despite Bradley's quirks, he is a mathematical genius and worked the LIBOR wonderfully. Each year, he gained banks hundreds of millions of dollars by trading financial products linked to the LIBOR. He was cherished by Wall Street, despite his dandruff and clothes. It was like this until the financial crash. Then he became *the villain*, the poster boy for everything bad that happened.

"When indicted, a person can choose to battle the government in court or to plead guilty and accept the best deal to reduce their sentence."

I nodded. This is common knowledge.

"Why was Bradley arrested instead of having his lawyer arrange his surrender?" I asked.

"Because he behaved stupidly. He had agreed to cooperate and testify against his boss and rival traders and brokers. He would accept a guilty plea with the promise of a short sentence at one of the low-security Federal prisons that resembles a summer camp. He might even have gotten only probation or house arrest.

"After accepting this deal, Bradly gave more than enough evidence incriminating himself and others to satisfy the government. I was happy, his lawyer was happy, and the prosecutor was happy. Then Bradley's *superior* brain began working and he changed his mind.

"He *couldn't stand* the idea of his daughters and others viewing him as a convicted criminal. He was smarter than everyone else. He now decided to go into court, battle the government, and win!"

"But that's *insane*. He had already vowed that he was guilty and given enough evidence to convict himself. He couldn't hope to win!" I burst out.

"No, he won't, but that's what he did," Jennifer said.

She finished drinking her wine, and we stared at each other in silence.

Chapter 93

"I should visit Bradley but he told me not to come, that I couldn't do anything. He'll be freed after tomorrow's bail hearing according to his lawyer."

"You're a lawyer. What do you think?" I asked.

The crisis had changed my role from teenage babysitter to adult sounding board. That my father is a lawyer had probably helped. It made me an informal member of the legal community.

"He *should* get out, with a high bail and agreement to surrender his passport and wear a GPS device on his ankle. He has family and business roots here and his case isn't murder. I can't remember an accused who was refused bail for a strictly financial crime. No case that I was ever involved with."

I looked at her quizzically.

"I was an assistant District Attorney for four years until joining Willis, Wanding, and Webb. It sounds like a joke but there's nothing funny about our clients. I try to them get off but don't feel guilty even though most of them are. I play a crucial role in America's legal system by trying to keep the government honest."

I nodded. Though my father hadn't handled many criminal cases he had said much the same thing: that a lawyer must never be confused with their client.

"They're probably keeping him isolated in jail. His case is high profile and the government wouldn't want him injured. Do you remember the Strauss-Kahn case?"

"The French politician who was arrested for attempted rape?" I asked.

"Yes. They kept him isolated and watched continually after his arrest. It was considered that he would have become the next French President were it not for his arrest," Jennifer said.

"What happened to him?"

"After posting bail, he was placed on house arrest and ordered to wear an ankle monitoring bracelet. Later, holes were found in his accuser's story and all charges were dismissed. A civil lawsuit followed, he settled the case to avoid the embarrassment of testifying, and the woman allegedly walked off with a million dollars. She won and Strauss-Kahn's career was destroyed."

"A mixed blessing, so there's always hope," I said.

"In most cases but not after the accused has confessed, as Bradley did. *Dumb, dumb, dumb!*" Jennifer said, angrily.

I said nothing. My father wouldn't have disagreed either.

Chapter 94

Jennifer moped for next hour. When she went to her bedroom to nap, I phoned Kimberly to tell her what was going on. I said that I would be staying here for a few days and asked her to E-mail the class notes to me. Apart from her advanced computer and math classes we took the same required courses.

I asked Liz to send me the notes for my other classes. She was a new friend who lived in Manhattan and commuted to school. She had asked me over for dinner with her family and I promised to set a date once my life had calmed down.

I became preoccupied with Jennifer's worries: the peril of prison that Bradley faced, and the legal fees which could bankrupt the family.

There was also the S&M gear that I had seen. I found it hard to believe that Jennifer had willingly engaged in such activity, particularly when considering the marks on her neck which she took care to conceal. If publicized, her legal reputation would be destroyed by scandal. Having a criminally charged husband was bad enough for any lawyer.

Child Protective Services might even investigate and custody of their children could be lost. They hadn't been easy births; Jennifer had difficulty conceiving.

"After years of doing it the old-fashioned way, we entered the expensive world of fertility medicine. Consultations, shots, pills, tests, and hours of tearful waiting in doctor's offices with no certainty of success. The HCG injections were the worst. Do you know what that is?"

"No."

"HCG, human chorionic gonadotropin, is a hormone that supports the normal development of eggs in a woman's ovary and stimulates their release during ovulation. It's used with fertility problems but left me feeling bloated with stomach pain.

"HCG must be injected under the skin or into a muscle. I lay on the bed as Bradley counted down from four to one before injecting me. Once he hit a vein and the needle shot back out. Blood spattered, we both screamed, and he began again. Countdown with a new needle and another shot. But it was worth it! We have two beautiful, smart children. They *are* smart, aren't they?"

"They're *really* smart," I agreed, with an assured tone. No mother will accept another reply.

"Yes, and we now have this," Jennifer said, raising both hands in a gesture of helpless despair.

"I understand why you told me about your fertility treatment," I said.

"Why?"

"Because fertility and legal problems are identical in one respect," I replied.

"What's that?" Jennifer asked, with a puzzled tone.

"They have only one possible outcome: either you succeed or you fail."

"Yes, that's true," Jennifer said, sadly.

I tried adding a hopeful note to the gloom that had enveloped us.

"My dad said that because you can't predict a jury's verdict, it's not over until it's over," I added.

Though Jennifer nodded agreement, her worried look had remained.

Chapter 95

Some women eat or clean when they are worried. After napping, Jennifer cooked. Cooking is my worst skill and something in which I have no interest. So after listening to her mind-numbing description of how her children's favorite cookie (chocolate-chip-raspberry-shortbread) was prepared, I pleaded a headache and went for a walk.

Once outside, I was unsure where to go. Water is restful, I decided, and walked to Carl Schurz Park. Jennifer had told me during my hiring interview that it overlooked the East River.

The Park was serene and the sight of passing ships reminded me of the Greenwich waterfront. Thoughts of Jennifer's and Kimberly's troubles left my mind. I was thinking about Erika when my phone rang.

"I was just thinking of you," I spoke into the phone.

"We're psychically connected. What's happening?" Erika asked.

I told her of my new babysitting job. Of Bradley's arrest, Jennifer's bruised neck, and the S&M gear that I discovered.

"It feels creepy," I summarized.

"Each to their own. Do you feel safe?" Erika asked.

"So long as I keep my eyes open," I replied.

"Then quit," Erika advised me.

"I need the money."

"You don't have to work. Your biological parents are rich and would give you whatever you asked. I would too. *We are sisters,*" Erika said.

Erika and I have been best friends for years and consider each other sisters. She also knows my background: that I've lived with adoptive parents since birth and first learned about my real parentage as a teenager.

"I'm grateful, but accepting money wouldn't be right. It would hurt my adoptive parents and sisters. That I could spend freely while they..."

I didn't have to complete the sentence. The meaning was obvious and Erika understood. We had gone through so much that it was as if we had shared a childhood together.

"What's your boss' last name?" she asked, and I told her.

"That's what I thought. One of my father's hedge funds lost money because of him. My dad is furious and would like to see him hung," Erika said.

"Him and the rest of America. Give my best to Clarence," I said, before hanging up.

Clarence is her boyfriend. Erika and I have an informal competition as to who marries first.

Chapter 96

I would have enjoyed spending all afternoon strolling the Upper East Side but that wasn't what I was being paid for. I returned to the apartment a half-hour later.

Jennifer's cookies were out of the oven, and she was more cheerful.

"Bradley's lawyer called. Bradley is at Central Booking and OK. He'll be arraigned in the morning and his lawyer wants me in the courtroom. I'll need you here.

"He also said that it would be best if the children stayed in the apartment for a few days. Reporters will mob the building, hungry for comment from a family member of America's number one financial criminal. Photos of his children would be even better. Do you remember how Bernard Madoff's family was treated?"

I did. The Madoff swindle had created the biggest financial headlines until LIBOR. A movie, *Blue Jasmine,* was even based on his life. Madoff pleaded guilty to save his family but this hadn't helped. He and his wife lost their assets, everyone disowned them, and an innocent son killed himself.

I knew how relentless the press could be even with those whom they favor. My biological father is a British national hero.

Jennifer didn't know how to tell her children and I suggested that she play it by ear.

"Children don't want a long explanation. Say that their daddy is dealing with grown-up things and meanwhile they have school and their friends to worry about. Then ask something ordinary, like what to have for dinner. It should work," I advised.

Jennifer looked at me for several moments before speaking.

"You're more than a mere babysitter," she said, calmly.

"I'm no different from any other. But I've been caring for children for years beginning with my sisters," I said, modestly.

"I made a good choice in hiring you," Jennifer said.

Her phone rang and she opened it.

"It's the lawyer. I'll have to take this but you can stay," she said.

I tried to appear not to listen but couldn't avoid hearing her scream, *"No!"*

Chapter 97

Jennifer's face was drawn with fright when she ended the call.

"What happened?" I asked.

Jennifer sat down before answering.

"Bradley may not get out of jail. The prosecutor will oppose bail, arguing that he's a flight risk because of his money in offshore accounts. The lawyer believes that they're trying to soften Bradley, so he'll plead guilty and testify against others. His lawyer will appeal but that takes time. For now, he'll be jailed at Rikers Island. Did you see the article about it in today's *Times*?" Jennifer asked.

I shook my head. I do read newspapers but only online and on weekends. Jennifer rummaged through *The New York Times* until finding the proper page. She handed it to me.

The article told of a corrections officer who, after opening the cell door for one inmate, was grabbed by another and thrown to the ground. Two other prisoners slashed his face, head, and arms.

"If that happens to a guard, how can Bradley hope to survive? His only exercise is moving a computer mouse," Jennifer said.

"Bradley is high value and the authorities wouldn't let him be harmed. All jails have a hospital unit and they'll probably house him there," I said, reassuringly.

My knowledge of jails is small but was more than Jennifer's.

"You're a lawyer and know how to fight. You must keep strong for him and your children," I said.

I felt uncomfortable speaking like this since Jennifer was much older than me. But someone had to screw up her courage and I was there.

Jennifer stared at me before speaking.

"You're an unusual girl," she said.

"Maybe just one with a bigger mouth than most."

Jennifer managed a tiny smile.

"Do you have a bank account?" she asked.

"Yes," I replied, though being puzzled by her question.

"I'm going to pay you in advance for the next three months. The government may freeze our assets to pressure Bradley and I don't want you to suffer. I'll write you a check for four thousand dollars. Draw against the money for hours worked and for expenses when you take the children out," Jennifer said.

"That's very trusting. Are you sure that you want to?" I asked.

I never had so much money.

"Yes, I'm sure."

Jennifer took a checkbook from her purse and wrote the check. I had passed a Chase Bank branch while walking to the apartment and would deposit the check there. I suddenly felt rich.

"For luck," Jennifer said, apropos of nothing, as she handed me the check.

"Luck doesn't just happen. It's when opportunity meets preparation," I replied.

"What?"

"Another of my dad's sayings," I said, though not identifying which of my fathers had said it. Describing Vladimir's involvement in my life was too personal a matter to share with Jennifer.

"That's true. He's a wise man. I'm taking a nap. Maybe I'll have a cheerful dream," Jennifer said, before leaving the room.

Chapter 98

Events went as Bradley's lawyer had feared. The prosecutor opposed bail, the judge agreed, and Bradley was ordered to remain in custody until his trial, which could take months.

His lawyer immediately appealed this decision to a higher court and believed that their decision would be favorable. Meanwhile, America's newspaper editorials regretted that Bradley couldn't be executed and wanted him jailed for life.

Being the object of such hatred wears a person down and Jennifer did her best to keep Bradley's spirits high. This was challenging considering the awfulness of prison life.

Career criminals view jail as a disliked but definitely possible part of their existence, like having predictable work hours on a job. Their attitude is that if you do the crime, you should be willing to do the time. When jailed, they are amongst their kind of people, sharing worse food but usually better health care services than they received outside.

White-collar criminals are not like this. They may not consider what caused their arrest to be a crime since with certain financial transactions there is a legal gray area. Or if they did, they hadn't expected to get caught since many of them don't.

Furthermore, even if indicted, they usually accept a plea bargain which demands a financial penalty but no jail time.

No banking big-shots were jailed after the 2008 financial crisis that they caused, and the penalty for the major player in the earlier Savings and Loan Bank scandal was to be forced into retirement with hundreds of millions of dollars to keep him comfortable.

Jennifer decided to keep the children out of school for a while. Even their innocence and youth hadn't protected them from acquiring angry looks and hushed comments in the apartment house elevator. Cries for Bradley's execution erupted regularly from picketers but police kept them from the building's entrance.

While Jennifer conferred with Bradley's lawyer, I helped the children with their homework that had been E-mailed to them. When this was completed, I tried to maintain their spirits through activities: playing games like Sorry. and Chutes and Ladders, and Connect Four; and reading to them from children's books that I had bought online.

Groceries and other needed purchases were delivered and we stopped going out. We came to share Bradley's imprisoned existence, which Jennifer described after her visit to Rikers Island.

Chapter 99

Jennifer had been understandably nervous.

"Getting to Rikers Island was the first problem. I don't have a car and was told that driving wasn't a good idea anyway. I went by bus, actually two buses. They were the first that I'd ridden in years.

"The Q101 originates locally, at East 59th Street and Second Avenue. It takes you to Hazen Street and 19th Avenue in Queens, which is the entrance to Rikers Island. At Hazen Street I transferred to the Q100 which travels across the Rikers Island Bridge to the jail's Visit Center.

"The view from the Bridge is captivating. It's a very *New York View* with planes taking off from LaGuardia and boats heading to and from the Long Island Sound. I arrived at a little after 10AM.

"I didn't know if there was a dress code but figured that it would be best to dress down, in the rattiest clothes that I had and without makeup or jewelry. I was visiting as a wife and not a lawyer. It was good that I did since I made friends on the bus. They were obviously poor and if I had dressed as I usually do..."

Jennifer's meaning was obvious. The other women's clothes had likely resembled mine.

"Mabel was visiting her husband. He's been charged with murder and has been in Rikers for four years. After finding a scalpel in his cell, they banned him from contact visits as punishment. Now they can't touch when she visits, a Plexiglas separates them.

"When Mabel learned that this was my first visit, she gave me good advice. She said that visitors get treated like inmates, and that the guards don't want them back. She said that she worries about her husband when he doesn't call since there are many scalpels floating around the jail and face slashing has made a comeback.

"She tries to visit him at least twice a week but it's hard for her mother to watch her toddlers since she has medical issues.

"She told me to put money in Bradley's account. He can use it to buy food, and for phone calls which cost about a dollar a minute.

"Annie, who sat in in back of us, leaned forward and chimed in. 'My man told me that the worst day in jail is the first,'" she said.

Chapter 100

"I'll paraphrase what she and Candice told me. They're not educated but definitely have street smarts," Jennifer said.

I listened closely. It's street smarts, not school learning, that can save your life.

"A new prisoner is in a state of shock and realizing that they are actually in jail takes time. They feel isolated, lonely and confused. Prisoners can write letters to family and friends and there are card phones to use but relationships suffer.

"Jails are dangerous places. There are violent gangs, and anger and humiliation are regular features. In a jail, as contrasted with a prison where one is sent after sentencing, there is no motivation for good behavior since there is no early release.

"The risks aren't only physical. Prosecutors place undercover agents in jail to get information from inmates by befriending them, and fellow inmates may give prosecutors information in exchange for leniency in sentencing or an early release."

"Bradley is smart enough not talk," I interrupted.

"He's definitely smarter than anyone there but must be shocked out of his wits too. Who knows what he might say," Jennifer replied, before continuing.

"When Annie finished speaking, Mabel added more good information. She said that being locked up is only as stressful as you make it but that other inmates are a great part of the stress. There are always weirdos who, unlike on the outside, you can't get away from.

"Mabel said that killing time is the most important thing to do while in jail. The TV in the day room is mostly Spanish novellas so the best thing to do is to read."

Jennifer paused to sip wine. She had begun drinking more since Bradley's lock up and particularly after a visit. She was permitted three visits per week and used all of them.

"Then Candice, who had sat beside Annie, prepared me for what would happen at Rikers. She was dead-on correct," Jennifer said.

Chapter 101

"The first thing that you're ordered to do after getting off the bus is to line up against a gate. There are signs stating that one must not bring electronic devices, weapons, or drugs inside the building. I left my phone in a locker. They take quarters and I had none but Annie had a pocketful and made change. She said that I could bring in money and packages. I had brought nothing except money, not knowing what Bradley needed.

"After going through the first metal detector you go to registration where you get something like a boarding ticket with the inmate's information on it. I had been told to bring Bradley's case number and where he was being housed.

"We then boarded a bus and were taken to housing. There, I went through another metal detector and was ordered to remove everything else: food, pen, watch, papers, earrings, and to lock them in that locker. If you bring packages for an inmate there's a window to have their stuff tagged. That wasn't the last of the security checks. I was frisked by a female correction officer before entering the waiting room.

"I sat and eventually Bradley came out. I wasn't sure what you were allowed to do but saw others hugging and that's what I did. I didn't want to let him go but we had to talk.

"I said what I was sure that his lawyer repeated when he visits: to speak of his case with no one but him.

Bradley looked annoyed when I said this, as if I considered him an idiot. But no one can be sure how they'll behave in jail. It's that weird a place.

"'How are things going?' I asked.

Bradley didn't reply immediately. Then, after waving his hand contemptuously, he asked. 'Do you really want to hear?' I nodded and he told me.

"'The floors are dirty and I've seen bed bugs the size of roaches. Wherever you are there's the smell of body odor, bleach, and Beefaroni. The staff are rude–clerical, guards, and professional alike–with none caring what you think of them. The place is a dump.'

"I put on my cheeriest smile. 'Is there anything good about the place?' I asked.

"Bradley thought for a moment before answering.

"'Well, to be honest, some guards *are* nice and most have the same attitude as the prisoners: wanting to get through their day with as few bothers as possible. Several have heard about my case and asked for financial advice. I told them that I was a computer geek and knew nothing about investing.

"'One guard gave me good advice. He said for me to say that I was Jewish no matter what my religion is. Jews get a box of Matzos and a bottle of grape juice each week from the Rabbi. He's a good guy who lets you use his phone.

"'There are gangs and plenty of tough guys but enough non-tough guys to balance the population and make things survivable. It's generally safe so long as you mind your own business, avoid hanging out in groups, and don't owe anyone anything. That leads to trouble.

"'The biggest problem is how to survive total boredom. The Rabbi suggested that I teach math to inmates studying for their GED, or a computer coding class. He said that he could arrange it."

"'Do it!' It'll help keep you sane until your lawyer gets you out. He's hopeful," I said, with greater assurance than I felt.

"'I just might. My first teaching job,' Bradley said, with a nod and the hint of a smile."

Chapter 102

The following months passed quickly. I spent most of my time at Jennifer's apartment, attending classes only for exams. That I did well reveals how unimportant class attendance can be. But I had always learned best from books, the class notes that I borrowed were excellent, and Kimberly is a wonderful math tutor.

Jennifer had met Kimberly when she tutored me at Jennifer's apartment. Thereafter, she and her daughter, Julia, became regular visitors. They were welcome additions to the compressed life that reporters had forced on the family.

The worst news was that the Court of Appeals had rejected Bradley's application for bail. Thus he would remain locked up until his trial, which was months away.

A new plea bargain had been offered by the prosecutor. It would require Bradley to testify against his co-workers, pay a huge fine, and serve a prison sentence of between five and ten years. His lawyer advised him to seriously consider this offer: recent financial crimes had gained three times that length of imprisonment.

But Bradley dismissed the offer out-of-hand. He still felt confident that he would sway the jury by telling his side of the story. I didn't think that *any* story could explain away his earlier confession but said nothing. I was, after all, merely the family's babysitter.

Jennifer had returned to work. Money was needed to support the family and to pay Bradley's increasing legal expenses. Their assets had paid for the expensive apartment and into college funds for their children. Tapping their retirement funds would involve paying a large tax penalty.

Bradley had taken the Rabbi's suggestion of teaching. One of his classes was elementary math, to help prisoners pass the GED exam and get a high school diploma. His other class taught computer coding, an ability that could be learned in several months. Demand for these skilled workers was so great that even the stigma of an arrest might be overcome.

As time passed, the number of reporters and picketers outside the apartment house grew fewer. Surprisingly, the next news article about Bradley was positive. It contained his photo above a glowing review of his coding class and the Correction Department's hopes for its graduates. Rikers needed good publicity. Days before, three guards were arrested for murder.

"The girls are so proud. They made copies of the article and put them in envelopes with happy face stickers. They slip them under apartment doors while playing in the building," Jennifer said, as she handed me one of them.

Chapter 103

Public opinion is fickle. The newspaper's article about Bradley's class was picked up online and attitudes about him changed. His claim of innocence was now taken seriously.

Some even regarded him as a hero, improbable though this may seem. Bradley was no longer a mere financial crook. Instead, he had been a warrior against regulatory agencies that stood in the way of high-tech progress.

His earlier "confession," this was now labeled with quotation marks, was re-interpreted as being the rambling of a frightened, naïve genius. Columnists compared Bradley to Aaron Swartz, the twenty-six-year-old computer prodigy who killed himself after being threatened with thirty-five-years imprisonment for seeking to make scholarly documents freely available.

Swartz' death had been widely mourned: "Aaron's insatiable curiosity, creativity and brilliance; his reflexive empathy and capacity for selfless, boundless love; his refusal to accept injustice as inevitable–these gifts made the world, and our lives, far brighter...He used his prodigious skills as a programmer and technologist not to enrich himself but to make the Internet and the world a fairer, better place."

Bradley too was being turned into a saint. When I questioned how this change of opinion could occur so rapidly, Jennifer explained.

"Bradley's company hired a public relations firm. If the jury finds him innocent, the company wins too," she explained.

Family life became more normal with the children's return to school. They had been nervous the first day but the only comments from classmates were that they were glad to see them back. Nothing was said about their father.

My babysitting income decreased but I didn't mind. Earning money off another's misery is no way to live a life.

It often seems that one worry begins just as another worry leaves. After Bradley's situation improved, my mind had returned to what Mother Marie told Kimberly: that no matter how powerful the wickedness, righteousness will overcome it in the end.

Kimberly sensed that evil approached but not what it could be. Yet nothing happened and her life blossomed. She loved being a mother to Julia, and had been offered high-status consulting jobs though being only a college sophomore.

"Everything is going like clockwork. Let's drop the worrying today," I said, as we left the campus.

Julia's birthday was the following day and Kimberly was satisfying Julia's wish: to eat at a "grown-up restaurant" of her choice. Which, surprisingly, turned out to be The Russian Tea Room.

I wondered how she had even heard of it. Ask almost any child where they want to eat and they'll say

McDonald's or Burger King. Maybe Taco Bell for those with a more sophisticated taste. But *The Russian Tea Room?*

"Annushka told her," Kimberly said.

Annushka was Julia's personal bodyguard. A tall, slim, woman of about thirty, she looked like an Upper East Side soccer mom but was a veteran of the Russian streets. Abram, Erika's bodyguard, said that she was equally skilled with a knife and a pistol and always carried both.

"Having Annushka for her name is almost a joke. It means gracious and merciful," Abram added.

Kimberly was depressed as we went to pick up Julia. Only after she had shared her dream of the previous night did I understood why.

Chapter 104

The Russian Tea Room was opened nearly ninety years ago by members of the Russian Imperial Ballet. It is down the street from Carnegie Hall and a favorite of the entertainment industry. It's appeared in classic movies, *When Harry Met Sally* and *Manhattan*. Madonna once worked there as a coat-check girl.

The restaurant's décor was over-the-top, in the old European style with gold veneer throughout the walls and ceiling. The lighting was dim and the colors were red and gold. There were showcases with knick-knacks for sale, and so many photographs that I didn't know which to look at first.

The waiter seated us in a large red booth with red cushions. Annushka gave up speaking Russian to the waiter for he didn't understand.

We had arrived in time for the Afternoon Tea. Kimberly allowed Julia to choose from the children's menu, which had little Russian about it. Her choice was the usual children's favorite though with a Russian touch: peanut butter and jelly on blini (a thin pancake).

For dessert she chose a red velvet cupcake with sprinkles, and hot chocolate with whipped cream and marshmallows. Julia was happy, Kimberly was happy, and Annushka smiled.

Kimberly and I had the smoked salmon with chive cream cheese and cucumber while Annushka had the curried chicken salad with raisins and pecans. Kimberly drank tea, I drank water, and Annushka had coffee.

"This is Manhattan's version of Russia," Annushka said, as we left the restaurant. It seemed a good evaluation.

Later that day, Kimberly shared her disturbing dream.

"You were in it," she began.

I waited silently.

"I was in a room surrounded by angry, yelling women and felt very alone. 'Why am I here?' I cried, but my question was ignored. Then I saw you. You were standing at the door, trying to force it open against some massive force. I tried to reach you but couldn't because of the crush of people. I woke up, soaking wet."

I asked Kimberly the same question that Erika asks me when I tell her my troubling dream.

"What do you think that the dream could mean?"

Kimberly looked thoughtful before speaking a Yoruba religious phrase. I knew it well for it was one of Mother Marie's favorites: "Bi owe, bi owe, ru Ifa soro." Paraphrased, this means, *God speaks through proverbs*. And through dreams too? I wondered.

Chapter 105

I didn't say anything although knowing that dreams reveal what a person is thinking. The unconscious part of Kimberly's mind insisted that danger approached and Mother Marie was convinced of this too. Her advice once saved my life and, years later, had recalled my English father to life. I would never ignore what she believed. Still, we could do nothing except wait and worry.

Jennifer had invited Kimberly and me to celebrate Thanksgiving with her family. But that would be a purchased event: buffet at the Grand Hyatt Hotel on 42nd Street, like Erika's Thanksgiving fête at a fancy Greenwich restaurant.

My mother suggested that Kimberly and Jennifer's families come for Thanksgiving dinner at our house. It was too small to put them up for the weekend and Erika came to the rescue. The dinner would be at my home and Kimberly and Jennifer and their children would stay at Erika's.

Despite the nasty hovering reporters, Jennifer had mixed feelings about leaving New York City. Bradley was imprisoned here, and she was his wife.

Bradley decided the matter by insisting that she go. He said that he was busy with work since his students never left. Though a lame excuse, it came from the heart and worked.

Erika made plans, ranging from which bedroom would be occupied to the weekend's activities. Though meaning well, she can be a bit bossy.

The morning of Thanksgiving, Erika sent her father's largest SUV to pick us up. It was a gloriously cool, sunny day. Despite the heavy traffic, the trip from the City went smoothly and took under an hour. The children played video games while the adults chatted.

Kimberly remained tense with worry but Jennifer seemed more relaxed than at any time since we first met. She spoke of her college years at Princeton, how she and Bradley had met, and his encouraging her to attend law school despite her fears.

Princeton is a highly selective school. Only the *really* smart are admitted so I wondered about Jennifer's self-doubt. The reason for this became clear when she revealed her childhood. Both of her parents had been abusive drunks and she was their only well-functioning child. Her older sister was a drug addict, a graduate of many rehabs and jails.

After that disclosure, Jennifer napped for the rest of the journey. Kimberly and I soon followed her lead.

Chapter 106

Surviving on Social Security Disability payments and Food Stamps isn't easy for a family. Putting on a large Thanksgiving spread would be hard for my mother. I knew this and so do my closest friends. Every Thanksgiving, whether she's a guest or not, Erika sends my mother a five-hundred-dollar gift certificate for Greenwich's Whole Foods. Her note says that her father gives this to each of his employees and that Erika has spent so much time at our home that she feels my mother deserves it.

People who don't know Erika well have criticized her. They say that she's bossy and ignores the opinions of others. But this typifies many smart people and no one has ever denied that Erika has a big heart. And she never looks for thanks either!

After settling everyone at Erika's house, we arrived at mine just before noon. I made introductions and, before one of my younger sisters would ask their usual tactless question of who would be sharing *their* room, I said that the guests would be sleeping at Erika's house. No one likes giving up their room and young kids are the most selfish.

After this crucial question was answered, my youngest sister, Claudine, asked if the girls would like to see her room. Jennifer's daughters, Alexandra and Kristina, looked hesitant but followed Kimberly's daughter, Julia, and all trooped upstairs.

"We've been scouring used-book stores for old Nancy Drew mysteries. She wants to show her collection," my mother said, proudly.

One of her Godly commandments for children is to read and this became our life-long habit.

After the children left, the atmosphere became awkward. It was as if there were a huge elephant in the room that no one wanted to refer to. The elephant was Bradley. Publicity had made his name a household word and curiosity abounded. But there is such a thing as tact and my father has it in spades. His simple question reduced the tension in the room.

"How is your husband doing?" he asked Jennifer, and she colored.

"I've visited clients in jail. It isn't easy for them," my dad said quickly.

Jennifer relaxed, and leaned back. My father had insisted that she sit in his recliner. It was his favorite and the most comfortable chair in the room.

"The fear and boredom of the early days nearly drove him crazy but he's OK now. Or as OK as one can be given his situation. He's very bright and, in the past, didn't do well with those who aren't and would dismiss their comments with insults.

"But teaching the prisoners has changed him. Judging from his stories, he's extraordinarily patient with them. He gives them his all and they love him, if that's not too strong a word.

"I hate saying this but being in jail has made him a better person. He has greater self-control and is more thoughtful. Our marriage is stronger than it's ever been."

Jennifer's sense that she is amongst friends is why she can share such intimate feelings with us. It will be a good weekend, I told myself.

"He's proud of his students and they're proud of him. It may be improper to say, but he's become almost Christ-like," Jennifer added, with a hint of embarrassment.

My mother stared at Jennifer and spoke softly, almost to herself.

"As iron sharpens iron, so one person sharpens another. He who tends the fig tree will eat its fruit. Proverbs 27:17. There is a great power silently working all things for the good."

Chapter 107

There couldn't have been much change from the Whole Foods five-hundred-dollar gift certificate though their Thanksgiving dinner wasn't out of the ordinary.

It was the traditional turkey with New England stuffing, mashed potatoes, green beans with almonds, cranberry-orange relish, and butternut-squash soup. For the vegetarians, there was a small soy-based turkey shaped like a real turkey. I ate this.

There was also a boneless salmon platter garnished with slices of cucumber and vegetables.

For dessert there were commercial pumpkin pie, apple tart, and cookies baked by my younger sisters. My mother's talent for baking extends to them.

My older sister, Melody, spoke of applying to law school. After graduating from college and rejecting the menial jobs offered, she followed our father's advice to gain an applied degree.

Melody had graduated from New York University's Cinema Studies Department a year before, hoping to be a film critic. Martin Scorsese, the director of *Goodfellas*, and Joel Cohen, the director of *Fargo*, were earlier graduates.

After meeting them at a seminar, it was as if she encountered God and there was no turning back. Except, my dad advised, one must also pay bills. Thus, Melody would train as a lawyer. There were far more jobs for an entertainment lawyer than a movie reviewer and she would make better contacts too.

My father told shocking but funny stories of how some lawyers had tried to get business. One sent flowers to the mother of a dead child, enclosing his business card. The mother then received a call from a spiritualist, "Sister Carol," stating that God wanted her to call the lawyer.

Another lawyer, seeking accident cases, had sprinkled his business cards on the pizzas that he sent to Emergency Room orderlies.

"To succeed, a person must be willing to think outside the box," Melody observed.

"Yes, but not too far," my father replied.

We then wrestled with Melanie's ethical and social dilemma. What to do if she likes a boy that she has been told likes her but has a girlfriend going to a different school.

During this discussion, Jennifer's phone rang. Another of my mother's Godly rules forbids taking calls during dinner but this doesn't apply to guests. Jennifer looked at the phone's screen and smiled.

"It's from the jail. It must be Bradley. I have to take it," she said, happily, and left the room.

A minute later, our lively conversation was ended by Jennifer's piercing scream.

Chapter 108

A person's life can change in an instant. You're crossing the street and a drunken driver knocks you down. Thereafter, if you survive, your life is greatly changed even with the best medical treatment. The death of a loved one has a similar outcome: life is never the same afterward.

With Jennifer's scream, the bubbling dining room conversation stopped. I was closest to the door and reached her first. Her face was white as she slipped to the floor. I knelt beside her. Obviously, something huge had happened.

"What is it?" I asked.

As the adults gathered about her, Jennifer was too stunned to speak. Then, after recovering, she ordered, "Send the children upstairs."

My mother asked Melanie to do this and she instantly obeyed, realizing that then wasn't the time for arguing.

When the children were gone, Kimberly slowly stood and faced us.

"Bradley is dead," she said.

"What happened? Was it a heart attack?" my father asked.

Though young, Bradley's life had been filled with stress.

"No, he was murdered," Jennifer said.

Her tone was matter-of-fact. She was apparently still in shock.

No one spoke while Jennifer was helped to the living room. There, she lay on the sofa and closed her eyes. Our Thanksgiving celebration was over. My mother got Jennifer a glass of water. As she sipped, her explanation slipped out.

"The killer wasn't anyone that Bradley knew or had met. He was just one of those crazies who winds up in jail instead of the mental hospital they need. As Bradley passed him in the corridor, the man stabbed him in the neck. Inmates tackled the killer and held him down while another inmate tried to stop the bleeding. Bradley was dead by the time medical aid arrived."

Jennifer began sobbing.

"He became a good man. I must go to him," Jennifer said, and she began to get up.

My mother placed a restraining hand on her shoulder.

"He is gone but you must be here for your children. It is they who need you now," she said, softly.

Kimberly whispered in my ear an ancient Yoruba proverb: "Aye l'oja, orun n'ile." ("The world is a marketplace. The spirit world is home.")

Chapter 109

Jennifer didn't tell her children of their father's death right away. She felt that they deserved a carefree weekend in view of all that they had experienced. She asked my mother to care for them that weekend and my mother readily agreed, promising to keep the TV off. The children would accompany Kimberly to Manhattan on Monday.

The news of Bradley's death gave my house a mournful atmosphere. Late that evening, after Jennifer had left, Kimberly and I went for a walk. Greenwich Avenue isn't far from my house but all of the stores except for the restaurants were closed for the holiday. We sat in the small park on the Avenue and moped.

"Bummer," I said, apropos of nothing.

Kimberly looked thoughtful and nodded.

"Could this be the evil that Mother Marie foretold?" she asked.

"I don't think so. Her advice was given to you and you've never met Bradley," I replied.

Kimberly nodded agreement.

"Maybe there are details about his murder online," she said, opening her phone.

She pulled up *The New York Times* website and began reading. After several minutes she handed me her phone.

The article described both the murder and Bradley's life. He was educated at Harvard and Princeton, was a star in the computer field, and had worked at several multi-national banks. The criminal charges against him were detailed, along with praise for his work as a teacher at Rikers Island. Bradley's funeral would be attended by the Chief of Corrections and the Mayor. His office had already released their eulogy.

"They've turned him into a hero," Kimberly mused, as I read on.

"The City needs one. What happened is awful: a famed, protected defendant being murdered." I said, returning the phone.

"Read the eulogy. It sounds like they're preparing him for sainthood," she remarked, returning the phone to me after scrolling to another page.

"It is a delicate matter to speak of this City's loss, the premature death of a genius. His faults were overshadowed by the good that he did during his final months, which will triumph over his death. While hope expanded his soul, an invisible hand drew the curtain over his life and shut him from our view. Though we grieve, he has found peace in the arms of a forgiving God.

"His life has helped others weave theirs, even as he has departed for where the great and good have gone before him. The dignity that invested his character at his late hour has taught us how to live. Let his image remain with us and direct our actions."

"*Wow!* I hope they say that about me after I die," I said.

Chapter 110

I had become close with Jennifer's children and she wanted me with her when she told them of Bradley's death. The younger child, Alexandra, cried but not her older sister, Kristina. Kids learn *everything* in a family and I wondered what Kristina knew of her mother's abuse by her father.

Jennifer was shattered but unbroken.

"I must remain strong for my children," she said, and I nodded agreement.

With Bradley's death, the prosecutor's case fell apart. Their freeze of the family's financial assets ended and Jennifer remained a wealthy woman. The proceeds from Bradley's large life insurance policy, which had been purchased just before his arrest, would add to the family's financial comfort. I wondered if Bradley had been considering an accident-appearing-suicide were he convicted but kept this thought to myself.

After the small, private funeral, a memorial was held for Bradley at the Mormon Church. There, a year earlier, a similar though premature service had been held for Odis, the brother of my friend, Missy. Later, he returned home after a ten-year disappearance.

At the memorial, Bradley's computer genius was lauded by a co-worker, and another humanized him with personal stories. The prison Rabbi described Bradley's dedication to his students, and a soon-to-be-released inmate expressed his gratitude. Reporters covered the entrance but in a respectful, subdued fashion.

Afterward, I returned with Jennifer to her apartment, feeling that my involvement with her family had ended. I played Chutes and Ladders with the children while she prepared the late lunch that I didn't remain to share.

Before I left, Jennifer hugged me and said that we must keep in touch. I agreed but wondered if we would meet again. She had decided to move to Burlington, a sophisticated town in Vermont where residents don't intrude or care about your past. If you don't create trouble, people won't bother you.

Vermont is noted for its lack of government regulation, "Freedom and Unity" being its official motto. The state has become the home of many ex-New Yorkers (like Senator Bernie Sanders) seeking a hassle-free lifestyle. Their satisfaction often doesn't persist after experiencing Vermont's demanding winter weather.

Chapter 111

Being a baby-sitter can wear you out. For some girls it's just a job, like selling shoes at the mall. But a *good* babysitter can't help but become involved with the child's family and identify with their problems.

As much as I hadn't wanted them to, Jennifer's abuse by Bradley and his arrest for fraud had become *my* worries too. I was sorry how it turned out but glad to lose these concerns. Though I would miss the children and Jennifer, from this time they existed as memories.

But I still needed work to cover my living expenses. Jennifer had insisted that I keep the advance she gave me so I didn't have to call the Barnard Babysitting Service for another referral right away. I hoped to be hired by a happy couple with one dutiful child but doubted my luck.

Meanwhile, my demanding school classes continued, my younger sisters still sought my advice with growing-up problems, and my worry about Kimberly remained.

I invited her to spend Christmas with my family but she had already made plans with her uncle. They were looking for the small electric car that would be Julia's main gift. It would be a sight that would paralyze any child with joy. No family dinner in Greenwich could compete with that.

My family, as was customary, attended Christmas Eve service at our local Mormon Church. The joyous hymns and upbeat sermon didn't reduce my unease, and the smiling faces made me feel worse.

I responded to my father's concern with a weak smile. He didn't buy it but had always allowed me the freedom to decide whether to speak of my distress.

My phone rang in the middle of the sermon. I had forgotten to turn it off. I noted that the call came from Kimberly and let it go to voicemail. I would listen to it later.

The church service ended at 9PM and we arrived home a few minutes later. I felt exhausted and immediately went to my room. Only then did I remember Kimberly's call. Her message wasn't the holiday greeting that I had expected. Though brief and spoken calmly, her words kept me and my father awake for the rest of that night.

"I've been arrested, charged with drug dealing and murder. I need a lawyer," she said.

Chapter 112

After my father become disabled by Lyme disease, my mother had insisted that he get enough rest, be in bed by 10PM and preferably earlier. As his health improved, my mother's enforcement of her rule slowly relaxed.

Before becoming sick my father worked hard, six days a week and often late into the evening. Having family dinner at six was a rule only for the children. It's not easy for a naturally active person to relax. Thus, despite his weakened state, my dad contributed articles to law journals. He also accepted occasional, often unpaid, law cases, but only those which were unlikely to require his court appearance. These activities kept him content.

So although the hour was late and it was Christmas Eve, I wasn't surprised to find my father typing away in his home office. I watched silently and considered what to say. I would be demanding a lot and knew it.

"Can't sleep?" my father asked with a smile, looking up from his work, his fingers hovering above the keyboard.

"Dad, I love you terribly but must make am awful request," I said.

That got his attention. The smile left his face and he became serious.

"Sit," he said, softly, and I did.

"I just read Kimberly's phone message that she left two hours ago. She's been arrested for drug dealing and murder and is in jail. She needs a lawyer," I said.

I remained calm though my voice trembled. Kimberly had become a sister to me and I cared deeply.

"Your friend, Kimberly?" my father asked, showing the same astonishment that I felt.

"Yes," I replied.

Instantly, my dad's attitude became all business. Holiday or not, Kimberly's situation was an emergency and needed managing *then*.

"Did Kimberly say where she is?"

"No. Her message was brief. She sounded calm but must be in shock," I replied.

"OK," my dad said, drawing out the word as he thought.

"Those arrested by the New York Police Department are taken for initial processing to the precinct where the arrest occurred. They are then taken for further processing to Central Booking. It's located at the criminal court in their county, which for Kimberly is Manhattan and called New York County.

"Arraignment before a judge usually happens within twenty-four hours but who knows when that'll be. The system tends to get backed up, and it's a holiday too.

"One usually can't see the arrested person until their arraignment but we can't wait. I once helped the teenage son of an NYPD Bureau Chief who moved to Greenwich after retiring. He'll know the right people to get things moving. Get your coat!" he ordered.

"*What*?" I asked, nervously, feeling that events were moving too quickly for me to get a handle on them.

"We're driving to New York," my father said.

Chapter 113

While dressing, I heard my parents arguing and knew what it was about. My mother didn't want my father taking a demanding case and he insisted on doing so. I left my room and waited downstairs.

"Mom doesn't want you to go," I said.

"She worries, but not working is driving me crazy. She doesn't realize how much healthier I am. I've been walking two miles a day for the past three weeks," he said proudly.

I was impressed.

"You're nearly marathon material," I said.

He returned my smile, then became serious.

"I have to call Jack before we leave. He's the retired officer. Check that the car starts," my dad ordered, tossing the keys to me.

I had gotten my driver's license just after turning seventeen. While waiting in our ten-year-old car, I tried to think of what to tell Kimberly before reminding myself that legal advice was what she needed most. My sympathetic words could wait.

Besides, what could I tell a girl who had already survived so much: the death of her parents, a feared deadly illness, and childbirth. Kimberly didn't need words. She needed powerful friends, those that my father and Vladimir could provide. I made a mental note to call him.

My father loves cars. His favorite was the Chevy Camaro that he had driven as a teenager. Our old Malibu was no match but he did his best as we raced along the highway into New York City.

"Jack made calls. Kimberly is being held at the 24th Precinct on West 100th Street and that's where we're going. She'll be there for a few more hours before being sent to Central Booking. Jack told the Precinct Captain that her's is a sticky case. If handled badly, it could ruin careers and to treat her with kid gloves. He told her that her lawyer is coming, and that Kimberly has dual citizenship and Brazil's Consul must be notified," my father said.

I let this information sink in before turning to what was left unsaid.

"Her case will be a media nightmare and the trial could take weeks. Do you feel up to it?" I asked.

I worried more about my father's health than Kimberly's legal representation. Her wealth, and the case's attendant publicity, would have lawyers clamoring to represent her.

"Neither of us believes her guilty. Getting the charges dropped will be the first goal. A jury trial, with even the best lawyer and defense, is always a crap shoot.

"Still, she may not want me as her lawyer so my duties could end within a few hours until she can hire another. But she needs a lawyer now and finding one on Christmas won't be easy."

"The time of a miracle," I said softly.

"An arrest for murder doesn't drop from the sky. A miracle is exactly what Kimberly needs," my father said.

Chapter 114

My father didn't try to find parking on the street. Finding convenient street parking in Manhattan is as likely as finding a four-leaf clover. He parked in a garage and we walked two blocks to the police station.

There, my father introduced himself to the desk sergeant and was told that he had been expected. Another police officer led us to an interview room where we found Kimberly in the company of a female police officer.

I felt relieved to see that Kimberly looked nearly herself: expensively dressed though without her usual perfect makeup. I reminded myself of her core of strength. But did she now resemble brilliant crystal, stunning but cracking? I waved slightly and said nothing. It was her lawyer's job to do the talking.

"Kimberly, I am licensed to practice law in both Connecticut and New York State. Do you accept me as your attorney? You can change attorney at any time," my father said.

"Yes, and my uncle will pay your fee. He's away, on a friend's yacht with Julia. They're returning in four days," Kimberly replied.

With that obligatory matter settled, my father turned to the police officer.

"I wish to speak with my client alone and want your assurance that all recording devices are turned off," he said.

"None are operating. I'll be just outside. Can I get you something to drink? We also have bagels left from a community meeting earlier," the officer said.

Kimberly asked for coffee, and my father asked for water for him and myself. He reached for his wallet.

"It's on the house," the police officer said, before leaving.

I threw Kimberly a smile and left, knowing that a client must speak with their attorney alone lest their discussion lose the privilege of confidentiality.

Trying to relax while accompanying the officer to the vending machine, I remarked amiably, "I'll vouch for this station to my friends. Being arrested isn't as nasty as I had imagined."

"For the other prisoners it is. The Captain has already gotten three calls about her but once she leaves here..."

The police officer didn't need to finish her statement. Its meaning was crystal clear.

Chapter 115

The police officer directed me to the community room where I could wait. It was gaily decorated with holiday ornaments and a table was covered with the remaining snacks: bananas and apples, bagels, cookies, and donuts.

I sprawled on a comfortable chair in a corner, munched on a bagel, and took out my iPhone to continue reading a novel that I had downloaded from the Greenwich Library. Considering Kimberly's situation, I couldn't have chosen a more fitting book.

The Firm tells of a poor law school graduate who chose the job of his dreams. It offered a far higher salary and much better benefits than his other job offers. This included a new BMW to replace the wreck that he had been driving.

Though the job is in sleepy Memphis, which doesn't compare with New York City, Mitch and his wife, Abby, are initially happy. Then two of the firm's lawyers are killed in a mysterious boat explosion, and Mitch learns that other lawyers have also died under suspicious circumstances.

These events make sense once Mitch learns that the law firm, though having some reputable clients, is an immense criminal enterprise that uses lawyers to assist in tax evasion and money laundering.

Mitch wants to quit but knows that other lawyers who have tried to leave have wound up dead. Will he?

A man came close. He was dressed in gym clothes, a black t-shirt and black trousers. My eyes riveted on the crudely drawn swastika and skull tattoos on his muscular arm as he reached toward me.

"Welcome to my world. We'll have fun together," he murmured into my ear.

As his stinking breath enveloped me, I jerked upright, feeling a touch on my arm.

"We're leaving. Are you alright?" my father asked, noting my fright.

"I'm fine. I fell asleep and was having a nightmare. A thug grabbed for me and I felt your touch," I said.

"This can be a nightmarish place," my dad said, softly.

I said nothing, and thought of Kimberly.

Chapter 116

"A gigantic hole, ripped in the fabric of ordinary life," I said to my father, as we walked toward our car.

He stopped walking and turned toward me.

"What is?" he asked.

"The brutalizing aspect of being jailed. People would react to it in different ways and I fear its effect on Kimberly. She doesn't come from the streets," I said.

"You're becoming a poet," my dad said.

I appreciated the compliment but felt too upset to return his smile.

"What happens next? How soon before she'll be released on bail?" I asked.

I expected to receive an answer and wasn't disappointed. This information wouldn't conflict with what Kimberly had told him in confidence.

"What's happened so far is procedure. The arrested person is brought to the precinct for initial processing and interviewing. Thankfully, Kimberly was aware that she shouldn't speak without her lawyer being present and didn't.

"Her next move will be to Central Booking on Centre Street. She would be there already if it weren't for the calls that had been made on her behalf. The prosecutor wants everything done exactly right which includes notifying Brazil's Consul General of her arrest.

If he wants her seen immediately, her transfer will be delayed. I didn't realize how important her family is in Brazil. Her arrest will stir up a global media circus."

I listened without commenting. Such events were way out of my league.

"At Central Booking, which is located in the basement of the Manhattan Criminal Court building, Kimberly will wait until she can appear before a judge for arraignment. Meanwhile, they'll check her fingerprints and she'll be interviewed by the Criminal Justice Agency to determine her ties to the community. You won't be able to see her but she may be able to use a pay phone in the holding cell.

"The law requires an arrested person to be brought before a judge within twenty-four hours. This is generally done in New York City though it took a lawsuit to bring it about. I'll be at a nearby hotel until her arraignment later this morning. Do you want to stay with me or return to campus?"

"Can I go to the arraignment?" I asked.

"Yes, and that would be best. Kimberly will need all the support she can get. It's too bad her uncle is away. I'll speak with him as soon as he returns. She approved payment for our hotel expense, and for the others."

"What other costs will there be?" I asked.

"The usual in a criminal trial: our investigation, the copying of documents, possible travel. This case is a big one for the government and they have unlimited resources."

"Teenagers are the best detectives," I said.

"Huh?"

"They're masterful interpreters of human vibes," I answered.

"I'll keep that in mind," my dad said.

Chapter 117

Finding a hotel room on Christmas morning would not be easy in any American city. What I did is what people do nowadays. I went online to Expedia and chose a medium-price hotel. Since the expense would be paid by the client, I could have chosen a classy hotel but didn't. Kimberly was my friend, and my dad has ethics.

Despite my budget choice, he questioned the hotel's cost. People who have been poor can't easily spend money even when it's not theirs.

But though being cheaper, this hotel also had better reviews that many of the more expensive ones. And when I called, the receptionist sympathized with my story of being stranded. She promised we would be pleased with the adjoining rooms that she reserved and we were.

The hotel was on Greenwich Street in downtown Manhattan, not far from the Criminal Court Building where we would shortly have to be. Young couples going to the hotel's twentieth-floor rooftop bar accompanied us in the crowded elevator.

The rooms *were* comfortable but had the impersonal look of commerce. Each room had a queen-size bed, a desk and chair with enough lighting for working, a vase of flowers, and free Wi-Fi. A large photograph of Manhattan hung on one wall and a colorful abstract decorated another.

The bathroom contained the usual free toiletries. Its stylish black/white/gray color scheme might cause headache in the sensitive. Our fatigue prevented any criticism that we might have made.

The room wasn't as comfortable as my dorm room, to which I had added personal touches. But it would be for just one night and Kimberly has it immeasurably worse, I told myself. These were my thoughts before falling asleep.

Chapter 118

Because of my family's poverty, it had been many years since we ate at a hotel. I suggested this for breakfast but my father decided otherwise.

"Hotel meals are expensive and we could do with fresh air," he said.

While finding a restaurant isn't hard in Manhattan, choosing a good one can take time. But we lucked out. Two minutes after leaving the hotel, I spied an eatery. It being busy is always a good sign and, as it turned out, the diner was clean, the waitress was friendly, it had free Wi-Fi, and the prices were cheap for Manhattan. What more could any traveler want?

I would have preferred more vegetarian options but Kimberly's breakfast was certainly worse.

"Eat up. It may be a long day," my father suggested, and I did.

I ordered orange juice, oatmeal with blueberries, a toasted whole-wheat bagel, a veggie burger, and milk. My dad had grapefruit juice, pancakes, and a cinnamon-raisin bagel.

The service was quick, we ate fast, and forty minutes later we were on our way to the Criminal Court Building where Kimberly's arraignment would be held.

This building has been a regular feature in TV series and movies and is well-known. The huge, gray structure, which would be right at home beside Rome's Coliseum, instilled gloom. Kimberly will need our support, I thought.

"The holding cells are behind the courtroom where prisoners are arraigned. Beside them are interview booths for lawyers to speak privately with their clients before their hearing. You'll have to wait in the courtroom with the spectators. The proceedings have become a tourist attraction and you may meet interesting people," my dad said.

After making our way through the security procedures, my dad went one way and I went another. Apart from the judge not having arrived, the courtroom looks like those that you've seen in shows. It was filled with curious, smiling tourists and worrying prisoner families.

I sat in one of the few empty seats, beside a poorly dressed woman in her forties. She stopped dabbing her eyes with a crumpled tissue and turned toward me.

"Is it your boyfriend?" she asked, in a low voice.

Chapter 119

"No, a girlfriend. We live in the same college dorm," I replied.

The woman nodded, as if the arrest of a student were an everyday occurrence.

"Was she shoplifting?" she asked.

I answered though it was none of her business. She was clearly upset, wanted someone to talk to, and Kimberly's arrest would be front page news anyway.

"No. She's been charged with drug dealing and murder," I said.

The woman's eyes widened at this unexpected response.

"My boy did eleven years for manslaughter. He was arrested last night for assault. He said that he's innocent but a cop has it in for him."

"Eleven years is a long time," I said, with as much sympathy as I could muster. Her son didn't sound likable.

"Prison is hard. Leon, my son, told me that the way to survive is by not thinking about the sentence. You get through one day at a time and when you wake up, another day is behind you. The days add up and then the weeks and the years."

The woman nodded, as if Leon's conclusion was an article of faith. I hoped this information wouldn't be relevant for Kimberly.

"I'll pray for him," I said, and touched the woman's hand.

She grasped my hand and continued holding it as we watched the assembly line justice.

I tensed as Kimberly was brought into the courtroom.

"Is that your friend?" the woman asked, and I nodded.

"She's beautiful," the woman said.

"Yes," I agreed, thinking that good looks hadn't made her life any easier.

The legal procedure was brief. The government attorney described the charges and stated that Kimberly held both Brazilian and American citizenship. He said that she had great financial resources and, being a college student, had no ties to the community. In view of the murder charge and risk of flight, he asked that bail be denied and Kimberly be remanded for custody until trial.

My father argued that Kimberly had an exemplary reputation at Barnard College, that she had never been arrested, and was the mother of a young child. The notion that she engaged in drug dealing and murder was ridiculous, he insisted.

"Your client is *a mother*?" the judge asked.

"Yes, of a five-year-old girl," my father answered.

"And she is nineteen?" the judge asked.

"Yes, your honor."

Everyone did the math. Kimberly was thirteen when she conceived. That this is *not* evidence of an excellent character seemed the general conclusion.

"Bail is denied considering the charges and risk of flight. The defendant is remanded to the custody of the government until trial," he ruled.

Kimberly was immediately led away, without our opportunity to exchange a word. I feared that she would need Leon's advice.

Chapter 120

Vladimir once told me that a person lacking fear is a person without imagination. Kimberly is brilliant and has plenty of imagination so I knew that she must have felt terrified as she left the courtroom.

"What now?" I asked my father, as we approached the elevator.

"She'll be going to jail on Rikers Island. I'll appeal the judge's decision but that takes time. Considering the murder charge, I'm not hopeful."

"She *can't* go to Rikers!" I insisted, even as I knew how irrational my statement was.

"The law can be an ass," my dad replied.

"When can I visit her?" I asked.

"Not until she's settled in which will take a few days. Rikers' terrible reputation is mostly due to the larger men's section. A recent news article described a women's drama group that's taught by a famous acting teacher."

I nodded, having nothing to say. I felt that I had to do something but didn't know what.

"I'm going to speak with the District Attorney now, to get acquainted and pick up information. I arranged lunch with Brazil's Consul General. Maybe diplomacy can push the law. Kimberly needs something off the beaten track," my dad said.

After we parted, Leon's mother caught up to me and touched my arm.

"My son is going to Rikers on a pre-trial detention. I spoke with him for a minute. He said it's not so bad there so long as you have friends who'll make sure that you don't get messed with," she said.

Her words failed to reassure me. While walking outside, my father's statement, that Kimberly needed "something off the beaten track," echoed in my mind. That, and the need to assure her safety.

Jails, whether women's or men's, are violent places, filled with angry people who don't want to be there. Neither my father nor the District Attorney could guarantee Kimberly's safety. So, when alone, I phoned the one person that I knew who might accomplish this.

Chapter 121

In the fourth grade, I met a girl who had three fathers. One was her biological father that she never saw and two were step-fathers who occasionally entered her life. She called all of them "daddy."

I also have three fathers but didn't learn about two of them until I was a teenager. They are, in the order of when I first learned about them: my uncle, who adopted me with my aunt just hours after my birth; Peter, living in London, who had been a spy for Britain's Secret Intelligence Service (SIS); and Vladimir, a former general in Russia's Presidential Security Service, who now runs a private security company based in Berlin.

Clearly, my adoptive father is not my biological father but I'm unsure about the others. My biological mother, Lena, had affairs with both men when I was conceived and a DNA test was never performed. So, after learning of my existence, both men considered me their daughter and I don't object. The only thing better than having one great father is having three great fathers, I tell myself.

My English and Russian fathers co-own a business. All this might cause you to think that my family could star on *Dr. Phil,* the TV show specializing in divorced fathers who marry their teenage son's girlfriend and people like that. But our family celebrations are parties, not feuds.

Vladimir knows many important people. Some were met while battling terrorists and criminals in

Russia; others he knows through his other business partner who is a retired CIA official. They go fishing together too. Yes, life can be strange.

Berlin time is six hours ahead of New York and I hoped to catch him at his office. He's lately been kept up at night by the baby that he had with his girlfriend, Ulrika. She is a former officer in Germany's Special Forces, the *KSK Kommando Spezialkräfte*. Vladimir also has grown sons and a wife living somewhere in Russia. His life is as complicated as mine.

I dialed Vladimir's private number and he picked up on the second ring.

"One moment please," he said.

I heard an ongoing conversation in Russian before he returned to me.

"When will you visit? Your sister longs to see you," he said, in an emotional tone.

Russians are an affectionate people and family is important to them.

"I promise to come as soon as the school term is over. But there's a problem," I said.

Vladimir immediately became all business. Solving problems is what governments and rich people pay him for.

"Tell me about it," he ordered.

I explained the situation in a few words.

"Kimberly is our client. We must assure her safety. I hadn't known of this," he said, almost apologetically.

"It just happened. She's on her way to the jail on Rikers Island," I said.

"I've heard of it. It has a notorious reputation though not as bad as the prisons in Russia."

"Kimberly is your friend?" Vladimir asked, having sensed my emotion.

"She's a *best* friend who has already suffered more than anyone should in a lifetime. She has a daughter too," I replied.

There was a moment of silence before Vladimir spoke again. While standing in the lobby of the skyscraper from which I called, I watched the pedestrians. They looked happy and untroubled

"There is a man that you must see immediately. You are to offer up to ten-thousand-dollars a week to insure Kimberly's safety. Tell him who I am and that I don't tolerate failure. No one is available to accompany you but you will be safe. Stay by your phone. I'll get back to you."

I had my marching orders.

Chapter 122

I didn't know how long it would be before Vladimir called so I left the lobby and looked for a place to hang out. Two blocks away, I found it: a nearly empty pizza joint that sold the usual. I ordered French bread and a cup of vegetable soup, and chose a table farthest from the others. When my phone rang, I nearly choked on the bread.

I quickly opened the phone and heard sobbing. It was obvious that this wasn't the call that I was waiting for.

"Margaret?"

"Yes, it's me. What's wrong?" I asked.

It was my sister, Melanie. Another teen crisis had arisen.

"Mom wanted me to stay home. I have a fever," she said.

This fact anticipated my question: how she could be calling during school hours?

"How do you feel?"

"I'm OK."

"What's up?" I asked quickly, wanting to hang up to leave my phone free for Vladimir's call.

"Nell promised to come over yesterday but didn't. She said she wasn't feeling well. This morning I found out that she had a sleep-over at Joanne's house last night. She's my best friend but maybe I should drop her."

Melanie faced everyone's occasional problem: What to do when the people you love hurt you and how to find your way back up.

"Do you want my advice?" I asked, since her question had just been implied.

"Yes."

"OK. You have a right to be upset but don't delete her from your contacts yet. Maybe she wanted to branch out on her own and didn't know how to tell you so she lied. To clear the air, tell her how what she did made you feel. If she apologizes and promises to be upfront in the future, keep her as a friend. If not or she gets angry, maybe you should look for a new best friend."

"*Hmm,*" Melanie said, chewing over my hard-earned advice.

"I'm expecting a call and have to hang up. Can I phone you later?" I asked.

"Whenever," Melanie said, calmly, now that her crisis was over.

I hung up and returned to my food. Vladimir phoned five minutes later.

Chapter 123

"Victor, the man you must see, will meet you in two hours at his home on Staten Island," Vladimir said, sounding annoyed.

"*OK,*" I replied, slowly.

"I don't like you going there alone."

"Does he know that I'm your daughter?"

"Yes."

"Then I'll be in no danger. He wouldn't dare harm me."

I wasn't as confident as I hoped to sound. Criminals aren't completely sane and can behave foolishly.

"What is he like?" I asked.

As they say, forewarned is forearmed.

"My information is second-hand. He's about my age, and charming. He has three daughters, and a son who is a little older than you."

"OK," I said.

He is an ordinary man, I told myself, now feeling more confident.

"He's reputed to have murdered nine people in his younger days and ordered many more killings. Don't be swayed by his charm."

"I won't," I said, as my nervousness returned.

"Use the key that I gave you. Take whatever you feel you might need."

Vladimir is cautious when speaking on the phone.

"OK. I'll call you afterward."

"At any hour," he said, after telling me Victor's address.

The key that Vladimir referred to opened a safety deposit box in a bank on Church Street, a short walk from where I stood. My appointment with Victor was in two hours, at 4PM. Traveling to the southern tip of Manhattan and taking the ferry to Staten Island wouldn't take long. Nor should the taxi ride to Victor's house.

The bank that I entered was a private bank, and had surveillance cameras throughout. The manager had refreshments brought. I nibbled on a cheese Danish while he checked my identity. The account was a numbered account with access limited to three people: one was a woman possessing a particular eye color, height, and fingerprint.

After I passed inspection, the manager called for an attendant. He led me to an elevator and we descended to a sub-basement. I wondered if the bulge beneath his suit was a pistol.

When we reached the vault area, another man opened a steel gate that protected rows of safety deposit boxes. He opened mine with two keys, one being the key that I had provided. I was then led to a small room where I could inspect the box's content privately.

"Ring the buzzer when you're finished. I'll be just outside," the man said, before closing the door.

The metal box was about twelve by twenty-four inches. Inside, lay thick, clasped manila envelopes and two small cardboard boxes. I removed thirty one-hundred-dollar bills from one of the envelopes, a corporate credit card from another, and the contents of one of the cardboard boxes.

I re-clasped the envelope and replaced it and the empty cardboard box in the safety deposit box. Then I rang for the attendant, rode the elevator with him to the lobby floor, and walked quickly from the bank. I had shopping to do before meeting Victor.

Chapter 124

During a party in Greenwich, to celebrate the completion of my first year at Barnard, Vladimir took me aside. He gave me the key to this safety deposit box and told me what it contained: cash, a corporate credit card, and some other things that I might need in an emergency. A fingerprint was required to permit me access to the box.

I considered his request odd but taking my fingerprint took only a moment. He said that two other people were also allowed access to the box. I sensed that I shouldn't ask who they were.

What Vladimir hadn't said was that the safety deposit box contained two unusual guns. I was familiar with both of them. Ulrika, Vladimir's live-in girlfriend, had instructed me in their use while we were in Japan.

Both guns use the same 7.62x42mm SP-4 cartridge and are nearly silent when fired. The revolver, an OTs-38 Stechkin, holds five rounds and has an effective firing range of one-hundred-and-fifty feet. This gun had an attached laser sight. The other gun, a semi-automatic PSS Silent Pistol, holds six rounds and has a shorter effective firing range.

Should I carry a pistol to the meeting? I asked myself. The severity of New York City's gun laws told me "no." If arrested, I would certainly be jailed. Kimberly and I would become legendary as the only Barnard students to spend their sophomore year in jail.

But Victor was a killer and meeting him unarmed seemed the greater risk. I took the flatter PSS pistol. It was easier to conceal, though not with what I wore. This was another reason why I had to go shopping.

At a chic boutique on Fulton Street, I chose a Max Mara print. It had side pockets deep enough to hold the pistol. To this purchase I added an elegant bag by Dolce & Gabbona and gold earrings encrusted with tourmaline, sapphire and diamonds. My sneakers would also not do so I let the salesgirl talk me into buying Gianvito Rossi Sandals. "They're on sale for only seven-hundred-dollars," she said.

I left the store feeling the confidence that wearing exclusive clothes gives. I felt guilty at their expense but told myself that, if appearance was important, I had transformed myself into a negotiator that Victor would find hard to reckon with.

I had also become the store's valued customer for whom no favor was too great. I changed in the dressing room and left my old clothes in my backpack. I parked it with the sales clerk, saying that I would pick it up later that day.

The manager's smile was blinding as she led me to the exit. A quick twenty-one-thousand-dollar purchase will have this effect in most stores.

Chapter 125

My next task was getting to Staten Island. I doubted that any taxi would take me there from Manhattan. Doing so would involve wasted, unpaid time during their long return. So I turned to Uber after associating their app with the corporate credit card from the safety deposit box. I had used their service the year before while babysitting. Then, the child's mother had paid the charges.

I entered on the Uber app that my travel destination was South Ferry, not Staten Island. I would negotiate that part of the trip, and the driver's waiting time at Victor's home for my return trip, in person.

The driver came promptly and we reached South Ferry in fifteen minutes. Then a problem arose: I hadn't known that the Staten Island Ferry didn't carry cars.

The Ferry ride took twenty-five minutes. A row of taxis waited at the dock. I entered the nearest and spoke Victor's address. Upon reaching it, I made my offer.

"I have an appointment here and must return to Manhattan quickly after it's over. I will pay you two hundred dollars waiting time for each hour that my meeting takes. I will pay you four hundred dollars in advance. You can keep this even if my meeting takes only ten minutes, and it may be brief."

The man's eyes gleamed. He might have considered stranding me after being paid but I wasn't stupid.

"Here is the initial four hundred dollars for waiting," I said.

I showed him four crisp one-hundred-dollar bills and then tore two of them in half.

"You'll get the other halves when my meeting is over. As I said, it may only take a few minutes."

The driver, Roy Q. Barnes, according to his license, smiled and pocketed the money. I left the taxi and walked toward the house.

Chapter 126

While on the Ferry, watching the slowly receding Manhattan skyline, thoughts of Kimberly kept intruding. Kimberly handcuffed. Kimberly in the orange jumpsuit whose sight became popularized in *Orange is the New Black*. Kimberly being raped in the shower.

These black thoughts persisted until the taxi stopped at Victor's home. Then I tried to force them from my mind. I couldn't waste energy worrying about Kimberly. I had to end such thoughts to negotiate effectively.

Victor's house wasn't as grand as I had imagined. There was no gated presence protected by scowling guards. Instead, it resembled my family's home in Greenwich: a large Victorian structure with a door knocker instead of a bell.

I used the knocker, and looked back toward the taxi to be sure that it was still there. A minute went by. After I knocked again, the door was opened by a dark haired girl of about five.

"Can I help you?" she asked, in an adult tone.

I told her my name and why I was there.

"Grandpa is busy in the kitchen. Come this way, please," she told me.

My entrance occurred without the frisking that I had feared. Why did I risk bringing a gun? I asked myself, feeling silly.

In the kitchen stood a man who I assumed was Victor. He was speaking to a girl of about eight, and smiled at me before continuing.

"You soak the bread crumbs in the milk, add the meats, egg, onion, salt and pepper, and mix thoroughly. This mixture is then shaped into balls of about one and one-half inches in diameter and rolled in the flour," Victor instructed.

"We're having Swedish meatballs for dinner," Victor said, turning toward me.

The scene was as homey as one could imagine. Could Vladimir have sent me to the wrong person? I wondered.

Victor placed the meatballs in the refrigerator, and shooed the girls to their room. "Grandpa has business with this nice lady. Maybe she'll stay for dinner," he said, as he took off the frilly apron.

"I was told that you're Mormon and don't drink coffee. Would you like juice or water?" he asked, in a pleasant tone.

I accepted a juice box and he poured coffee for himself. Then he led me to his home office.

"They're my granddaughters. Their parents are in Florida for a week and I love it," Victor said.

His grin was infectious and, despite what I knew of his background, I couldn't help liking him.

I sipped my juice and he sipped his coffee.

To give myself time to think, I complimented the ethanol fireplace in the corner. It was made wholly of wires.

"Victor nodded approval, and smiled.

"It's a Giulio Iachetti creation. He calls it a *wireplace*," he said, and the smile left his face.

"I like to know who I'm dealing with. Tell me about yourself," Victor ordered, in a far less friendly tone.

Chapter 127

"I'm nineteen. I couldn't have accomplished much by my age," I replied, modestly.

"I did a lot by the time I was nineteen," Victor said.

I nodded.

"I've done a few things. I grew up in Greenwich and am in my second year at Barnard," I said.

"A rich bitch."

"Not really," I said, maintaining my friendly tone and ignoring his contempt.

"I was adopted at birth by a lawyer who became disabled by Lyme disease. I live in a house that's owned by an old family trust and our family survives on Social Security Disability payments and Food Stamps."

"You dress well for someone like that," Victor said.

I wasn't angered by his words. Continued suspicion has enabled him to survive his brutal world, I told myself.

"I've known Vladimir for years but first learned that he was my father a year ago. He paid for these," I said, gesturing across my dress.

Victor sipped his coffee. I placed my juice box on the table and slipped my hand in my pocket. The pistol's touch comforted me as I remembered Ulrika's advice: A gun is like toilet paper. When you need it, you need it bad.

She had also told me that one shouldn't bring a knife to a gunfight. I still didn't think I would need this gun but was glad that I had it.

"Tell me about Vladimir," Victor said.

I breathed deeply before replying. Vladimir's nature had always puzzled me.

"To understand Vladimir, you must understand the Russian people. They are loving, but cruel to those who betray them. Family is important to them. If you harm someone they love, the wound must be avenged.

"Vladimir was a general in Russia's Presidential Security Service. He now runs a security company in Berlin with two partners. One worked for the CIA and the other for the SIS, Britain's Secret Intelligence Service.

"Thirty years ago, Vladimir's friend was killed while on a mission in Syria. Vladimir took revenge with his unit of KGB Spetsnaz, Russian Special Forces. When they caught the men that killed him, they cut off their balls and stuffed them in their mouths. I don't know if this happened before or after they died. No Russians in Syria were harmed after that."

"He told you that story?" Victor questioned.

"No, his girlfriend did. She trained me in Tokyo where I helped Vladimir. His son said that no one could doubt that I am Vladimir's daughter," I replied.

"You must have been told who I am. Weren't you afraid to meet me?" Victor asked, with a smile and condescending tone.

Despite what I had just told him, I sensed that Victor still considered me a dumb college kid. I didn't mind personally but Kimberly's life was at stake. I decided that I had to say something startling, to end our babbling and get down to business. If Victor couldn't–or wouldn't–help Kimberly, Vladimir must find someone else.

I was also irritated by Victor's manner. In my mind, though an obviously loving grandfather, he was simply a thug, unworthy of mine or Vladimir's attention.

"No, I wasn't afraid. If you harm me, Vladimir will have you and your entire family killed. I also brought a friend," I replied.

"I don't see anyonc," Victor sneered.

"A very good friend. Do you know what a PSS is?" I asked, speaking slowly and deliberately.

Victor shook his head.

"It's a Russian 7.62mm silent pistol. It speaks softly, like the cough of a dying person," I said.

I lifted the pistol from my pocket and held it in my lap.

"I don't think that I'll need it," I said, calmly.

The atmosphere between us deepened until Victor lifted it with a real smile and raised his arms in mock surrender. I replaced the pistol in my pocket.

"Damn, I like you! Stay for dinner and meet my son. He's a student at Princeton," Victor said.

Chapter 128

I answered Victor's invitation with a smile. I would decide whether to stay after we completed our business, which I turned to. I described Kimberly, and her situation.

"Vladimir will pay you five-thousand-dollars a week to insure Kimberly's safety at Rikers Island with an initial bonus of twenty-five-thousand dollars. Her lawyer is trying to get her released on bail but may not be successful.

"The District Attorney is up for re-election. He lost his last big case and views this one as his rescue. I don't doubt that Kimberly is innocent and was framed. We've hired investigators but just now her safety is the biggest issue," I said.

"My contacts at Rikers are costly. You know of the investigation?" he asked.

"Yes," I replied.

The story of corrupt Rikers' guards had been national news.

"It will cost ten-thousand-dollars a week," Victor said.

I looked at him coolly without blinking.

"I have my orders. Vladimir won't pay more than a thousand dollars a day,' I said.

"*Done!*" Victor said, after a long stare.

"Thirty-two-thousand-dollars will be wired into your account tomorrow. This will cover the bonus and first week's payment. Thereafter, seven-thousand dollars will be wired into your account each Monday until Kimberly is released."

Victor continued smiling, and nodded.

I felt pleased at having saved Kimberly money though it didn't matter considering her wealth. But my years of living in poverty had left its mark.

"Will you stay for dinner?" Victor asked.

"I'd love to. Your family is charming. There's just one more thing. Vladimir also told me to say that he buys success and doesn't accept a refund for failure. He felt sure that you would understand," I said.

"That is my policy too. I would not do business any other way," Victor said.

Though his tone was friendly as we left the room, his smile, which hadn't been a real smile, didn't return until we neared a closed door.

My smile disappeared when I heard the crashing of furniture and screams from within the room. I slipped my hand into my pocket. The cold grip of the pistol warmed me.

Chapter 129

Feelings can twist your thinking and that's what happened with me. Victor was a monster. I had threatened him with Vladimir's words and become frightened. That was all.

The room that we entered held no torture chamber like the one that had imprisoned me in Tokyo. Instead, there were two squealing children and a young man. They chased after two small electric trains scooting along the carpet. It drove as if human, from one direction to another after bumping into an object. A small table had been overturned by a joyous child.

The girls calmed down and the man straightened himself after we entered the room. They smiled as Victor introduced me.

"Margaret is the daughter of a business associate. She's staying for dinner," he said.

The silence that followed caused me to wonder whether many strangers had received this invitation.

"That looks like quite a toy," I said, hoping to relax the atmosphere and start a conversation.

"They're WolVol Electric Trains, this year's most popular toy according to what I read. I bought them as an early Christmas present for my favorite nieces. I'm Anthony, *Tony*, if my father forgot to tell you. People get forgetful at his age," the man said, with an infectious grin.

"Please! Don't tell *all* this family's secrets," Victor said, with a feigned mournful look and playful shake of his finger.

I was surprised how by quickly Victor's mood had shifted from threatening to affectionately playful. But was this different from mine? I asked myself.

I brushed such analysis from my mind. This was not the time for it. Victor would be better as a friendly ally than if suspicious. I faced Tony and turned on the charm.

"Your father told me that you're at Princeton," I said.

"I was lucky to be admitted," he replied.

I liked Tony's modesty.

"It *wasn't* luck. Anthony made the highest SAT scores at Stuyvesant High which is the best high school in America. Princeton is lucky to have him," Victor said, proudly.

"What are you studying?" I asked.

"I'm not sure. Probably pre-law but I may go into politics. I interned with Boehner last year," Tony replied.

Representative Boehner was the former Speaker of the House and one of the most powerful figures in Washington until he retired from Congress.

"That's impressive!" I said, and meant it.

Tony is smart and ambitious and handsome. He *may not be* like his father, I thought, with approval.

My boyfriend, Randy, seemed far away. Could I be comfortable as Victor's daughter-in-law and a politician's wife? I asked myself.

Chapter 130

I knew this fantasy about Tony was crazy. I intend to marry Randy so why am I thinking about marrying Tony? I wondered.

But I should think about this puzzle later. Now, it was important to get through dinner. Then to return to Manhattan, inform Vladimir of the agreement with Victor, and visit Kimberly. I should also check in with Randy, Erika, and my family. Busy days awaited me.

I remembered the taxi driver as we entered the dining room.

"I have a taxi waiting. I'll have to speak with the driver," I said.

"He's probably gone. They're not good with waiting," Tony said.

"I made it worthwhile. I said that I'd pay him two-hundred-dollars an hour while waiting and gave him four-hundred-dollars in advance. I tore two of the hundred-dollar bills in half and said that he'd get the other halves when I returned," I explained.

Tony laughed but the gleam in Victor's eyes bothered me. His estimate of me had risen and I was of two minds about that.

I went outside and gave the taxi driver the two halves. He gave me his cell phone number and said that he would wait at a nearby diner. I could call him "whenever." He would make several week's earnings that night.

Despite my doubts, I enjoyed the dinner. Victor was a widower who enjoyed food and cooking was his hobby.

Being a non-coffee-drinking/non-alcohol-drinking Mormon had made me an unusual guest. Stating that I was vegetarian too might have sent him over the edge, and would have upset the girls who had helped make the meatballs. I repressed my convictions and ate them.

It was a real family dinner. Victor told of meeting the Pope as a child when visiting Rome with his father. Tony told of visiting the White House with Boehner, and the girls chattered away.

The older girl asked if I had sisters and I spoke of my adoptive sister, Claudine, who is their age. I said that she had lived in the South West and loved Nancy Drew mysteries. But I grew too comfortable and revealed too much.

"Her love of mysteries is understandable considering what she went through," I said.

The girls ignored that statement but Victor and Tony looked at me with interest.

"I'll tell you later," I said, indicating the children.

Later, was after gorging on Victor's Christmas Spice Cookies which the girls had helped bake. After they were put to bed, I spoke of the murder of Claudine's mother, the attempt on Claudine's life, and the bombing of her therapist's office.

"She's gone through a lot but is a sturdy kid," I concluded.

Both men simply stared.

Chapter 131

Tony offered to drive me to the Ferry but I refused.

"I told the taxi driver that he would be taking me," I said.

But the real reason was that I feared being alone with Tony. He is *that* attractive, and the aura of power has a seductive effect. Ask any politician.

I phoned for the taxi driver to pick me up, made my goodbyes, and left Victor's home. The driver came promptly. I paid him at the Ferry, and added another two-hundred-dollar bonus. I said that I might have more work for him in the future.

"Wherever," he said, with a grin, and bowed as he opened the door for me.

The rest of the day was uneventful. I changed back into my daily clothes at the store and carefully packed my purchases in my backpack. Next came the trip to the bank, to return the pistol and credit card to the safety deposit box. By 8PM I was back at the dorm, feeling exhausted.

I immediately phoned Vladimir to describe the agreement with Victor. I also told him of my expensive purchases.

"I needed a better appearance to negotiate well. We agreed on three-thousand-dollars less than he originally asked." I said proudly.

"You did good work but he's keeping most the money. In his world, money flows toward him and not down," Vladimir said.

"I'm holding a bit over two-thousand dollars. For an emergency if something comes up that need be done quickly. I'll hide it in a travel pouch," I said.

I felt uncomfortable keeping the money but Vladimir responded, "Good thinking." For his large company, that sum is donut money.

"Victor has an impressive son," I said, apropos of nothing. Tony was still on my mind.

"Anthony, yes, he's the next generation."

"Is he like Victor?" I asked, trying to sound merely curious.

"Maybe, but I know little. It's rumored that Victor had his wife and her lover murdered. It's not known whether Anthony knows this or suspects it."

I felt too stunned to say anything.

"*Don't* become involved with Anthony! With such a father, one can't be sure how deeply the roots have sunk," Vladimir warned.

"No, I won't," I promised.

When our conversation ended, I thought that his judgment could also be placed on me.

Chapter 132

I had another unsettling thought after our call. Victor had a strange look when I told of Claudine's mother being murdered. Was this because he had killed his wife?

Thankfully, school demands quickly engulfed me: I had to finish an essay and to study for a calculus exam. These removed other matters from my mind until my Greenwich father phoned.

"I'll be speaking with Kimberly at Rikers tomorrow. Can you come?" he asked.

"Of course!"

"Be outside your dorm at nine. I'll pick you up," my dad said, and hung up abruptly.

Working full-time on Kimberly's case had energized him, turning him back into the hard-charging lawyer he had once been.

I doubled-down on my schoolwork and finished a little before 2AM. The math exam was that evening. If I missed it, having been at Rikers would provide me with an unbeatable excuse, I joked to myself.

After turning out the light, I remembered an important task. Both Kimberly and I follow the Santeria faith. Victor would protect her as best he could but his power was nothing compared with that of the Gods. Kimberly could not offer sacrifice to them so I must do it for her.

I thought of the ancient Yoruba proverb: *Riru ebo ni i gbe ni airu ki i gbe eyan* (It is the offerings of sacrifices that brings blessings. Neglect of sacrifices blesses no one). And its consequence, for which one prays: *Ebo fin, Eru da* (The offerings are accepted, evil forces depart.).

I turned on the light and wrote myself this reminder. I would not rely on memory for this vital task.

I stood outside Brooks Hall for ten minutes before my father arrived.

"What did you do yesterday?" he asked, as soon as I had buckled up.

"Not much, shopped for some things and then studied," I replied.

My answer was deliberately vague. The worlds of Vladimir and Victor were far different from his. Luckily, few have greater deceiving ability than do teenagers with their parents.

We talked little during the trip; the congested Manhattan traffic demanded his concentration. I studied my calculus text, being absorbed in it until he suddenly spoke.

"Your mother called me this morning. She was feeling jittery after reading in the *Greenwich Times* that there have been forty-two robberies so far this year. I told her that 'residential burglary' could mean many things, even a bike being stolen from a garage."

His comment seemed fitting for our destination.

Chapter 133

Despite my father being at my side, my unease grew. There is a thin line between the civilized and the primitive and we were entering another world. A place where strength and street smarts but not intelligence count most, and where the rules aren't always followed.

The prisoners were locked in and so were we. We needed permission to use the bathroom or to leave the facility.

My father had been informed that parking at Rikers was limited and using public transportation was best. Thus after driving to Long Island City, we rode the Q100 bus to the jail.

The bus passengers wearing suits are probably lawyers and the others are probably prisoners' relatives, I told myself. It was a neither here nor there thought. I was trying to keep calm by making what I expected seem logical.

A painful memory from Tokyo had entered my mind: being locked-in with a monster, of which there were many at Rikers. I felt afraid and reached for my father's hand, just as I had when I was younger and more easily afraid.

"Feeling nervous?" he asked, with a concerned look.

I didn't speak but simply nodded, fearing that my voice would crack. American and Japanese officials had praised my actions in Tokyo but it had been an evil time.

"There's nothing to be afraid of, child."

The voice arose from in back of us.

I turned, and tried to smile. The woman was about my father's age, stout, and looking weary.

"It's a scary place," I replied honestly.

"Much more for the prisoners than for us. You'll be safe. The guards watch visitors like hawks, and especially a girl as pretty as you."

"Thanks," I said, with a grin.

Compliments go a long way with me.

"Are you visiting your son?" I asked.

I hoped to reduce my anxiety by speaking with this woman.

"No, it's my daughter," she replied.

"Has she been inside long?" I asked, deliberately avoiding using the word "jail" and adopting "street" lingo.

"Ten months. I come twice a week after my shift ends."

"Your shift?"

"I'm an ER nurse. I work night shifts to be free to visit during the week and avoid the weekend crush. It's actually a pretty place during the summer. The island gets the breeze off the Long Island Sound."

The woman reached into her large handbag and offered a business card.

"Call me when you visit so we can come together. It's less lonely that way," she said.

"Thank you," I replied, taking the card.

Jennifer had said me that friendships are frequently made while riding this bus. I learned during the London bombing that disaster brings strangers together. When I had told this to Kimberly, she said that such behavior "gives one hope for the human race."

Her painful life has made her old beyond her years, I thought. But, unlike this woman's daughter, I couldn't imagine Kimberly surviving ten months at Rikers.

Chapter 134

Our admittance to Rikers went exactly as Jennifer had described when she visited her husband. I went through the procedure calmly until a correction officer's question jolted me.

"Are you packing?" he asked.

When translated, his question meant: "Are you carrying a gun?"

I quickly looked up but this question hadn't been meant for me. He had asked it of someone in back of me. I turned and saw a man dressed in military uniform.

"Only when I have to and this isn't one of them," the man replied, with a smile.

The guard nodded and the line moved on.

In order to maintain client-lawyer confidentiality, my father had to speak with Kimberly alone. While waiting in the visiting room, I apparently looked suspicious. A correction officer singled me out and frisked me before repeating the visitor instructions: "Hugs, handshakes, and some kisses are permitted but no more!" I smiled meekly.

When later describing Rikers to Erika, I told her that what had most struck me was the unmistakable smell of bleach and body odor. That, and the rudeness of staff who didn't seem to care what visitors or inmates thought of them.

Rikers isn't a place that anyone wants to be and this affects attitudes. But, as Jennifer's husband had joked when trying to reassure her, along with his residency plan came free medical care, river and city views, and the use of a gym with more recreation time than anyone could want.

I wanted to leave and to take Kimberly out with me. It may have been Vladimir's genes that caused my thoughts to cycle through escape schemes though probably none of them would work. The required skills aren't yet taught at Barnard.

Kimberly finally came. My father sat at a distance while we spoke, sensing that we wanted to alone.

Kimberly sat gingerly, as if trying to avoid pain.

"Are you alright?" I asked, feeling concern.

Kimberly's face contorted before she replied. Her disjointed tone increased my fear.

"In the shower...a woman..." she mumbled.

I waited silently for Kimberly to catch herself.

"She...*liked me*. A guard was watching and stopped her."

"Are you afraid she'll bother you again?" I asked.

"No, not her. I heard that her wrists are broken. The Gods work in strange ways."

No, Victor is doing what he was paid to do, I thought. But I wouldn't tell Kimberly about Victor while we were in Rikers.

"I'm glad. I'll offer sacrifice," I said, instead.

"To Ogun," she asked.

I nodded agreement. Ogun is a powerful God in the Santeria faith. He is The Great One of the Other World, the protector of those who are being injured.

Kimberly looked into my eyes.

"How is Julia?" she asked, in a quivering voice.

Chapter 135

Kimberly's question is the first demand of any parent whose child is away, and I wasn't sure what to reply. I might say that Julia was with her guardian and so must be OK but knew that this vague answer wouldn't satisfy her.

Kimberly hungered for the assurance that I had just seen Julia and she was fine. But Kimberly most needed the truth about this and everything else. Only accurate facts would gain her freedom.

"Julia is still on the boat with your uncle. My father has been unable to reach him but it should dock today. What should we tell Julia?" I asked.

Kimberly became calm. Solving complex problems was part of her nature and relaxed her. It was her equivalent of playing a video game, and why many people play them obsessively.

"There are two issues: what she must be told, and where she will live until I'm out. What kills me is that she's lost me as a mother right after I began behaving like one. Tell her that I love her and will always love her. Tell her that though we must be apart for a while, I'll write her often. Writing to her will help me keep sane.

"My uncle is a good man but his business affairs demand travel. Plus, he's never been a parent and she must be shielded from reporters and TV. He couldn't do these properly so Julia can't live with him. Can she stay with your parents?"

I didn't hesitate though realizing that I should gain their approval before replying. Julia was already friends with my youngest sister and my mother would love to have her. Being a mother had been her major goal in life and she had always wanted a larger family. Now her older children were becoming independent and she was losing this role. Moreover, having been a teacher, she could teach Julia until she returned to school.

"Yes, of course. My parents would love to have her," I said, after just a momentary hesitation.

Kimberly let out the breath that she had been holding.

"There's just one more thing. You remember our agreement if something happens to me?"

My mind momentarily went blank before remembering. Months before, I had agreed to be Julia's godmother.

"*Nothing will happen to you!*" I said firmly.

Kimberly's reply was a slight wave about the room.

Regardless of where we are, she must now be told about Victor, I told myself, and then did in a low voice.

"Vladimir has arranged for your safety. Your attacker's injuries were no accident," I said.

Kimberly looked as if she had sensed this.

"He provides good security," she said, and I nodded

"Now that's been settled, where did these crazy charges come from?" I asked.

Kimberly took a deep breath before answering.

"It's just politics, and convenience too. Your father told me that news stories about me are coming. I'll be compared to *Griselda*, America's Cocaine Godmother and Queen of Narco-Trafficking who was murdered a few years ago. Being photogenic can be a curse," Kimberly replied, with a wry smile.

"Who in Hell is she?" I asked loudly, and a guard moved closer.

I don't often curse but Kimberly's statement had blown my mind. My astonishment grew as she explained.

Chapter 136

"Griselda Blanco was a monster and that we were both born in Cartagena, Colombia is being used against me," Kimberly said, without the hint of a smile.

"That's crazy!" I said.

"Tell it to me. My birth there was an accident. My father was inspecting a petrochemical plant that he owned and my very pregnant mother had accompanied him. She had labor pains in a restaurant where I wound up being born three weeks early. My father became friends with the restaurant's owner and he still sends me birthday cards."

I leaned back. This sounded like a long story.

"Griselda was a pickpocket before turning to prostitution and the drug trade. She's reported to have made her first killing at eleven but this story may be a myth.

"She was an important member of the Medellin cartel until falling out with them. She had accepted payment for a drug shipment, then tried to welsh by murdering the messenger and saying that the money hadn't been delivered. The dead woman was the niece of another cartel member and it became open season on Griselda. She managed to get away to New York City.

"In Queens, she and her second husband–her first had died mysteriously–began a cocaine business. She fled America after being indicted in 1975 but later returned to

Miami. She was the most notorious killer in the Miami drug wars and had her own execution squad, the *pistoleros*. She became furious at her chief killer after he didn't follow her order to murder all the members of a family. Police found the young children trying to awaken their dead parents."

Kimberly paused, and I shuddered. Her story and the jail's atmosphere had gotten to me.

"Griselda's killing spree become bad for the drug business. The other gang leaders put out a contract on her but she survived six assassination attempts. She was finally arrested and sentenced to prison. The murder cases against her collapsed on technical grounds.

"After being released, she was deported to Colombia where she was killed in a drive-by shooting. Two of her three children were also murdered. Her youngest, favored son was named 'Michael Corleone' after the *Godfather* movie gangster. He was raised by his maternal grandmother."

"That's interesting but what does it have to do with you?" I asked, speaking slowly.

Kimberly made a smile that wasn't really a smile.

"Absolutely nothing but that's not what the District Attorney thinks and the public will salivate over: A teenage, South American criminal who murders innocent Barnard students. You can't beat that for a headline. It could get me the needle if the Feds indict me too."

Chapter 137

Kimberly looked like she had reached that degree of tiredness when one can hardly carry a thought.

"You won't forget about Julia?" she asked, as her eyelids drooped.

"No, of course not," I replied.

"I'm sorry. I'm not thinking straight," Kimberly said, apologetically.

"I'm amazed that you're thinking at all considering what's happened. But you have great people fighting for you. My dad is a wonderful lawyer and Vladimir can reach many officials."

"Yes."

Kimberly's voice was weak but who would expect otherwise? Her image had changed from envied Barnard student to hated murderer.

My dad once said that things that seem terrible at night usually seem better in the morning but I didn't see Kimberly's situation getting better. Moreover, losing the willpower to go on destroys both body and mind. I tried to think of something hopeful to say.

"If lost in the wilderness, go back to where you started and begin again," I blurted out, without thinking.

"What did you say?" Kimberly asked, suddenly fully aroused.

I repeated what I had said.

"Yes, that's what must be done. Study every piece of evidence. There *must be* a mistake somewhere," she said.

"Or you've been framed."

"Or I've been framed," Kimberly agreed, as the visiting hour ended.

We hugged, and I reassured her about Julia. I suddenly remembered what I had meant to tell her though in the scheme of things it wasn't much.

"Say that you're Jewish! The Rabbi is a nice guy and will let you use his phone. You'll also get grape juice and a box of matzo each week," I said.

I had spoken in a rush since the guards had begun hustling people out.

My suggestion wouldn't change anything but it aroused her smile and that was something.

"Will do," she said, before being led away with the other prisoners.

A minute later, I looked to my father for comforting words.

"Don't despair. Great things are always being done by people too stupid to realize that they are impossible," he said, in a serious tone, before smiling.

"And keep blundering around. You have a talent for doing the wrong thing in the wrong way at the wrong time and coming up with the right answer," he said.

Outside in the cold, I clung to him as we stood shivering with the group, awaiting the bus to Queens.

Chapter 138

The bus was quiet. I didn't talk with my father nor were the other passengers saying much. A jail can depress even the most optimistic person. Only when we were settled in our car did I speak.

"Kimberly wants her daughter to stay with us in Greenwich. Her guardian travels and Julia must be shielded from reporters and TV. I realize that I should have asked you and mom first but I told her that it would be OK," I said, in an apologetic tone.

"That's no problem. We'd love having her," my father replied quickly.

It was coming onto the evening rush hour and he was absorbed in negotiating the heavy traffic. When cars were stopped at the entrance to the bridge, I changed the subject.

"What is this craziness? How has Kimberly become the poster child of evil. What evidence is there?" I asked.

My agitation expressed the incredulity that I felt.

My father sighed and looked about the road before answering. The cars showed no sign of moving. He turned toward me.

"The present evidence is indirect but the D.A. has told me that positive DNA results are expected. As much as I hate to say this, at heart it seems to stem from police embarrassment, and politics too.

"The case of two dead students has gone cold. They're suspected of having been involved in drug activity but Barnard isn't eager to aid the investigation. Applications have plunged because of parent fears and big-shots on their Board are pressuring to get things back to normal.

"Kimberly has been chosen to provide closure. Suspicion creates a wrong interpretation of everything. She holds foreign citizenship, often travels to South America, and everyone knows what their biggest export is.

"Direct suspicion at any honest person, slander them with distorted facts and the public will believe. The normal assumption of innocence will change as the concept of guilt beyond a reasonable doubt disappears.

"Also, the District Attorney is running for re-election. His poll numbers have fallen since botching his last high-profile case and winning this one could put him over the top. So instead of doing his job by evaluating the lack of evidence and reconsidering the case, he's plowing ahead to give the *appearance* of justice.

"Moreover, crime has risen in the City and the Mayor has become increasingly unpopular. It's important to change this, and for the District Attorney to be re-elected of course. Kimberly is just a bump in the road."

"And she be damned," I said.

"And Kimberly be damned," my father agreed.

"Not if we can help it!" I said, signing on to provide whatever help I could give though recognizing that it probably wouldn't count for much.

"Prosecutors always say, 'I believe in my case,' but it'll all depend on the DNA evidence, whatever that might be," my father said.

The traffic began moving and my father looked away from me.

Only as the car stopped at Brooks Hall did I dare to ask the question at the center of my mind.

"Could Kimberly really be executed?"

Moments passed before my father answered.

"Yes. She could be executed under several federal statutes. God help her, she could," he said, softly.

Chapter 139

My father is smart and has been described as a gifted lawyer. Despite this, I checked what he told me. I had always believed that, except for charges like treason and states like Texas, people are rarely executed. So the first thing that I did upon returning to my room was to fire up my iPad and browse to the Death Penalty Information Center.

I had expected to find possibly two crimes for which the death penalty could be imposed but was wrong. Forty-one statutes prescribe execution and the charges against Kimberly clearly fit within two of them: 18 U.S.C. 1111, First-degree murder; and 18 U.S.C. 1512, Murder with the intent of preventing testimony by a witness, victim, or informant. There could be others but I stopped looking.

The ringing of my phone whisked me from my depression. It was my father. Kimberly's uncle and Julia had returned. He asked me to pack for Julia and to accompany her to Greenwich.

I showered quickly, to remove the jail-house odor from my nostrils and clothes. Twenty-five minutes later, with my hair still damp, I stood on Broadway and waited for my Uber driver to arrive.

He had the hearse-looking Japanese car that has massive space for passengers and luggage. Kimberly's uncle didn't own a car so making travel arrangements to Greenwich were up to me.

The Uber fare for the three miles to the apartment was charged to my dad's business credit card. I negotiated with the driver.

"I'll need you for the rest of the day. A child is moving to Greenwich and I must pack for her. Would you wait for us and take us there?" I asked.

I understood the driver's hesitation. I was young, dressed in my usual shabby clothes, and might be doing something seedy. But I had expected this reaction. What had worked on Staten Island should work in Manhattan.

I took out a roll of hundred-dollar bills.

"Tell Uber that you're feeling sick and are going off duty. I'll pay you five-hundred-dollars to drive us to Greenwich, one-hundred-dollars for each hour that you wait, and an additional five-hundred-dollars to drive me back to Barnard. There, I'll give you a two-hundred-dollar bonus. All-in-all it shouldn't take more than six hours. You pay for gas and tolls."

As I spoke, suspicion left the man's face and he beamed. I would be paying him more than a week's earnings for less than a day's work, and away from the madness of Manhattan traffic too. I gave him a hundred-dollar bill and tore five other hundred-dollar bills in half.

"Here is the money up front. You'll get the rest and the other halves of the hundred-dollar bills upon my return to Barnard," I said.

The driver couldn't do enough.

Chapter 140

Julia's move didn't go as easily as I had hoped. Like with every mother substitute, a child wants the real thing. The explanation Kimberly had created, that she was on a business trip and would write to Julia regularly, didn't satisfy.

Julia had experienced little mothering in her life. Her grandmother died when she was barely two, her step-mother had largely ignored her, and her real mother had only recently engaged with her. Though I did my best, Julia suffered.

Her eyes glistened with tears. Mine did too as she repeatedly asked, "Where's mommy? When is she coming?"

While holding her in the car, I repeated the excuse that sounded like a lie even to me. The Uber driver tried to help by telling stories of his young daughter but our efforts didn't work. Finally, Julia became exhausted and fell asleep. A few minutes later I nodded off too.

There hadn't been much to pack. Most of the clothes that Julia would need were in several suitcases that were brought from the yacht. I threw more pajamas and underwear and a few stuffed animals into a plastic bag. Whatever else she needed could be bought. Shopping would help to get Julia's mind off her absent mother.

Our arrival in Greenwich went smoothly. My mother hugged Julia and she was reacquainted with my sisters. She was shown the room that she would share with her bodyguard. It was my room but I didn't object. I would be busy in the City and could use a sleeping bag when I visited.

I hugged each member of my family and gave my longest hug to Julia. Then I left quickly, saying that I had a taxi waiting. Even before closing the door, I heard Julia's grief-stricken wail, "Where's mommy?"

The driver's smile disappeared when he saw the black look on my face. As we drove from Greenwich, I vowed that whoever had caused Kimberly's and Julia's suffering would pay. No matter how dirty the deed, I would do it. And the Gods would smile!

Chapter 141

My vow, that the Gods would smile when I exacted punishment, reminded me of my promise to Kimberly: to give sacrifice to *Ogun*, a great spirit of the Santeria religion that we followed.

Though often called pagan and heathenistic, the Africa originated religion of Santeria is similar to its Western counterparts. It is even older and had voiced the belief in one God thousands of years before Judaism and Christianity arose.

The many Gods to whom Santeria followers pray are akin to angels, intermediaries between humans and The Being, *Olodumare*. These, such as Ogun, are viewed as helping with the survival of people and nations. Santeria angels are called *orisha*.

Santeria is neither a cult nor occult but a religion. Like all faiths, it recognizes the insubstantial feelings and thought processes of humans that religions take seriously.

Santeria has basic beliefs and practices. One principle is that there are supernatural beings and forces that can create and destroy. Each orisha, or angelic force, demands a particular worship and sacrifice. One may achieve their destiny (*ayanmo*) by living a moral life, following ritual, and giving offerings to the angels. Kimberly had asked that I give sacrifice to Ogun since she could not do this in prison.

Ogun represents divine justice and truth on Earth. He is known for his keen insight into the human heart and can be a liberator or executioner.

But I also intended to pray to *Shango*. Though speaking only once and tending to be temperamental, he helps with legal problems and has the power to make things better. Shango's symbol is a double axe for he is fierce in retribution.

Kimberly is a Santeria priestess and will understand, I told myself, as I checked the Botanica's address on my phone.

"Pull over! We're making a stop in the Bronx," I yelled to the Uber driver.

Chapter 142

The driver stopped on the side of the road. He didn't want to go to the Bronx.

"I can't go there. It's dangerous! Gangs attack police stations," he said, in an agitated tone.

I remained calm. He was afraid and needed reassurance. I'm a news junkie but hadn't heard *that* bulletin.

"Where did you hear this?" I asked.

"It was in a movie."

"A movie?"

The driver nodded despite how ridiculous his statement was.

"Look, it must have been an old movie and the Bronx has changed since then. It's smartened up and become a hot place to live. We're going near Fordham University, with college kids like at Barnard," I said.

I wasn't sure of my facts but expected that the driver knew less about the Bronx than I did.

"I'll give you another two-hundred-dollar bonus when we get back," I said.

That settled the matter. The driver nodded and asked for the store's address. He fiddled with his GPS and pulled into the traffic.

The store's size calmed us both. I had expected a tiny hole-in-the-wall covered with obscene graffiti but it was huge and clean. This former supermarket was now a Costco catering to spiritual needs.

Shelves were filled with candles, incense powders, and statuary. Some, perhaps big sellers, were silly: aerosol sprays to attract love or gain a fortune. I touched a plastic bag of dead vampire bats, then searched for what I needed. For reverence to Ogun, as Kimberly had asked, Eucalyptus and Motherwort; and Sacred Ficus and Camwood to seek aid from Shango.

These would be used for spiritual bathing before prayer. I placed myrrh, frankincense, a white cotton sheet, a white cotton cloth, and white candles in my shopping basket. I scanned the shelves for whatever else I might need

"Can I help you?" a voice inquired from behind me and I jumped.

"Thanks, no, I was just thinking."

"You are a believer?"

Salsa music blasted through the store. All of the other customers were Latino and African-American. With my long flaming red hair, I stood out like a unicorn and had become an object of curiosity.

I stared into his eyes and spoke in an ancient tongue.

"Aye l'oja, orun n'ile," I said. ("The world is a marketplace. The spirit world is home.")

"Ka maa worisha. Iṣe Olorun tobi," he replied. ("Let us keep looking to the orisha. God's work is great and mighty.")

He bowed, and walked away. I paid for my purchases and left the store.

Before leaving, I had walked through its bookstore. Opening a random book, my eyes locked onto a Yoruba ethos that startled me: "It is a grave tragedy to die young so we pray." I instantly thought of Kimberly.

Chapter 143

While I shopped, the nervous driver had waited beside his car though the scene, except for the race of most passersby, was no different from Greenwich: strollers enjoying an outing.

At Brooks Hall, I paid him the money that I had promised.

"I may have further trips for the same pay. Would you be available?" I asked.

I received his broad smile and a card with his cellphone number.

"Day or night!" he said.

At the residence, I responded briefly to the greetings of acquaintances, then rushed to my room though not to do school work. I had more important tasks.

The herbs that I purchased were for spiritual bathing, to sanctify myself before prayer. Unfortunately, dormitory bathrooms weren't set up for this. There was no bathtub for me to leisurely soak in the herbal mixture. Sponge bathing in my room must do. But I believed that this would be acceptable to the Gods since my other preparations followed tradition.

I laid out the white sheet to later wrap myself in and the white cloth to cover my head. Then I cleaned the immediate space with myrrh and frankincense and lit the white candles.

After showering with natural soap and shampoo and returning to my room, I wiped my body with the spiritual bathing solutions that I had prepared. Then I patted myself dry, wrapped my body in the white sheet, and covered my hair with the white cloth.

I set out the offerings: small quantities of the Gods' favorite foods. The residence walls were thick; unholy sounds would not interrupt my prayer. I prayed first to Ogun and then to Shango.

My knowledge of the Santeria faith was limited but I did my best. Some words I spoke in the ancient Yoruba tongue but mostly in English. The Gods are kind and will accept my failings. It is the spirit that counts, I reassured myself.

"ASE MOJUBA ORISA," I sang, in a low voice. ("Authority, I pay homage to the selected head.")

"Mo fe bo." ("I want to worship.")

My first prayer was to Ogun.

> "Ogun the powerful one,
>
> Sufficiently great to stand before death.
>
> The strong one of the earth,
>
> The great one of the other world,
>
> The protector of those who are being injured.
>
> Ogun support me."

I next prayed to Shango.

> "Shango do not quarrel with me.

I am not one of them who is against you.

Protect us from misfortune,

Let us experience the calm

and gentle things of life."

With my head bowed, I kneeled and waited, losing track of time. My eyes closed and I felt myself hurtling through space. Lightning flashed and I experienced a pulsing force that was neither light nor sound nor heat. This was accompanied by changing shapes that nevertheless seemed the same.

I felt myself drawn into them, a speck in the universe of time. Something that I could not define was taking place. Then all disappeared and my soul returned. Words throbbed within me, those for which I had prayed: "Ebo fin, Eru da. Dide dide lalafia." ("The offerings are accepted, evil forces depart. Arise, arise in peace.")

Kimberly had gained the support of the Gods. I wondered what would happen next.

Chapter 144

Life went on as usual for the other students at Barnard. None had been close with Kimberly and her arrest was soon forgotten. The event had merely been another weirdness in a city filled with them. They were stressed with their current hook-up and final exams. I remained obsessed with Kimberly, and how much I had changed.

Victor had taken my threat seriously when I showed the pistol. Had I now become a murderer? I asked myself, before instantly dismissing this notion. I would not have killed him unless my life were endangered. But would I have murdered all witnesses afterward: his innocent grandchildren and son and the taxi driver? Was my life so valuable? Could any God forgive that evil?

Obsessing what might have been destroys a person. I am just nervous and the cure is to lose myself in work, I thought. But I couldn't think of anything else that I might do to help Kimberly. It was as if I were running in a race without knowing its length or where I ranked.

As I opened the thick calculus text to study, I had another thought. Math is highly organized for understanding advanced topics requires the knowledge of basic concepts. Organizing my life will calm me, I told myself, and began studying.

Soon after awakening the next morning, I wrote a list of what I had to do. After calling home to see how

Julia was doing, I would phone Randy for an update on his life. When my exams were over, I would visit Kimberly. I knew how much she must be suffering and how welcome my visit would be.

Three days later, I couldn't help thinking that the Gods had favored me though believing that they wouldn't intervene with trivia. My exams had covered *exactly* what I studied. Though the grades wouldn't be posted for a week, I knew that I had done well. My scholarship was safe for another term!

I left my last exam with a worn-out but upbeat feeling. I entered Brooks Hall with the intention of napping until a voice called my name. Upon seeing the unexpected face, I was so surprised that I blinked hard and stared.

Chapter 145

"What are *you* doing here?" I asked.

My tone wasn't friendly but his appearance had rattled me and I spoke impulsively.

"I'm sorry but I wasn't expecting you," I apologized, a moment later.

"Obviously not. Can we talk?" he asked, with an infectious grin.

"Sure."

"But not here."

"There's a diner on the corner," I suggested.

I quashed my instant thought to invite him to my room. Yes, Tony is *that* attractive.

We walked in silence to the diner, like two old friends for whom silence had become comfortable.

There, I ordered one of my favorites, blueberry pancakes, and he ordered a cheeseburger. He had a hard time getting started but I waited for him to open the conversation. Before speaking, he glanced about the half-filled room as if he were afraid of being seen with me.

"My father said that I should be more like you, that he would want you as a daughter," Tony said, with a slight smile.

Despite the smile, I knew that he felt hurt. Honesty and not tact is needed now, I told myself, so I spoke the truth.

"I don't consider that a compliment. Your father is a monster," I said.

"There's a primeval darkness in each of us, a kinship with every filth. He has more than most."

Tony's ready agreement surprised me. It's not easy for a child to reject their parent no matter what they've done.

"You're not like your father," I said.

"No, and I avoid him and my relatives as much as possible. Girls bolt when they hear my name. I may enter a monastery."

I burst out laughing as Tony bit into his cheeseburger.

"What did you say that so impressed him?" he asked, a moment later.

I wasn't proud of what I had said and didn't want to reveal it. But I also felt that Tony had to know if we were to be friends.

"I had a business proposition for your father and he wasn't taking me seriously. He threatened me, and I showed him a pistol. I said that I would kill him if he tried to hurt me and that if I were hurt, my father would have him and his entire family killed. Your father had been testing me. He smiled, and we did business," I said.

Now it was Tony's turn to stare.

"Your father must be something too," he said slowly.

"He's nothing like your's. He's a former Russian general, and family is very important to Russians."

There was a pause in our conversation before I spoke again.

"Why are you here?" I asked, in a calm, measured tone.

Chapter 146

Tony sipped more water before replying.

"There was a photo of you with Kimberly's lawyer in the *Daily News*," he said.

"Yes."

The photo appeared to have been taken with a telephoto lens. It wasn't a good picture but I was recognizable.

"I want to help Kimberly. I don't like people being screwed," Tony said.

I ate some pancake to give me time to think.

"How can you help her?" I asked.

"Kimberly's public image needs help. I know reporters from my time as an intern in Washington. They'd love the story: a beautiful Barnard student battles the City from her Rikers Island cell. I can see a movie coming," Tony said.

I couldn't help smiling but sensed that Tony's interest in justice wasn't his only motive. Helping to free Kimberly could propel his political career, and might give him a stunning girlfriend too. They could have gorgeous kids, I thought.

"OK, but I don't want your father or any of his friends involved. That would be her kiss of death," I said.

"Agreed."

"How do we get started?" I asked.

"By watching a movie, to get you in the right frame of mind."

"Huh?"

"Did you see *Broken City*?

"No."

"That doesn't surprise me, It's well-acted but poorly written. Trashy, and with stupid coincidences."

"So why should I see it?"

"Because it shows what we're up against, the world that we'll be operating in."

"Where's it playing?"

"It's not. I have it on DVD. We can watch it at my apartment."

I stared without saying anything until he got my thought.

"No, it's not a 'Come to my place and we'll watch a movie' bit. If you could scare my father, I'd never put a hand on you. Besides, we're like brother and sister."

I felt momentarily hurt though having the same feeling. Then a thought occurred to me.

"Are you adopted?" I asked.

Tony looked stricken.

"How did you know?" he asked, slowly.

"Because I'm adopted too. I learned my real parents only recently."

"I'm still looking for mine. I'm getting close but Italian families are close-mouthed."

I nodded. Adopted kids know this instinctively.

"One more thing. Kimberly is wonderful girl. Please don't hurt her," I pleaded.

"If I do you'll kill me? I'm sorry. I'm nervous and that was a stupid thing to say."

"No, I won't kill you. But I'll be very disappointed."

Only later did I realized why I had said this. There seemed a part of Tony that had never grown up and nothing is worse for a child than to lose respect.

Chapter 147

Since Tony is single, I had expected for his apartment to be a studio but it was a large three-bedroom. When I remarked on this, he said that he had inherited the co-op from his grandmother and left it unchanged except for buying a new bed. I readily understood. Sleeping on the bed of one who has died would be a bit much.

The furniture was large and heavy in the old European style. We watched *Broken City* while seated on a fringed, thickly cushioned, heavily carved sofa.

Tony was right. The movie wasn't good but it did rouse us into battle mode for what we had to do since Kimberly's predicament was similar.

Broken City tells of a New York City detective, Billy. He is arrested for the murder of Mikey who was believed to have raped and murdered sixteen-year-old, Yesenia. Evidence is buried and Billy is cleared of murder with Mikey's killing being accepted as self-defense. Billy is proclaimed a hero though forced to leave the Police Department.

I won't bore you with the rest of the movie. It's enough to say that political corruption is rampant, the characters are detestable, and there is an implausibly happy ending. We hoped for better with Kimberly.

"Do you want to meet Kimberly?" I asked, as Tony shut off the video player.

"It would be best. My getting a fact wrong would blow the media stories," he said.

"Much in her past could increase sympathy. She can tell you what she would feel comfortable having publicized. There's her daughter to consider," I said.

Tony spoke after a few moments of silence.

"It's amazing that people believe what's being said about her. She's rich, a college sophomore and a mother. It isn't plausible that she would be involved in drug dealing and murder," he said.

"Terror attacks and the increase in crime have scared people. Many aren't thinking logically, and her beauty and wealth matter too," I said.

"How?"

"Envy causes people to wish that the privileged fall," I said.

At that, I became lost in my thoughts and missed what Tony spoke in a soft voice.

"What?" I asked.

"If you don't expect justice you'll be a lot less disappointed," he repeated.

I simply nodded.

Chapter 148

After returning to my room, I phoned my father. He had to be told of my plan to visit Kimberly with Tony. I also wanted the latest news about her case and to learn how Julia was doing.

This didn't happen right away since Claudine answered the phone. But hearing her goings-on provided me with some of this information.

"Julia is sad. She misses her mother," Claudine said, after telling what she felt that I needed to know about her life.

"Yes," I replied.

"When will she see her?"

I was silent until an idea entered my mind.

"Maybe soon but I'll have to speak with dad first. Is he there?" I asked.

"Daddy, it's Margaret for you!" Claudine yelled.

"How are you?" my father asked, immediately.

"Fine. My friend, Tony, wants to help Kimberly get favorable publicity. He's a Princeton student who interned with Boehner in Washington and knows many reporters. I'd like to visit Kimberly and thought that he and Julia could come. Claudine said that Julia is sad."

My father mulled over these suggestions. Being a lawyer, he knew of possibilities that I was ignorant of and one wrong move could prove disastrous.

"I can't see that your visit would do any harm. There's no judicial gag order and leaks have flooded from the D.A.'s office promoting their views.

"Julia isn't eating well and we're worried. We've made an appointment for her with Claudine's therapist but she really needs her mother. Do you know the visiting rules?"

"No."

"OK. There can't be more than three visitors at a time so you and Tony and Julia will be OK. Go online and check the visitor schedule. It goes by the first letter of the inmate's last name, and there is no visiting on Mondays or Tuesdays.

"Bring ID, a driver's license is OK. I'll send you a copy of Julia's birth certificate though that shouldn't be necessary. I'll also send my letter approving the visit but that shouldn't be needed either.

"Don't bring anything. The rules about what's allowed are complicated and I've placed money in her account so she can buy what she needs. When do you plan to go?"

"As soon as possible. Wednesday?" I asked.

"OK. Julia's bodyguard will bring her into the City. She'll pick you up in front of Brooks Hall at noon for the drive to Rikers. Visitor registration begins at one and you can stay as late as nine if you wish. Afterward, Julia will be driven back to Greenwich. Do you have any questions?"

"Is anything new?" I asked.

"You didn't see the news?" my dad asked.

"No, I was busy with tests," I said, and felt my stomach sink.

"Kimberly's DNA was found in the murder room."

"So what? Everyone visits in the dorm," I objected.

"But Kimberly told the police that she had never been in that room A bag containing *Shatter*, a super-high-potency marijuana, was also found there and Kimberly's fingerprints are on the bag."

Chapter 149

While driving to Rikers, the mood in the car matched the gloomy weather. Though battling DNA and fingerprint evidence seemed impossible, I still believed Kimberly to be innocent and that the world would come to believe it too. I just didn't know how this would happen.

I sighed, and Tony picked up on my mood.

"What?" he asked.

"What's come out in the news," I replied.

"Unpleasant facts create welcome opportunities," Tony said.

"*Huh!* Who said that?" I asked.

"President Roosevelt, during the early, dark days of World War II."

Julia raised her head. I had introduced Tony to her when we picked him up in front of his apartment building. Thereafter, she had turned within herself, leaning against me and occasionally dozing.

"I'm going to see mommy?" Julia asked again, despite having been reassured several times.

"Absolutely!" I replied.

Then I told her the truth, that Rikers would not be the hotel that she was probably expecting.

"Julia, you're now a big girl so I'll tell you what's happened. Your mother has been arrested and is in jail. That's where we are going to visit her. But she's done nothing wrong and people are working to get her out.

"The jail may look scary but you will be safe. Lots of children will be there to visit their mommy or daddy. Do you understand?"

"Why is she in jail?" Julia asked, though I sensed that she understood what I had said.

"Because the police have made a mistake. We're going to find out the truth," I replied.

After considering this silently for several moments, Julia looked up and smiled.

"You're a detective like Nancy Drew?" she asked, excitedly.

"Yes, I'm exactly like Nancy Drew and everything turns out happy in her life," I replied, and couldn't help smiling.

My answer contented Julia. She turned away and looked out the window for the rest of the journey. The clouds grew blacker and the rain increased as we approached the jail.

Chapter 150

The annoyances that had irritated me during my past visit to Rikers didn't bother Julia. She took everything in stride, as if it were merely more adult silliness that she had to endure. But the guards are friendlier when there is a child about too.

We arrived just as visiting hours began and were the first ones through the security procedures. Then we sat in the visitor's room and waited for the prisoners to be brought in. Julia noticed Kimberly first.

"Mommy!" she screamed, and soon they were in each other's arms.

Tony and I stood back. I introduced him when Julia began dozing in Kimberly's arms, smiling and content.

"Tony is a friend. He knows reporters and wants to help. He attends Princeton and had an internship in Washington with Representative Boehner, the last Speaker of the House. You need more favorable news stories than you've been getting."

Kimberly stared at Tony for a long moment.

"Why are you interested in me?" she asked, suspiciously.

"Because I don't like people getting screwed," he replied, holding her gaze.

"And why do you believe that of me?" Kimberly asked.

"You're a computer geek. I know the criminal world and you wouldn't survive there for a day. You're not of them," Tony replied.

"What's your last name?" Kimberly asked, after a pause.

Tony told her.

"Your father is *him*? The crime boss?" she asked, with raised eyebrows.

Tony nodded, before adding, "I'm adopted," as if to say, I don't share his genes. Don't judge me by him.

"Then you must know that world. Thank you for believing in me. I'm innocent and have no idea how my DNA and fingerprints were found in that room. That was an even bigger shock than finding myself here," Kimberly said, with a small wave about the room.

"But be careful. Decent intentions can be dangerous," she added, with a small smile.

They suddenly became silent and I stared at them. It was as if they had entered their own private world, a place far from the grubby, noisy visitor's room. Apart from physical attractiveness, they seemed to share something else and Tony spoke what it was.

"There is a certain dignity to having survived a painful life," he said, softly.

Though being young and well-off, they both know what misery is, I thought.

Chapter 151

We stayed at Rikers for nearly three hours until even Kimberly looked exhausted. She spoke of the jail conditions and of the other inmates that she had met. I told of events at school and Tony spoke of his experiences in Washington. But it was Julia who occupied most of our attention with descriptions of her new friends and her new bedroom in Greenwich. When Kimberly got up to leave, Julia wouldn't let her go.

"I *must go* but Margaret will bring you again. You're a big girl and helping Margaret like Nancy Drew," she said.

When Kimberly became tearful, I touched Julia's shoulder.

"Come. Tony is hungry and I promised him that we'd go to McDonald's for lunch," I said, in a playful tone.

Julia released her grip on her mother. As Kimberly and I hugged goodbye, she whispered in my ear.

"Did you give offering?" she asked.

"To Ogun, as you asked, and to Shango too."

"What was the response?"

"Ebo fin, Eru da. Dide dide lalafia." ("The offerings are accepted, evil forces depart. Arise, arise in peace.")

"*Bless you!*" Kimberly said.

Her step seemed lighter as she left the room.

McDonald's did its usual magic on Julia. I let her order whatever she wanted despite my commitment to healthy diet. She chose the Chicken McNuggets, strawberry yoghurt, and fat-free chocolate milk. I comforted myself with the thought that eating one meal of nearly anything has no effect on health.

Tony chose a Double Quarter Pounder with Cheese, and a McCafé Frappé Chocolate Chip. His eating habits are another reason why we could never be a couple. The restaurant had an all-day breakfast policy and I chose Hotcakes, Fruit and Maple Oatmeal, and orange juice. Oatmeal is oatmeal and the pancakes weren't bad either.

"What's next?" Tony asked, between bites, as Julia played with the small Star Wars figure that came with her meal.

"I don't know. I feel that I must do something but don't know what," I replied.

"The physical evidence against her is overwhelming. She must feel hopeless," Tony said.

He seemed upset and I stopped worrying that he would hurt Kimberly if they became a couple.

"No, she's not. Kimberly is a Santeria priestess like her mother. She has led a good life and believes that the Gods favor her and will save her," I said.

Tony stopped eating and stared. Julia put down her toy.

"I had a dream. There were waves and flowers," Julia said, brightly.

"Was it scary?" I asked.

"A little but I felt better when I woke up. The man dressed in white told me that everything will be OK," Julia replied.

"Who did?"

"The man dressed in white. There were women too. One wore a necklace with seven blue beads, and the other held purple flowers."

I explained this to Tony. Julia seemed to have no need of explanation.

"Julia's dream means that the Gods are banding together to rescue Kimberly. Yemayá is a Goddess, the protector of women. She lives in the oceans and her favored number is seven. Oyá is the Guardian of the Gates of Death and favors wine colored flowers. Obatalá is the most powerful of the Gods. He is known as the King of the White Cloth," I said.

When I finished my explanation, Tony's stare had become one of incredulity.

Annushka, Julia's Russian bodyguard and our driver, hadn't spoken that day. She had waited in the car when we entered the jail. Now she muttered something in her native tongue.

"What?" I asked, a bit rudely. It had been a hard day.

"I'm sorry," she said, apologetically. "It's an old Russian proverb: 'God sees the truth but won't tell soon.' An American would say, 'The mills of God grind slowly.'"

Chapter 152

Annushka first dropped off Tony and then me. I hugged Julia and she smiled when I told her that she was now a detective. I made a mental note to buy her a toy detective's kit. When they left, I stood leaning against the building, thinking not about crime but of love.

I had been simple-minded. Because Kimberly and Tony were beautiful people, handsome and educated, I had assumed that they would make an ideal couple. But this was high school fantasy of a Homecoming King and Queen.

Tony's astonishment when I described Santeria beliefs and his eating habits would clash with Kimberly's lifestyle. Moreover, while she was a loner, he hoped for a political career and needed a fitting wife which Kimberly couldn't be. So either one of them would have to change drastically or, more likely, both would seek romance elsewhere.

After concluding this, I considered Kimberly's legal catastrophe. I wanted to do more to help but, apart from providing her with emotional support, I had no idea what.

It was with this frustration that I entered Brooks Hall and went to my room. After closing the door, I noticed that an envelope had been slipped inside.

It was greeting card size and sealed with a sticker of a Classic Mac's terminal window. Inside, was a photograph of Kimberly and four young men. All lay on cushions and bean bags, smiling and relaxed. They were obviously friends.

On the back of the photo was a printed label: "Your presence is requested by the *Followers of Dikē.* 10AM/Thursday/Brownie's." There was an E-mail address.

I knew that *dyke* was the belittling term for a lesbian but it didn't fit here. A lesbian society consisting mostly of men?

Going online, I learned that *Dikē* had nothing to do with sexual preference. She was an ancient Greek goddess, a daughter of Zeus who had ruled as King of the Gods. She was also the goddess of justice, and her best friend was Astraea, the goddess of innocence.

After only the briefest thought, I E-mailed my reply. I accepted the summons. I would go.

Chapter 153

Every school has celebrated institutions. *Brownie's* is one of Columbia University's. Nestled within the basement of a historic building, Avery Hall, it's long been a graduate student hang-out.

Vastly different from a Starbucks, it resembles an art gallery that has gone to seed. Its subterranean atmosphere has walls that need painting. A fire-hose in the staircase leading to it detracts from even this "charm."

Brownie's contains a mix of four-person tables and bench-style seating. Its prices are lower than off-campus, and two-thirds of Barnard's Diana Center Café. Because of this and its cheap drinks, it gets crowded during the school-term. I had often studied there when the isolation of my dorm room got to me. Now, though being the only hang-out open on campus during the school break, it was just half full.

I arrived at two minutes after ten, looked at the photo, and scanned the room. Five men were seated at a long table. All wore hoodies of different style and length. They had obviously been waiting for me since all stood as I approached.

Their hoodies were worn in a grown-up way: paired with dark chinos, a top coat, or a refined bomber jacket.

Two of them had a mustache and the others had beards. Two of the men were short, two were a little taller than my 5'10", and one man towered over us.

It was he who spoke first. His surprising upper-class English accent reminded me of *Downton Abbey*. This up-ended my anticipations and I wondered what would follow.

"Margaret, how pleased we are that you join us. Come, sit here," he said.

He smiled invitingly and indicated the chair beside him. I returned his smile and sat. All then sat and I awaited an explanation. This came from a short Black man who seemed to be their spokesman. He surprised me by speaking with the same crisp English accent. I later learned that he was a citizen of the British West Indies.

"Kimberly spoke highly of you and, apart from us, you are her only friend. We respect her because, like you and us, she refuses to be anybody but herself. We have worked with her on projects and know her well. She despises drug use and cannot be a murderer. We have vowed to rescue her, regardless of what we must do. Family is all that we have and we are family. Will you join us?"

I felt so moved by these words that I was unable to speak. I had been feeling alone and helpless, lost and lacking a path. Now I would not be alone though the road remained unclear.

With tear-filled eyes, still unable to speak, I nodded and extended my hands which were immediately joined by the others.

Unlike boys, girls cry when they like someone. None of them laughed when I cried. They waited silently. When I finished drying my eyes, each raised a glass of water and I joined the softly spoken toast: "To Kimberly, whose goodness–and our help–will guide her home."

Chapter 154

Though the men tried not to show it, they were equally moved by the toast. Small talk followed during which each man introduced himself and told something of his life.

"How did you all meet?" I asked.

"Well, since we're all geniuses, no one else would socialize with us," the tallest man, Creighton ("Call me Cray") replied, with a grin.

George, the man from the British West Indies, spoke seriously.

"Cray's right. We're not social but it wasn't that. We met at Hack the Planet last year, Silicon Valley's most important hackathon to which one must be invited.

"Kimberly was there and we've hung together ever since. She's spectacularly gifted and I don't compliment readily."

George returned to his sandwich. Silence reigned until he spoke again.

"We've been in contact with Kimberly," he said.

"*How*," I asked, with surprise.

I felt taken aback, having assumed that Kimberly would have told me everything during our meetings at Rikers. What else didn't I know about her? I wondered, but didn't share this concern.

"She followed your suggestion and attends Jewish services. The Rabbi trusts her to use his phone. With it, she can speak freely since it's not bugged like the prison phones. But she can use it for only ten minutes each time."

Cray, the tallest man, spoke again. His nickname was *Hoops* though he had never played any sport. He avoided exercise except for taking long solitary walks, from the Columbia campus to the New York Public Library on 42nd Street and back again.

"Kimberly suggested several things to help her. How far are you prepared to go?" he asked me.

They still consider me an outsider, I thought.

"I enjoy uncovering secrets," I replied.

"That's not what I asked. What she suggested is illegal. We could all wind up at Rikers. Would you go that far?"

Those who had been eating, stopped and stared. They awaited my reply.

"When things are going disastrously, it's sometimes best to toss the rules. Kimberly has been a good friend. I'm in her debt and I always pay my debts," I said.

I raised my glass of water for another toast. The gesture was dramatic but it seemed the moment for drama.

"A smart person can usually find room between a rock and a hard place. You're all super-smart and you'll find it," I said.

We clinked glasses, and got down to work.

Chapter 155

Getting down to work meant making plans and my "brothers," which is what they insisted they had become, seemed clueless. No computer problem would scare them but I doubted that any could survive a reality show.

I reminded myself that each person has strengths and weaknesses and that Kimberly's problem was unique. So I put in my two cents, hoping that it would be worth far more.

"Kimberly has two battles: against the public view of her, and two apparently undeniable pieces of evidence. Her DNA was found at the murder scene where she denied being, and her fingerprints are on a bag of drugs.

"I've begun work on the first problem. A friend, Tony, knows reporters and will try to get sympathetic stories published. Attacking the physical evidence is trickier," I said.

"Working that out will take time. Get some food. It's on us. We do private work on the side and have a kitty for expenses," George said, handing me a twenty-dollar bill.

Living in poverty had made me super-sensitive about accepting money but I shelved this feeling and took it with a simple "thanks."

It was too early for a salad and apart from salads, Brownie's has few vegetarian options. I ignored my partiality and chose a roasted turkey with brie and cranberries on a multigrain roll.

After I returned to the table and had taken several bites of my sandwich, Roy had a suggestion.

"We need data to work, the raw police and DNA findings, not just their publicized conclusions," he said.

"No problemo," John said, though his only Hispanic element was frequenting Spanish restaurants.

"Hacking government agencies is John's specialty. He interned at the NSA and they've offered him a job," Cray explained.

"No way. I plan to go legal and be rich," John said, with a grin.

"And you'll do it! Just don't forget to share the wealth with your buddies," came Cray's playful response.

Silence descended over the table as we ate. The restaurant began filling up.

"I have to get going. What would you like me to do?" I asked, as I stood.

"Just watch your back. We're going up against powerful people who don't like to lose. There'll be serious pushback if opposition is sensed," George said.

"So they'd better not find out. It's good that we're working together. Company and a shared resolve help to keep moody fears at bay," I said.

They were quiet as I walked away.

Chapter 156

Later that day I received an E-mail from George. He suggested that we meet every other weekday at 10AM at Brownies to review developments and I replied, "OK." Brownies is closed on weekends.

My immediate thought was that they wanted to keep tabs on me, fearing that our activities would endanger me. It's good to being watched over, I thought, with a sense of contentment.

The next day, Tony E-mailed me a copy of a favorable news article about Kimberly that he had gained. I loved it, and was sure that the prosecutor wouldn't. The writer was well-known for her civil rights battles. Her sentiment was more than we had dared hope.

"No objective observer can avoid questioning why male and female defendants are treated so differently for committing similar crimes. A twenty-year-old man was recently indicted for murder and drug dealing. Though having extensive criminal ties, he was released on two-million-dollars bail into his mother's custody after surrendering his passport and agreeing to wear an ankle bracelet.

"Yet a nineteen-year-old Barnard student with dual American and Brazilian citizenship, a woman with a blameless record from a distinguished family, is being forced to languish in a cell after being accused of the identical crimes. This, despite Brazil's condemnation of her treatment as being 'a crime against humanity.'

"Kimberly is our sister. If you believe that a woman's life is equally as valuable as a man's, protest with me at City Hall at 11AM this Saturday. Women gained the vote a century ago. Obviously, some politicians still haven't gotten the message."

The columnist was president of the New York chapter of the American Civil Liberties Union. Kimberly's case had now become a prominent woman's cause.

Our next meeting at Brownie's was more relaxed. We had bonded and were comfortable with each other. Progress was reported but details weren't shared. It was felt that talking about work in progress would jinx it. I understood, having had the same feeling in the past. But at least they are optimistic, I told myself.

There was a long period of silence at the table. Their comfort was with computers, not people. I bridged this uncomfortable gap by speaking of my life: my family in Greenwich, and the summer I had spent in London.

"Your father was a spy," Cray declared.

"You've checked up on me," I replied.

"We like to know who we're dealing with. Your father is famous and the facts were easily gained," George said.

They walked me back to the dorm, forming a protective cocoon around me. As we approached Brooks Hall, Cray suddenly threw me to the ground. He covered my body with his as debris rained down from the explosion.

Chapter 157

Cray had meant well by throwing me to the ground but it was my instincts that saved me. While falling, I automatically turned my head to a side and covered my face with my arms. Falling directly onto Broadway's concrete sidewalk would have given me a broken nose or worse. Still, as I said, Cray had meant well.

Brooks Hall is an eight story, red brick building with limestone and terra cotta trim. While brushing fragments from my clothes, I saw that this decoration now littered the street. The building's sturdy, 1907 construction hadn't prepared it for explosion.

The next few minutes were a blur of screams that gradually lessened until the secondary blast. We ran west toward Riverside Park with swelling police and fire engine sirens speeding us along.

Once in the Park, we searched each other for injury but found only scratches. I went through a bombing in London the year before and had hoped never to experience it again.

Cray turned toward me.

"You won't be able to stay at Brooks," he said.

"No, I'll be in Greenwich until the term starts. I'll give you my number. It'll be crazy here for a while. Do any of you need a place to stay? My home is packed but I have a friend who can put you up," I said.

Erika's house has twenty-two rooms and thirteen bathrooms. Finding a spare bedroom there is never a problem and her father enjoys knowledgeable guests.

No one took up my offer. Either none of them needed it or, being loners, could tolerate the togetherness of being a houseguest. But, I told myself, they're grownups and I'm not their mother.

"What could have happened? A gas leak?" I asked.

"That's doubtful. However much the residents complain about dormitory living, they praise the maintenance. No, it wasn't a gas leak and I think I know what it was. While I hope no one was injured, the explosions just might free Kimberly from Rikers," George said.

I simply stared, expecting that more explanation was coming.

Chapter 158

"Have you ever heard of *Glass* or *Ice* or *Tina*," George asked.

"No," I replied.

"They're all names for the same thing. *Glass* is enormously valuable, worth $10,000 to $30,000 a pound. It's a street drug, crystal methamphetamine, a colorless, odorless form of d-methamphetamine which is a powerful stimulant.

"Crystal meth has a higher purity level and produces longer-lasting, more intense effects than d-meth. In a small dose, it improves concentration, arouses physical activity, and destroys appetite.

"But if used for a long time it can cause violent behavior and hallucinations. The drug has become popular on college campuses.

"John has gained access to confidential police reports. Asian crime gangs are battling Mexican drug cartels to become the major seller of Glass on the East Coast."

"OK, so?" I asked, as George paused.

I wasn't sure if he was catching his breath or heightening the suspense as some story-tellers can't resist doing. The others seemed annoyed too.

"Glass is made using a 'washing' technique: dissolving powdered d-methamphetamine in a solvent like acetone or denatured alcohol. The mixture is allowed to evaporate in a refrigerator and small crystals are created. These are collected and dried on a paper towel.

"The purity of the product depends on the amount of washing and the operator's experience. It's a dangerous procedure since vapors from the solvents are unstable and can collect during the evaporation. These may explode when the appliance's light turns on as the door is opened."

I immediately understood.

"You're thinking that a person who was making Glass caused the explosion. And that producing the Glass locally, at a cut-rate price, gave unwanted competition to the established drug gangs and caused the murder of the two students," I said.

George nodded agreement and the others looked thoughtful.

"Or, that they died while testing a bad batch on themselves," I added.

"It's been known to happen," George agreed.

"But even if you're right, how does the explosion free Kimberly? The prosecutor could say that she was part of the operation, its South American connection." I said.

"Yes, but we can also theorize that evidence was planted to cause Kimberly's arrest as the ringleader so that the operation could continue. There are few better places to operate an illegal activity than a woman's dorm at a prestigious college.

"John will get into the prosecutor's files, to check the evidence and see what's being held back. The D.A. won't want to lose his publicity-rich case," George concluded.

Chapter 159

My phone began ringing. News of the explosion at Barnard and the fear that it involved a terrorist attack had erupted. First came my parents' call, then Randy's, then Erika's. I spoke only briefly to each, saying that I was unharmed and returning home. I had learned in London that connecting with loved ones was what people instinctively did after a disaster.

Despite my earlier reassurance, my mother had tightly hugged and inspected me when I arrived. Fragments from the explosion still lingered on my clothes and I looked awful. My sisters took this more calmly. Children view life as a series of calamities that quickly become insignificant, over-and-done-with memories.

My oldest sister, Melody, had graduated from New York University the previous June and decided to work for a year before beginning law school. My father found her a job as a para-legal, with a local law firm that did corporate work. "If you can stand the drag, you'll survive your early years as a lawyer," he had told her.

That evening, she and three friends were comfortably sprawled in our basement, nibbling on my mother's peanut butter cookies and sharing dating disasters. I joined them and listened. One can't know too much about dating.

Christine, one of my sister's co-workers, was twenty-nine and had already become jaded about men. She had an older, married friend, Dina, who thought that everyone should be married. Christine was her latest project.

"But her standards aren't the greatest. If she tells you that she's seen the man, it means that she's seen him at least once. If she says that you have a lot in common, it could just mean that you're both breathing," Christine said. Still, she gave her referrals a shot.

Claude was divorced, three years older, and worked for a tech company. He came to Christine's door bearing a gift: a plastic bag filled with phone chargers. They went for a drink and he talked about batteries.

James was Christine's next candidate. He was ten years older and said that he had never been married. He was into exercise and described his excellent health, how much he ran, and his aches. He was leaving for Tulsa the next day, said that he would call when he returned, and instructed her to never leave a message with his secretary. Christine concluded that James was only occasionally single.

"Snake" was Christine's last date from Dina. He brought her candy: a small baggie containing Hershey Kisses. He said that he was a writer and had prepared a list of questions to determine their suitability. Christine is a tall red-head. He asked what she would do if she were a carrot and he approached her in the market.

Christine had just stared at him, and none of us could think of a sensible reply. She shrugged when my sister asked her how she could allow herself to date a man called Snake.

"Well, I'd know what to do. During one dreadful dinner date, between stories of his ex-wife, his stomach problems, and the arrival of entrées, I excused myself to use the ladies' room, the one at my apartment," Pamela said.

I exhaled deeply. The explosions at Barnard seemed far away.

Chapter 160

In a good family, returning home is like falling into a soft mattress. Current worries disappear as run-of-the-mill problems demand involvement. But these were trivial when compared with my persisting concern of earlier years.

The symptoms from my father's Lyme disease had disappeared, as can happen with basically healthy sufferers. Still, he had been disabled for so long that it came as a shock.

While ill, my father had kept busy by reading law journals and writing legal articles in his home office. Now, he was up at six every weekday morning and out the house by seven.

He had rented space in the law office where Melody worked, leased a new car in place of our ancient Chevy, and bought clothes at Richards, the Greenwich store that outfits local moguls.

Known for making customers feel like family, they could easily spend five-hundred dollars on a casual shirt but love it too. Considering our long years of poverty, I didn't expect frivolous purchases by my father but knew that professionals who don't appear prosperous aren't taken seriously.

The large fee from Kimberly's case had brought prosperity to our family, and its notoriety brought my father other lucrative cases. His name and legal ancestry were now often in the *Greenwich Times*. There can't be better public relations for a lawyer than to be linked with a Chief Justice of their state's Supreme Court.

Being poor was a weighty burden and its lifting had a tonic effect on all of us. Minor squabbles disappeared and joy reigned as a daily experience. Family members no longer felt under house arrest to save gas money.

Though the gloom of Rikers Island got to me when visiting Kimberly, her spirits had risen. Word had spread among the Hispanic inmates that she was an *Iyalorisha*, a Santeria priestess. They now revered and protected her but our payments to Victor continued. An inmate can never have too much protection.

The protest at City Hall had been wildly successful. An estimated thirty-nine thousand women–and men– showed up, along with enough media that the event gained world-wide coverage.

This, and the recent explosion at Barnard with which Kimberly couldn't have been involved, raised fiery questions about justice. Had there been a rush to judgment? Was Kimberly innocent and her rights being trampled on?

These were good developments but, as Kimberly observed, "Being the poster-child for woman's rights won't get me out of here."

Chapter 161

During Kimberly's early weeks in jail, she had no visitors except me, my father, Julia, and Tony. This was how it remained until after the rally. Then, hungry reporters flocked to Rikers, seeking a banner-winning story of how its most publicized resident survived amongst New York's worst.

Brazil's Consul-General visited Kimberly too. Her experience had been portrayed in that country's press as reflecting another example of America's condescension toward the huge nation of Brazil. A rally supporting Kimberly was held in Rio de Janeiro and police were needed to keep protestors from storming the American Embassy.

"You are an inspiration to all Brazilians," the Consul-General had told her, before kissing her hand.

"*Edward* visited me too," Kimberly told me, in a spirited tone.

"*Edward?*" I asked.

"*You remember*: the policeman we met after seeing *Psycho*," Kimberly replied, slowly.

Now I did remember. He had phoned her the day after she slipped his card under her bra. This act had impressed me and obviously impressed him even more.

"He must consider me innocent. He wouldn't risk his career by visiting a murderer. Rumor of my innocence must be spreading in the Police Department," Kimberly said.

It *was*, but I didn't learn this until receiving an E-mail the following day.

"We've gotten hold of explosive facts. I've sent it to Tony to be passed to reporters. They'll bless him for it," George wrote, and I could picture his grin.

"What is it?" I wrote back.

"Check tomorrow's news," came his teasing reply that left me hanging.

My father knew nothing of the *Followers of Dikē* and I wanted to keep it that way. Lawyers are bound by professional ethics. I didn't want him placed in a vulnerable position and kept our conversation brief.

"I've been told that there will be important news about Kimberly's case in the papers tomorrow," I said, in a slow, deliberate manner.

"Huh?" my father asked, looking up from what he was reading.

"The stories should help with her case," I said, even more slowly.

I nodded, stared, and remained silent. My father got the unspoken message: that illegal activities had been conducted on Kimberly's behalf and he needed to be able to deny knowledge of them.

"Thank you for telling me. Sleep well," he said, with a small smile, before returning to his work.

I tossed in bed and was unable to sleep for much of the night. I could hardly wait for the morning to arrive.

Chapter 162

I finally fell asleep at a little after one and slept until five. The *Greenwich Times*, *The New York Times*, and *The Wall Street Journal* were delivered by six and I hovered in the kitchen until then. My father came downstairs a little before six, dressed in a bathrobe.

I rushed for the door upon hearing the newspapers hit the porch. Because of a recent terror attack, neither of us expected that Kimberly's story would be front-page news and we scanned quickly through the papers.

While the *Greenwich Times* had nothing, columnists in *The New York Times* and *The Wall Street Journal* said plenty. Their headlines told it all: "Justice Denied: Jailed College Student was Framed," read one title. The second was harsher: "District Attorney Hides Evidence of Jailed Student's Innocence to Aid his Re-election." Both stories were structured the same.

First, came a description of the Barnard murders whose perpetrator had gained the nickname of "the dormitory killer." Then, that Kimberly's arrest was based on the theory that she was a murdering drug overlord. The notorious cartel chief, Griselda Blanco, also known as The Black Widow, was used as an example.

The evidence against Kimberly was itemized: that she lied when stating that she had never been at the murder scene though her DNA was found there; and that a bag containing drugs had yielded her fingerprints.

Then came facts that the District Attorney had wanted hidden: "Informed sources, who did not wish to be identified, have revealed that following the explosion at Barnard, a thirty-one-year-old woman was treated at St. Luke's Hospital for severe burns. Fingerprints have linked this woman to the blast scene.

"Though denying involvement in any Barnard 'murders,' these deaths having been accidentally caused by testing drugs, the woman admitted to stealing plastic bags and trashed sanitary napkins to spread false fingerprint and DNA evidence. All reports containing this information were stamped, *Confidential–Not to be Distributed.*

"The woman, who has not yet been identified, had been using an unused attic room in Barnard College's Brooks Hall dormitory for her drug 'washing' activity which caused the explosion.

"Though far older than the typical student, she suffers from Turner's Syndrome, a genetic deformity that causes an immature, youthful appearance. A fake student ID card and key to the dormitory's rear door were found in her possession. The falsely imprisoned student is expected to be released shortly."

Two days later that's exactly what happened. Without notice, Kimberly was brought to the Warden's office, told that she was being released and ordered to collect her things. She left Rikers Island without fanfare, dressed in the clothes that she had been arrested in.

Holding a plastic bag containing her possessions, an astonished Kimberly quickly found herself standing at the bus stop outside the prison, awaiting the Q100 bus amidst other newly released inmates.

"I'd become an embarrassment to the system so they sped me out. I would have liked to say 'goodbye' to some prisoners but maybe it's best that I didn't. Envy and all," Kimberly told me later.

Chapter 163

Kimberly's first stop after getting off the bus was a public phone. Her cellphone had been left at home when she was arrested. She called my father, he told us about her release, and Annushka drove into the City to pick her up.

There were more tears than laughter when Kimberly arrived in Greenwich. We all knew that disaster had been too close.

Kimberly is sturdy but events had gotten to her. After hugging Julia, both went to sleep. When my mother looked in, Julia's arms were wrapped about her mother's neck.

Kimberly awoke four hours later, showered ("to wash the jail smell from me"), and came downstairs. By this time, Erika and her boyfriend, Clarence, had arrived. My boyfriend, Randy, couldn't come. His parents were gone for the day and he had to babysit his toddler sister. It's good practice for our married life, I consoled myself.

Messages begging for an interview with Kimberly began. She was now famous, having become a poster child against gender discrimination. Her painful experience reminded reporters of Amanda Knox, the college student who had been imprisoned in Italy for four years on a false murder charge. Book offers were undoubtedly on the way.

"School will be starting soon," I said, during a lull in the conversation.

"College is over for me. I no longer have the patience, and Julia needs me more than I need Barnard."

"But you're a genius with computers. What will you do?" I asked.

"Watch TV, eat and get fat," Kimberly replied, with a small smile.

Clarence's eyes lit up at the word "computers." He didn't know Kimberly and had barely paid attention to what had probably seemed "girl talk." Now, Erika nudged his leg. He turned toward Kimberly and spoke.

"Come join us!" Clarence said, forcefully.

"What?" she asked, with a puzzled look on her face.

"Both my parents have doctorates in computer science. Our startup has hedge fund investment, and you could come in on the ground floor. There are only four of us but even our office manager, Lydia, is a hacker. We're doing great things and would love to have you," he said.

"You could live in my house until you buy your own, and Julia already has friends here. Lydia is a young widow with five children and you can help each other," Erika chimed in.

And that's what happened.

Chapter 164

It took almost a week for the public craziness to die down. Four days after Kimberly's release, my father held a press conference for her at Greenwich's Homestead Inn.

When questioned about her future, she said that her most important task was to be a mother. She said that her harrowing experience had made her unable to return to college. She thanked her Barnard instructors for the knowledge that she had gained, adding that she had been recruited by a local startup where her computer skills would be valuable.

Kimberly closed her remarks by thanking the reporters, saying that it was their work that had secured her freedom and that America would lose its commanding role in the world were it not for their dedication.

On this stirring note, my father closed the meeting and invited all to attend the caviar/baked salmon buffet at the room next door. While reporters mingled, Kimberly quietly slipped away.

The next day, during girl talk with me and Erika in Erica's bedroom, Kimberly suddenly stood, said that she was tired, and left for a nap.

"She's been sleeping a lot. She's been affected more than she'll admit," Erika observed.

"Probably, but talking was always hard for her though she's gotten better," I said.

A ringtone filled the room and I reached for my phone.

"Margaret?"

The woman's voice was familiar but I couldn't immediately place it. Then I felt embarrassed at my memory lapse.

"*Ulrika*, how are you?" I asked, cheerfully.

Ulrika is Vladimir's long-term, live-in girlfriend and the mother of his baby daughter. He also has a wife in Russia that he hasn't seen for many years.

"Vladimir insisted that I wait to tell you until he was better. He's had a small heart attack and wants to see you. Can you come?" she asked, hesitantly.

"*Of course!*" I burst out, as fear enveloped me.

Erika stared at me.

"United has direct flights to Berlin. I'll arrange for an open ticket to be held for you at their Newark counter. Call and tell me when you'll be arriving. I'll have someone pick you up. Bless you," she said, before hanging up abruptly.

My mind felt scattered as I jumped up. Concern lit Erika's face.

"*What is it?*" she asked.

"Vladimir. He may be dying. I'm going to Berlin," I said, and quickly gathered my things.

Chapter 165

I have three best friends but only Erica knows my odd background. That Aunt Lena, my mother's sister, is actually my biological mother; and that my biological father is either Peter, a former British spy, or Vladimir, a former Russian general.

Lena doesn't know who it is since she had affairs with both men at the same time and a DNA test was never performed.

Upon hearing this, many people would probably conclude that I must have had an awful life but this isn't true. Including the couple who adopted me as a newborn, I now have five parents that love me deeply, which is surely a blessing.

In the deepest recess of my mind I might long for normality: to have only one mother and one father. But I never actually thought this, maybe because growing up involves learning to compromise between what is desired and the possible.

My adoptive parents know about Peter but not about Vladimir and they rarely met him. Moreover, they associate him with Erika since his business provides security for her family.

Thus, I lied upon returning home to pack some clothes. I told my parents that I was visiting a sick friend in New York City. Since the next semester began in two weeks, I would remain there. To ease their disappointment, I promised to Skype home daily and they willingly accepted this. My father's legal practice was booming, and my mother had two younger daughters to occupy her time.

Abram, Erika's bodyguard, drove Erika and me to Newark Airport. She insisted on this, not wanting me to be alone. It was all that I could do to keep her from accompanying me to Berlin.

At the airport, I checked in at the United Airline counter and picked up my ticket. It was three hours before departure and we looked for an appealing place to sit. The many attractive restaurants made choosing one tough for a vegetarian like me.

Erika hassles her father to eat healthy but is more relaxed about her diet. Abram eats anything but never while on duty. We walked the long corridor and read the menus posted on restaurant windows.

Chapter 166

I'm not a fervent vegetarian. You'll never see me picketing McDonald's to sell vege-burgers and I do eat fish and dairy. But I almost always draw the line at eating meat and this was the specialty of most of the restaurants that we passed. One specialized in "jerk chicken omelet," whatever that is. Other eateries offered Korean fried chicken, escargot and steak, veal, all manner of burgers, and something called gyoza.

Finally, just when we thought that we would have to survive on vending machine cookies and water, we stopped at the Flora Café. It had enough items to warm a vegetarian's heart: lentil soup, Greek salad, humus, and falafel.

I had the Greek salad and hummus, and Erika ordered the lentil soup and hummus. She insisted that Abram eat too, saying that it would be hours before they returned to Greenwich and she didn't want him fainting from hunger. He could keep one hand on his gun and eat with the other. If he needed more than one hand to protect her, she would hire another bodyguard, she added.

Abram sighed, and motioned for the waitress. He had apparently been through this before. He ordered falafel on pita bread, which could be eaten with one hand. While scanning our surroundings for threats, he courteously pretended not to listen though, having been Erika's bodyguard since she was a child, there was little about her life that he didn't know.

"How long will you be gone?" Erika asked, as we waited for the food to arrive.

"I don't know. I don't know how Vladimir is. I'll be staying if he's truly ill. If he's OK, probably just for a few weeks. He's my father and we've never lived together," I replied.

"He *may be* your father," Erika corrected.

"But he loves me like a father and has been important in my life. He's *family*," I said.

Though Abram almost never enters our conversations, he now did. What I said had touched him, and he muttered in Russian.

"What's that?" Erika asked.

"A Russian proverb about family. It means: 'Together, it's cramped; apart, it's boring,'" he said.

"You can't live with them and you can't live without them," Erika interpreted.

"Exactly so," Abram said, with a small smile.

Chapter 167

Erika and I didn't speak much since there wasn't much to say. Things were going well with our families, and Kimberly's life was settled. My only concern was Vladimir's health.

After leaving the restaurant, we sat in the departure lounge and watched the bustling scene. Two women sat behind us.

"Why is your nickname, *Diehard*?" one asked the other, in a puzzled tone.

I touched Erika's arm and nodded in back of me. We listened.

"Have you seen the movie?" the woman replied, with her own question.

"No."

"*Diehard* tells the story of a detective who visits his estranged wife at her job. While there, the skyscraper is taken over by murdering robbers. Though injured, he never gives up and finally defeats them. It's a great film."

"So?"

"Well, after we first met, Clinton, who is now my husband, did everything for me. He brought me flowers and took me to the best restaurants. He mowed my lawn, and bought toys for my daughter. I knew that it wasn't good to say this too soon but after three months of such treatment I told him that I loved him," the woman said.

There was a pause before the other woman asked, "What did he reply?"

"*Nothing, absolutely nothing*. You could at least say, 'thank you,' I said, and he did."

Both women laughed.

"That wasn't Clinton's only problem. Not only could he not say *love* but he couldn't say *marriage* except to say that he wasn't the marrying kind. He said he liked my company but also enjoyed being with other women and what was wrong with that? I could either accept it or walk away.

I loved Clinton and wanted him so I stayed. I hated myself for doing this but felt that I had no choice. It remained like this for the next year. He slept over two nights every week and on every weekend. I kept saying 'I love you' and he kept replying 'thank you.'"

There was another pause before the woman continued her story.

"One night I went to a party alone and met Mitch. He wanted to go out with me and I said 'OK.' Later, when Clinton stopped by, I told him to call me before coming over since I would be seeing another man occasionally.

"Clinton got mad. He said that he wasn't interested in sharing me and if that was what I wanted, we should call it quits. I replied that he had been seeing other women while dating me. He said that I had accepted it but that he couldn't accept this."

"*Men!*" said the other woman.

"I had four dates with Mitch. Clinton didn't call or drop in though I once saw him cruising the neighborhood. I felt lousy and told my daughter that I wasn't feeling well. I said that if Mitch phoned, to tell him that I couldn't talk. Later that night, she came to my room and said that she had told him this but the man wouldn't hang up. It was Clinton and he kept repeating, 'I love you.'

"He immediately came over and said that though he loved me and now wouldn't date other women, he still wasn't the marrying kind. But, being Diehard, I stuck with him for another year. Then when I threatened to get a job in another state, he finally proposed and we were married eight days later. We've been married twelve years and he tells me that he loves me every day."

A departure announcement came over the loudspeaker and the women rose and left.

Erika and I looked at each other.

"Men!" we exclaimed in chorus, and laughed.

Chapter 168

Diehard's story of her love success gave me the last smile that day. For the next hour, Erika and I sat silently while Abram watched protectively. When my departure announcement sounded, Erika hugged me tightly.

"Come back soon!" she said.

Her eyes looked troubled and I sensed that something was wrong.

"What is it?" I asked, though hearing more bad news was the last thing I needed that day.

"Nothing! I'll tell you when you're back," Erika said quickly.

She rushed away with Abram in pursuit.

I stood rigid for a moment, thinking. I must phone her after seeing Vladimir. Erika is strong; small bothers don't upset her.

Why can't things stay tranquil in my life? I asked myself, though realizing how simple-minded this thought is. Fate influences every life and only a coward or a fool tries to ignore it.

This insight calmed me until I remembered that it was Vladimir who had said it. My worry about him returned.

The distance from Newark to Berlin's Tegel Airport is nearly four-thousand miles and takes a little under eight hours. Ulrika remembered that I am vegetarian and had pre-ordered a vegetarian meal for me. This, the United Airlines' counter clerk had told me, was Indian and spicy, free of meat, poultry, fish and shellfish but included dairy products.

Aboard the plane, I was offered an amenity kit containing skin care products, a duvet and pillows, a noise-reducing headset, and a complimentary issue of *The Wall Street Journal*. Ice cream, fruit, and cheeses would come later, the stewardess assured me.

My seating companion was a woman in her late twenties. She stared shrewdly at me and immediately became supportive.

"Don't be frightened. Fear is being wise in the face of danger and you're safer flying than crossing city streets," she said.

"Thank you, but it's not the flying. I have things on my mind," I said.

"I've had that feeling. It's like when you know what happened to someone and made a vow that sticks with you," she said.

Her sympathetic tone had been filled with meaning.

"What happened to someone?" I asked casually, these seeming the significant words.

"Raped, and nearly killed," was the startling reply.

Her eyes told me that she hadn't been joking. She had known calamity and was for real. I asked the only reasonable question.

"What kind of work do you do?"

"I'm a New York City Police Detective-Investigator, Second Grade. That is, I was one until being fired," she said.

Chapter 169

I continued speaking with this woman I didn't know. Throughout my life I had spoken with strangers. How else can one learn?

Most British won't socialize without being formally introduced but she and I were American, and on an American airline too. She needed to talk and must have sensed that I would be sympathetic.

"I wasn't really fired but quit. I live on the Upper West Side and had worked as a detective in Manhattan. They downgraded me to street patrol on Staten Island. I had no future with the Department," she said.

I knew that becoming a police officer meant more than a steady paycheck. It meant gaining a close-knit group and desired identity.

"You must have had good reason to quit," I said.

"I did. I was threatened with jail," she replied.

These words surprised me too. She must have *some* story, I thought.

"It began with a rape case. A woman had been waiting for her boyfriend in the early morning. The rapist assaulted her so badly that she was hospitalized.

"A guy on the street got his license number. It was a Massachusetts plate and we tracked him down. The rapist was a Harvard Business School graduate and worked for an international consulting firm.

"He had been a football star in a Big Ten college, was drop-dead gorgeous, and all through his trial his beautiful girlfriend sat supportively behind him. The victim was a stewardess. She was intelligent, spoke clearly, and came across that way.

"But the jury was confused. They couldn't see how this all-American, great looking guy with a beautiful girlfriend could be guilty though rape has mostly to do with power and not sex. The jury acquitted him of rape, deviate sexual assault, and aggravated battery. They found him guilty of unlawful restraint.

"I was furious after the verdict but told myself that I had done my best. Outside the courtroom, a reporter that I barely knew whispered, 'He was acquitted because his girlfriend's ass is almost as great as yours,' and pinched mine.

"I didn't think. I just turned around and knocked him cold. A tourist filmed it and the scene went viral. You may have seen it on YouTube."

"No, I didn't," I said.

I felt moved. Her story was one that all women could identify with.

"Though the reporter didn't press charges, the Department felt that I had to be disciplined. I was demoted and quit. Technically, I wasn't fired but my career was over."

"Why are you going to Berlin?" I asked.

"To visit my grandmother, to get away for a while and clear my head."

"What will you do afterward?"

"I don't know. I have a degree in political science and could go to law school but the idea of being a lawyer isn't appealing."

Our conversation petered out and I began thinking. This woman, whose name I didn't yet know, was a good person who had been screwed. There had been times in my life when I needed a favor and been given one. Being someone's friend, even their temporary friend, is enough of a reason for doing this, I assured myself.

The woman had leaned back in her seat and closed her eyes.

"I have an idea that you may like," I said.

Her eyes opened and she turned toward me.

"My father owns an international security company. His partners are retired from the CIA and Britain's Secret Intelligence Service. They're always looking for good people and I could give him your name," I said.

"What's the company?"

I told her.

"*Your father owns it?*" she asked, with surprise.

"Yes. He's the major partner," I replied.

"But he's a Russian general."

"Long retired, and living in Berlin. He's a good man. He views people in terms of right and wrong and is committed to protecting those in the right. He helps others to achieve more than they believed they could. He is like that with me too and would be with you. Call him. You'll like him," I said.

I wrote Vladimir's name and telephone number on the cover of the *Hemispheres* inflight magazine and gave it to her.

"I'll tell him about you. What's your name?" I asked.

"Margaret, but everyone calls me 'Maggie,'" she said.

I couldn't help grinning.

"What?" she asked.

"Margaret is my name too but no would dare call me 'Maggie,'" I replied.

Chapter 170

We parted at Tegel Airport with just a handshake. We weren't yet on hugging terms. United Airlines was at Terminal A, a hexagon-shaped concourse containing a parking area, taxi stands, and bus stops in its middle.

Compared to most airports, Tegel's walking distance is short. The airport is small, crowded, and has a retro but marvelous design. It has minimal seating but is easy to find your way around. It is forty years old; the completion of Berlin's new Brandenburg Airport is long delayed.

Passengers scowled at the departure screens and tapped their smartphones in frustration. Tegel's only benefit is that it is a twenty-minute ride from the center of Berlin.

A man held a sign bearing my name and I approached him. He spoke in accented but understandable English.

"The madam waits in the car with the baby," he said.

We picked up my luggage, which I let him carry though it wasn't much. My visit wasn't for holiday.

A toddler can cheer even the most depressed. Ulrika's daughter did her magic and we spoke with her playfully before becoming serious.

"How is Vladimir?" I asked.

"Vladimir is being Vladimir. They wanted him to stay in the hospital for a few days but he insisted on going home," Ulrika replied.

"What was wrong with him?"

"You mean apart from eating lousy and working too hard?"

I relaxed. Vladimir's medical crisis seemed to be over.

"Yes."

"He had severe shoulder pain and I screamed until he went to the hospital. The doctor diagnosed it as a coronary artery spasm. That's when the artery wall tightens and blood flow becomes restricted. An angiogram didn't find any blockage, and it's believed that there was minimal damage to his heart.

"He was prescribed a nitrate and a calcium channel blocker. He was also told to change his diet and lose twenty pounds. I scream at him daily. Try to get used to it," Ulrika said.

As we traveled through Charlottenburg, an affluent borough of Berlin, Ulrika took on the role of tour guide. She pointed out the Charlottenburg Palace, the largest surviving royal palace in Berlin, and the Museum Berggruen that specializes in modern art.

When Ulrika became pregnant, their former apartment was enlarged by combining it with the apartment next door. It now has nine bedrooms and six bathrooms. It is on the fourth floor of a building that was constructed in 1910. Thankfully, there is an elevator.

"He's waiting for you in the study," Ulrika said, pointing toward it,

I suddenly felt nervous, like an erring pupil approaching their principal. Vladimir has that effect on people. But after taking a deep breath, my confidence returned. I was a grown woman, not a child, and had helped in his business.

The door of the study was open. My sneakers had been noiseless, and I waited silently until he looked up from his reading.

Vladimir was thinner than at our last meeting and all of his hair was now gray. Tears filled my eyes. I felt a flood of emotion as I sensed beyond any doubt that he, not Peter, was my biological father.

Vladimir rose from the sofa, spread his arms, and spoke in heavily accented English.

"Little daughter," he said, using the old-fashioned Russian endearment from parent to child.

I replied, in Russian, with the phrase that I had practiced with Abram, Erika's Russian bodyguard.

"Papa, I've come home," I said, and rushed forward into his embrace.